THE HOUSE
ON LOOKOUT
MOUNTAIN

PATCHWORK MYSTERIES

THE HOUSE ON LOOKOUT MOUNTAIN

JO ANN BROWN

Guideposts

New York, New York

Guideposts.org
(800) 932-2145
Guideposts Books & Inspirational Media

Cover design by Wendy Bass
Cover illustration by Joyce Patti
Interior design by Lorie Pagnozzi
Typeset by Aptara

Printed and bound in the United States of America
10 9 8 7 6 5 4 3 2

For Debbie Earthrowl

You are a blessing for our family.

How lovely are the messengers that preach us the gospel of peace.—Felix Mendelssohn

Family Patterns

Time to Share

Muslin Mystery

Timeless Treasures

Homespun Holiday

Pieces of the Past

Threads of Truth

Secret in the Stitches

Bound in Love

Yesterday's Secrets

Squared Away

Mystery on the Midway

A Quilt of Memories

The House on Lookout Mountain

THE HOUSE
ON LOOKOUT
MOUNTAIN

CHAPTER ONE

S arah Hart manually shifted her car into a lower gear as the road grew even steeper, and she heard the car's engine strain. There couldn't really be a house way up here on Lookout Mountain, could there?

That morning, Neil Lawton, an accountant in Maple Hill and a longtime friend, had called Sarah and asked if she would meet him at a house he and a business associate had recently purchased. He wouldn't answer Sarah's questions, but said he would explain when she got there, and that he could use her expertise. Sarah assumed he was referring to a quilt, but he had just repeated that he would explain when she got there.

Then he said the words that had set her curiosity afire: "Don't tell anyone else about the house, Sarah. We're trying to keep the whole thing confidential until we know for sure what we've got up here."

It was impossible for Sarah to resist a mysterious invitation like that. She was glad for an excuse to get out of the house. Since her father's funeral last month, she had savored the comfort of family and dear friends, sharing stories about her father that made her cry and let her laugh. Her grief hadn't dimmed, but Neil's phone call had her jumping into her car and heading up Lookout Mountain.

She eased on the brakes as another hairpin turn twisted her higher along the narrow road. She hadn't known there were any houses past the Morrisseys' tumbledown barns. Just cliffs and trees clinging to the sheer mountainside.

The road straightened. Sarah glanced at the page she held against the steering wheel. Neil had given her directions. *4.7 miles after Morrisseys'*. She chuckled. Trust an accountant to be that exact.

The engine strained again—louder this time—as the road rose at a sharper angle. She hoped she wouldn't meet another car. There were only a few places wide enough to pull over to let another car pass, and she didn't want to have to back down to one of them.

Sarah switched off the air conditioning to lessen the stress on the engine and rolled down the front windows. A blast of unseasonably hot air rushed into the car. So far, September had not heralded the return of autumn.

At exactly 4.7 miles, the trees thinned to reveal a gate set between stone walls. Not New England dry stone walls, but high masonry walls with thick stones confined in concrete. Two pillars, each about seven feet tall, framed the open gate. The dirt road between them fell back into bushes that looked as if they had been recently chopped back just enough to reopen the road and let her through. The whole thing looked like something a fairy tale villain would conjure around a castle to keep Prince Charming from his princess.

Sarah grinned. She couldn't wait to see what Neil's house looked like and find out why he wanted her opinion on it. Maybe he had found something interesting stashed in the back of a closet or even in a wall if they had begun renovations. She remembered the quilt she and her granddaughters had found in a hidden passage in her grandfather's old house that now belonged to Sarah's son and his family. Old houses held lots of secrets.

She drove carefully through the gate. The dirt road was rutted with potholes, and her silver Grand Prix bounced from one side to the other like a ship at sea.

She grimaced and slowed even further as briars scratched at the car. She straightened the wheel when, a quarter of a mile down the road, the car emerged from the overgrown shrubs.

Sarah's eyes widened at the sight before her. It wasn't a castle, but it was close. The three-story house had been sited to allow fabulous views of the valley, but trees and brush had grown up to block the vistas. Behind the house and its two wings, white pines reached high into the sky, surrounding the house with an ancient forest.

Windows were dull, empty eyes on the upper floors, and Sarah guessed the panes were dirty and filled with cobwebs. The ground floor windows were covered with rickety shutters. Weatherworn clapboards covered the façade on the lower two stories, but the top floor was timbered like an English Tudor house. Plaster had flaked off between the timbers, leaving gray spots that had dried to a driftwood color. Several chimneys sprouted from the roof, and half a dozen smaller buildings clustered to one side and behind the house.

Sarah stopped the car and looked back. The thick jungle of bushes and weeds she had passed through might once have been a vast expanse of lawn.

How could a house like this be forgotten by everyone in Maple Hill? A twinge ached in her as she wondered if her father had known about the house. He had served as a Maple Hill postman for years and knew just about every house in town.

Neil walked from around the house and hailed her with a friendly wave. The weather in Maple Hill was hot and humid, with the threat of thunderstorms every afternoon. Most people, stuck in school or at work, were tired and irritable and looked as if they had just run a marathon.

Not Neil Lawton. He appeared as cool and dapper as always. His only concession to the heat was a short-sleeved white Oxford shirt instead of his usual long-sleeved one. A conservative navy blue tie was knotted beneath his chin, accenting his movie star good looks. Half the girls had had a crush on Neil back in high school. Almost fifty years later, he still had a distinguished charm.

Sarah doubted she looked as fresh.

"You can leave the car right here," Neil said with a bright smile. "You're the last to arrive, so it won't be in the way."

She turned off the engine and opened the door.

"You found us." He held the door while she got out.

"Yes, but how did you find this house?" Sarah took her purse out of the car, heavy with her camera and notebook. She had almost brought her full quilting bag, not sure what she would need, but had settled for just the two items.

"I'll explain inside." Neil seemed to balance his weight on the balls of his feet like a sprinter getting ready for a race. "It's easier when you can see what we've discovered."

She nodded, even though her curiosity was ramping up with each passing second. "Can't wait. I had no idea there was a house up here. I wonder how anyone kept it a secret for so long."

"That's what we're hoping you can tell *us*," replied a deep voice to her left.

Sarah turned to look at a very tall, very thin, dark haired man. He wore designer rustic clothes that were supposed to make him look like an outdoorsman, but had to be brand-new. A wave of expensive cologne rushed from him, a scent better suited for a boardroom than the old house.

"This is Reginald Carruthers," Neil said, "my business partner on this project. Reginald, Sarah Hart."

Sarah smiled as she shook Reginald's hand. He wasn't as classically good-looking as Neil, but his smile was welcoming. He rubbed his hands together, and she wondered if he was as nervous as Neil was acting.

What were they anxious about? It wasn't like Neil not to make sure every "t" was crossed and every "i" dotted before he got involved with a project. She would have guessed he had gone over the house with a fine-tooth comb before the closing.

"Shall we?" Neil gestured toward the house. "Everyone's waiting."

"Everyone?" Sarah asked as she walked with the men toward a slanting porte cochere. The covered section of the driveway next to what must be the front door would have allowed company to arrive and enter the house without having to worry about the weather. It didn't have any of the Victorian extravagance of gingerbread moldings like the ones she had seen in Maple Hill.

Reginald didn't give Neil a chance to answer. While they climbed the steps to a wraparound porch that seemed like an afterthought on the magnificent house, he began apologizing for the briars and the rough road.

"We've got someone coming in to cut those bushes down," Reginald said. "They were supposed to come over this weekend, but didn't."

Sarah looked past him when she saw another man walking around the corner of the porch. He had a tweed coat folded over his arm. The sleeves of his white shirt were rolled up past his elbows as a concession to the unseasonable heat.

"Chester!" she said.

Chester Winslow's sparse silver hair glistened in the sunlight, and a broad smile creased his friendly face. He was a good friend who had helped her almost a year ago get a job writing a quilting column for *Country Cottage* magazine.

"Sarah's here," he called over his shoulder.

She stared as her daughter-in-law Maggie Hart and her friend Irene Stuart appeared behind Chester. Both Chester and Maggie were antiques experts and Irene worked at Maple Hill's historical society.

"Why didn't you tell me they'd be here, too, Neil?" Sarah asked after giving all three quick hugs. Chester's embrace lingered a second longer than the others, but she pretended not to notice. That would embarrass him, and she didn't want to do that to a friend. She wished he would think of her as just a friend too.

"Like I told you," Neil said as his gaze wandered from face to face. "We wanted to keep the word from getting out about this house."

"And why is that?"

"Let's go inside, and we'll explain." Neil opened the front door. It was a solid slab of wood. He bowed them in with an unsteady grin. Did anyone else notice that his fingers were trembling? Sarah didn't say anything, but this was so unlike the composed man she had known for years.

As the others followed Neil indoors, Sarah hung back with Maggie. Her daughter-in-law's auburn hair was pulled back in a ponytail, and she wore a light green, sleeveless shirt.

"If I'd known Neil had spoken with you too," Maggie said, "we could have driven up together. I was just saying the same thing to Irene." Her voice lowered. "Why do you think they're being so secretive? Do you think it was a ruse to get us to come up here fast?"

"You've got me." Sarah looked closely at Maggie's pinched expression. "Is something else wrong?"

"Nothing other than having twins with moods swinging in opposite directions. If Audrey is smiling, Amy is glum and vice versa. It's Amy's turn today to be a drama queen." She flashed Sarah a wry smile as she reached to open the door. "Actually she's been taking on that role a lot lately. Usually on days when her field hockey team has a game. I don't know why. She's doing great, and so is the team."

"They're teenagers now. It'll get better as they get older."

"Thank goodness," Maggie said.

"After it gets worse."

Maggie laughed. "I know it's part of their growing up. According to my folks, I wasn't the easiest person to be around when I was that age. I guess it's payback time for driving my parents crazy. I just wanted to give you a heads-up since they're going over to your house tomorrow after school."

Sarah couldn't help smiling. She enjoyed time with her grandchildren. She didn't get to see her grandsons often, because they lived in Texas, and now that Amy and Audrey were more deeply involved in school and activities, their visits to her house weren't as frequent as when they had first moved to Maple Hill last year.

"I'm looking forward to it," she said.

"I hope they'll both be up instead of glum."

Sarah's answer fizzled when she and Maggie stepped into the foyer. The house's interior was as startling as its exterior. Sarah had thought it would be dark and cramped with the shutters closed, but the ceilings rose more than a dozen feet from the maple floors. Light flowed down a staircase that slowly spiraled to the upper floors. Simple metal balusters were covered with dust, as was the wide banister. A thick newel post at the bottom was topped by what looked like an oversized wooden bowling ball.

Beyond the stairs, tall rectangular glass windows offered a view of an overgrown garden and the roofs of the barns on the far side of a stone wall. Some of the upper panes in the windows had been opened to let in fresh air.

"Does anyone else," asked Sarah, "find this juxtaposition of English Tudor styling and ultramodern design a little jarring?"

"It's like the Mad Hatter and the latest winner of some interior decorating reality show collaborated," Irene said. Her light brown hair fell forward onto her face. She brushed it back as she examined the windows, running a finger along the sash and glass. "These could be original. It doesn't look like something anyone from rural New England would design. What do you think, Maggie? Doesn't it have a more urban feel to you?"

"If the walls weren't bare," Maggie said, "I'd say it looks like a museum. Or maybe a fancy boutique hotel in New York or LA."

"Exactly." Neil stepped between them and the windows. As everyone turned to look at him, he said, "I'm sure you're all wondering why I invited you here today." He smiled. "I've always wanted to say that."

No one laughed, and Reginald cleared his throat.

"Okay, let me start over," Neil said. "Thank you for making the trip up here today. I apologize again for the state of the grounds."

Sarah glanced at Chester. She knew how much he loved his silver BMW. He must have been as curious as she was to risk scratching it on the briars. He stood with his arms folded in front of him, impatient to see what Neil and Reginald had to show them.

"I didn't even know there was a house up here until I got a call from Reginald," Neil said. "Just a little bit of background. We went to college together, and Reginald lives in Albany, New York, now. He heard about this property from a Realtor he's worked with before. He asked me to go in with him on it. He's a shrewd guy, so I did, even though he should know better than to invest with an accountant." He smiled at Reginald who arched his brows and chuckled. "We believe the house is close to a hundred years old, but we can't be certain because of the unique architecture. We decided to ask the experts." He smiled at them. "Chester, I remembered you from your antiques appraisal event at Maggie's store. We'd like both of your opinions about what has value and what needs to be sent to the dump. There's a lot of stuff, so we figured it'd be too big a job for one person. You two know more about antiques than I ever will. They're not my style."

Sarah smiled. Neil's office was stark white and metal with modern paintings that didn't match the view of the Maple Hill town green outside his windows.

"Irene, what you don't know about Maple Hill history probably isn't worth knowing," Neil said. "And, Sarah, you're an expert on quilting and textiles and solving mysteries."

"Mysteries?" Sarah asked. "What have you discovered?"

Neil again didn't answer her question. "You should know that our plans were to redo the whole place and turn it into a high-end resort and spa."

"Here?" asked Maggie, astonished. "You want to develop a luxury hotel on top of a mountain? The road is too narrow for two-way traffic."

"That can be rectified." His eyes glittered, and Sarah wondered what luxurious accoutrements he was imagining. "It's not as crazy as it sounds. Maple Hill is an easy drive from Boston, New York, and Albany. People who want to enjoy something a bit different and be surrounded by first-class luxury will come flocking. There are already several high-end resorts in the Berkshires."

Sarah nodded. That was true. Luxury spas had popped up during the last ten years, set side by side with small New England farmhouses. Visitors liked being pampered amid the mountains and the buildings that harkened back to a simpler time.

"But it sounds as if that *was* your plan," Sarah said. "What changed?"

Neil exchanged a glance with Reginald. "We're still going ahead, but we want some answers before we start renovations. When we got here, we found the house was completely furnished. We hadn't expected that."

"Actually," Chester said, "I'm not surprised. It couldn't have been easy to get furniture up here in the first place, and it might have been simpler to leave big and bulky items."

"That's what we thought at first," Reginald said. "But then we realized it wasn't just furniture. It looks as if the family who lived here just got up one day and walked away, leaving everything behind them."

"Why would anyone do that?" asked Sarah.

"That's what we're hoping you can tell us."

CHAPTER TWO

When Neil and Reginald walked down a hall past the staircase, Sarah and the others followed like a row of ducklings. Questions were a roller coaster in her brain—twisting and turning in every direction. Chester was right. There wasn't anything unusual about the house being sold furnished, though she was surprised Neil and Reginald hadn't been informed of the fact.

But what had they seen that made them invite her?

The possibilities ran through Sarah's mind as they walked down the hallway, passing several closed doors along it on both sides. It was wide enough so they could walk two abreast. Wallpaper hung in tatters near the high ceiling, more than twenty feet from the floor. The air was damp and stale.

A set of doors were open to their right. Sarah stopped to look into a large, formal parlor. The moldings were beautifully carved, but the ceiling light was starkly modern. A flowered rug was spread across the maple floor. A trio of paintings of snow-covered mountains were displayed, along with a woven tapestry of a similar scene.

Sarah went to look at the tapestry. The room was shadowed because shutters covered the windows. Light came in through broken slats, and the air was much cooler than in the hallway.

Neil crossed the room to a three-piece set of burgundy furniture. "The sofa—"

"Davenport," said Maggie with a smile. "That's what they called it in the nineteen thirties when this furniture was new." She ruffled the dark red fabric that looked like it had been given a crew cut. "An overstuffed davenport covered with burgundy mohair. We found one a lot like it on the back porch of our house when we moved in. I considered stripping it down, but a chipmunk family had moved in, along with a ton of acorns."

Reginald ran his fingers along the carved marble on the fireplace, then grimaced at the dirt on them. Shrugging, he pulled out a handkerchief and wiped his hand on it. The scent of his cologne grew stronger, then diminished when he shoved the handkerchief back in his pocket.

"This room," Reginald said, "we believe was for show. You know, the kind of room families never use, except when they've got company. Let me show you a room that the family must have used a lot." He walked out into the hallway, and they went with him. "I really hope you can help us figure out what happened to the family who used to live here. We don't have a clue."

Sarah looked at Maggie and Irene, but they both shrugged. So far, they hadn't seen anything out of the ordinary. The house had obviously been empty for years. It was dirty and dusty and smelled.

Neil stopped at a pair of closed doors just one room over. As he put his hand on one, he said, "This is the smaller of the two dining rooms. I suspect it was used for everyday meals while the bigger one on the far side of the kitchen was for special guests." He opened the pocket doors.

For such a grand house, the dining room was cozy, which meant it was no more than three times the size of Sarah's. The windows and lighting belonged to the middle of the twentieth century, but the furniture looked older. The wood had turned black with age and damp.

Irene and Maggie opened doors in the built-in cupboard and the sideboard. Two platters with blue willow patterns leaned against the back of the sideboard. Maggie carefully set them flat, so they wouldn't get jostled off. Her eyes sparkled, and Sarah guessed Maggie was interested in studying the china more.

Sarah walked to the table. It had been laid for eight people, though the table could have held more than twice that many comfortably. Plates were half-hidden beneath napkins. She lifted one, and quickly dropped it back to hide what might have once been food. Only bits remained. She glanced around, wincing. She hoped whatever vermin had eaten the food were long gone. Maggie's face was an odd grayish green, and Sarah guessed she was thinking the same thing.

"This," Reginald said, his voice as serious as an undertaker's, "is why we're curious about what happened to the family who lived here. It looks like they decided to go out for a walk halfway through supper and never came back."

"I've made some quiet inquiries around town," Neil said, "and nobody seems to know anything about the house or who lived here. How could a family live here and nobody knew?"

"I don't know about that," Chester said, running his hand along the back of a chair. "But I can tell you the house is only about seventy or eighty years old—"

"How do you know that?" asked Neil.

Chester hooked a thumb toward the window. "Look at the white pines along your garden wall and count the rings of branches."

Sarah did a quick calculation. White pines grew a new ring of branches each year, which made it easy to figure how old they were. She couldn't see to the top of the trees from where she stood, but she trusted Chester's estimate.

"But," Chester said, "The furniture in this room is older. I'm not saying for certain because I'd need to study it more, but that's my gut feeling. It has the patina of age, and it's a style earlier than the thirties or forties. As for the rest..." He smiled at Irene. "Family history in Maple Hill is your bailiwick."

"Are there other examples of what made you believe the family left quickly?" Irene asked.

Neil nodded.

"Can we see them?"

"Sure," Neil said. "But I'd like to hear Chester's reasoning for dating the furniture as prethirties, and then I'll show you."

While Chester tilted one chair on its side, Sarah looked at a still life on the wall over the sideboard. That food looked fresh enough to eat, but dust had packed down like felt on the frame. On the opposite wall a fabric hanging had faded until its colors were almost lost.

Chester directed the two men to look at some interesting aspects of the chair. He had pulled out his camera, reminding Sarah to do the same. She snapped photos of the room from one corner and then from another before focusing on the tapestry and bric-a-brac.

Maggie walked over to where Sarah was looking at some knickknacks.

"Chester seemed really glad to see you," Maggie said in not much more than a whisper.

"I'm glad he's here. He's going to enjoy digging up the history on all these things with you."

Maggie picked up a china dog and turned it over to see if anything was stamped on it. "Does he know you and Liam are an item?"

Sarah did enjoy spending time with Liam Connolly, who owned The Spotted Dog Café and Bookstore on the Maple

Hill town green. It was a favorite for locals and the leaf-peepers who would be coming to view the changing foliage by month's end.

"I wouldn't call us an item," Sarah hedged. "We've gone out a few times, that's all."

"There's a lot more to see," Reginald said, again the genial host. "Why don't we give you the lay of the land, and then you can decide which things you want to study in more detail?"

Irene was the first out the door, eager to see what else might suggest the family had abandoned their home. The others followed more slowly.

Sarah waited while Neil closed the door before she said, "It's a puzzling house."

"That's why we asked you to come here."

"But there are enough mysteries here without creating more." She smiled and caught his eye. "Neil, we've been friends a long time. All you needed to do was tell the truth, and I would have come up here without mentioning it to anyone."

"Even Martha?"

Sarah's smile widened. Martha Maplethorpe had been her best friend since grade school. Sarah had learned that Martha's insights into a mystery were solid, so she often discussed clues with her friend.

"You don't need to worry about that, Neil. Martha is busy, busy, busy with a project at church right now. I've scarcely seen her for the past week. And even if I had, Martha isn't a gossip. You should know that."

Neil drew in a deep breath and then let it sift past his tight lips. "I'm sorry, Sarah. I didn't mean to insult you or Martha. It's this house. I didn't know it would get this complicated. If we uncover something exciting, it could make a great marketing point for the hotel."

Sarah accepted his apology, but hurried to catch up with Maggie who was walking with Reginald. Irene and Chester followed them.

"Neil tells me that you have twins," Reginald was saying as Sarah came within earshot.

"Yes, twin girls," Maggie said.

"How old?"

"Thirteen."

"Not an easy age." His chuckle was sympathetic. "Our two daughters and younger son were born the same day. They went through every phase—good and bad—together. Now they're all married and have children of their own."

"Triplets? Wow!"

He nodded. "And our oldest son is barely two years older than the triplets. When we decided to have another baby, we had no idea we'd be blessed with three more. Neither my wife nor I have multiples in our families."

"We don't either," Maggie said. "It must have been a challenge to have four teens at once."

"Yes, but I wouldn't change a moment of it for the world."

"Me neither."

Glad to hear Maggie was feeling better about the twins' drama, Sarah smiled at Chester who paused to let her catch up with him.

"If I wasn't seeing this with my own eyes," he said, "I don't know if I'd believe it. All this beautiful furniture waiting for us to discover when and where it was made. Maggie looked thrilled about the china and porcelain, and I saw you looking at the tapestries. And there's a mystery to solve."

"Potential mystery," Sarah said. "People don't just vanish."

Chester pushed aside a piece of wallpaper that had fallen down enough to brush his head. "Someone has to know what happened. But it seems as though it's been covered up."

"That sounds like you think there's a conspiracy."

He grinned. "I'm not saying Elvis or a flying saucer took off with them, but you have to admit this is peculiar."

"*Really* peculiar."

Maggie, Neil, and Reginald had paused in front of a painting. It was, Sarah saw, a view of Maple Hill from high on Lookout Mountain, even closer to the peak than the house was.

"Neil," Sarah asked, "do you have an inventory of what's in the house?"

Both Neil and Reginald shook their heads before Reginald said, "The real estate listing simply said it was being sold with its contents."

"Would the Realtor have a list? Maybe if we look at that instead of being distracted by this collection of interesting items, we'll see some sort of pattern," Sarah suggested.

"That's a great idea, Sarah. I'll give Harriet a call," Neil said and reached into his pocket for his cell. "Harriet Richards had this listing."

Sarah recognized the name from seeing it on "For Sale" signs in Maple Hill and nearby towns. Ms. Richards was one of the most successful Realtors in the Berkshires, and she was the go-to person when the media wanted a quote about house values.

"Come in here!" Irene called from a room on the left. "You've got to see this!"

Sarah wasn't sure what to expect, but she followed Irene's voice. She stared at the room in disbelief. The family must have included small children. Toys were scattered on the wide board pine floors near floor-to-ceiling bookcases. Blocks had stood in a tall stack for decades. A rocking horse, worn and faded, had a blanket for a saddle. Both the blanket and the horse's mane looked like they had been gnawed. On the floor beside it, a doll sprawled. Sarah picked it up and propped it gently against the horse.

Sarah turned over a corner of the blanket and saw it was a flowered tapestry. It hadn't been handmade because the stitches were too even, both front and back. But someone must have tried to repair the tapestry because a trio of three-inch cotton squares had been sewn to the bottom. The bottom edges of the squares were shredded. She laid it down on the rocking horse gingerly and winced when the fabric unraveled more.

Flies buzzed against the window, and Chester opened the lower section and shoved aside the shutters. Instead of going outside, the flies zipped up to the ceiling to swirl around the hanging light. The open-topped globes were filled with dead flies.

"Stupid cluster flies," Chester muttered.

Sarah bent to pick up a small box with a tortoiseshell oval on the top. There was a key on the bottom—it was a music box. She turned the key, and a lighthearted melody brightened the room. She set it on a low table.

Chester picked it up and whistled. Both Neil and Reginald looked at him eagerly.

"Don't get your hopes up," Chester said, "but some antique German music boxes are very valuable." He lifted the oval to reveal a single golden bird with an ivory beak. "It looks like a Karl Griesbaum box. Early part of the twentieth century, I'd guess. If it is truly a Griesbaum, it could be worth several thousand dollars."

"And it was on the floor!" Neil said.

"Along with everything else." Maggie put a black stuffed dog on a shelf next to some old children's books. "What would make a family leave everything like this?"

Nobody had an answer.

Kneeling by a box beneath the open window, Sarah took out what looked like doll clothes. The fabric was rotting, but when she carefully turned a section of the garment so she could see the seams, she saw the little items had been hand-sewn. Beneath them were a trio of blonde dolls like the one on the rocking horse.

"Chester," Maggie said. "I don't know much about twentieth-century toys. What do you make of this?" She held out a metal truck painted with camouflage. It had a large cannon on the back. She turned it over and pointed to where it was stamped *Germany*.

He examined it. "I'd say this is midthirties. At that time, all the best toys were made in Germany. I'd wager that rocking horse and the dolls Sarah is taking out came from Germany too. This truck has to be from before World War Two."

"Why?" asked Neil as he peered over Chester's shoulder.

"During the war, factories switched to war production. After the war, Germany was divided for forty-five years. Anything manufactured during that time would have FRG or GDR on it. FRG for the Federal Republic of Germany. What we called 'West Germany.' East Germany was known as the German Democratic Republic." He grinned. "Sorry for the history lesson, but that's how I know this little truck was made before the war."

"Hey, Chester," Neil said with a smile, "this is why we wanted you to help us. Who knows what tidbit of information will help us figure out why the family disappeared?"

Sarah looked around the room again. It truly did appear that the family had gone away without taking anything with them. But why would anyone do that?

As if she had asked the question aloud, Neil said, "I can't begin to guess why a family would leave everything behind."

"Especially the children's toys." Maggie bent and picked up a stuffed bear. It obviously had been well loved because its fur was thin in patches. "I can't imagine my girls leaving behind their favorite toys."

"When my kids were young enough to have a bear as a best friend," Reginald said, "they would have insisted on taking him with them." He took the bear from her, glanced at it quickly, then placed it on a chair. "To be honest, they'd have insisted on taking *all* their things with them."

"Maybe they did take some things with them," Chester said. "If we could figure out what isn't here, maybe we could guess why they left."

"Trying to guess what isn't here could lead us on a thousand different wild goose chases," Maggie said. "Until we know if there's a house inventory list, we should concentrate on what *is* here unless something is obviously missing."

"One thing is obviously missing. Pictures," Sarah said.

Everyone turned to her.

"Look around," she said, spreading her hands wide. "In every room we've visited, there are beautiful paintings. We've seen knickknacks and books, but not a single photograph. If we're assuming this house is from the midthirties, there should be family pictures. Anyone who could afford to build this house could afford a camera."

"Or could have afforded to have a portrait done at the photography studio that used to be on the Maple Hill green," Irene said as she turned slowly. "Sarah, I think you're on to something here." Going to the bookshelves, she took down a leather volume with a gold-tooled title. She opened it and held it up. The first page had a two-by-three-inch rectangle torn out of it.

"That's just the right size for a bookplate." Maggie took the book from Irene and ran her fingers along the page. Small shreds of paper clung to her fingertips. "Whoever ripped out the bookplate didn't handle the book much after that. Maybe not at all, other than to put it back on the shelf."

Sarah selected another book and opened it. She had to peel apart the first pages, because they were stuck together with bits of rubber cement. The bookplate, or whatever had been glued in the front, was gone too. She returned it to the shelf, then picked up two *American Girl* magazines that had been left on the floor. One was dated February 1938, and the other was March 1940.

She pointed at the magazine's bottom corner. "The address label was cut off. Someone was making sure nobody would know who'd lived here."

"Covering their tracks?" Chester frowned as he considered his own question.

"It looks that way. But what made these people leave? Why did they abandon this house?"

"If you want my opinion, I'd say they were scared," Irene said. "People don't flee, leaving behind their things unless they're terrified."

CHAPTER THREE

Sarah wasn't surprised when Reginald suggested they split up to search for anything that could identify the family. "An envelope or a note stuck into something else might give us a clue," he suggested.

While Irene took photos with her cell and Maggie paged through more books, the men went toward the front of the house. Sarah walked in the opposite direction. The voices behind her faded as she went back along the hall.

Two small tapestries hung on either side of a closed door not far from the dining room. She hadn't noticed the tapestries before. Pulling her reading glasses from her purse, she put them on and examined the first tapestry. A unicorn knelt by a maiden in a bower of flowers and trees. The stitches were exquisite, even though the wool was thick and uneven. This tapestry must be far older than the one in the toy room. It might be the real deal. The unicorn was more yellow than white, and the maiden's green dress was faded except for a pair of crosses in black near the hem. Sarah almost didn't see the crosses because they blended in with the blue and white flowers scattered beneath the silvery trees.

With care, she tilted the tapestry to look at the reverse. The stitches were smooth. Not as perfect as the machine-made piece was, but whoever had made the small tapestry had been skilled.

Sarah searched for a tag or anything that might identify its age or origin. Nothing was on the tapestry or the sleeve that had been sewn on the back so the piece could be hung. With a sigh, she let it swing gently back against the wall. She pulled out her camera and took several pictures front and back of the unicorn tapestry and the one beside it.

The second tapestry also had an allegorical image. St. George stood with one foot on a gray dragon. His white surcoat was decorated with a cross that had faded to a deep pink. St. George was the patron saint of England. Were the tapestries English? She would have to do research to learn more.

Putting the camera back in her purse, she slid her glasses up on her head. She opened the door between the tapestries.

A short corridor led to the kitchen. Leaving the door open behind her, Sarah went to see if the family had overlooked something that would identify them in the kitchen.

Sarah flipped the light switch, unsure if the electricity was on. Three ceiling lights blinked on, then off, then came back on again. They continued to flicker as Sarah looked around. The kitchen was almost as big as the whole first floor of her house. The worn linoleum had no pattern left, and she couldn't guess what color it had been originally. Cabinets lined the walls, and four huge tables with thick wooden legs were arranged in the center. One table showed signs that someone had done a lot of chopping on it. A second table had what looked like flour or sugar ingrained in the top.

A white stove had burners all to one side. The other side was a flat surface with a single lid on it. Sarah lifted the lid to reveal a deep well the right size for a soup pot. Her grandmother'd had a stove like this. It had been from the thirties, if Sarah remembered correctly, so this one must have been new when the house was built.

A large pan and two pots sat on the burners, but they were empty. No signs of food clung to them. She opened the oven. A rusty cast-iron pan inside was crusted with something. She couldn't be sure if it had been food or not, even when she jabbed it with her fingernail.

She closed the door and frowned at the flickering lights. That was really annoying. The wires must be frayed. She turned off the lights, then went to the icebox.

A stain on the floor showed where water had overflowed the pan that was supposed to collect runoff when the block of ice melted. Had that happened when the family vanished, or had it occurred regularly? She remembered her mother laughing about how she and her friends would splash each other with the icebox overflow when their parents weren't watching.

Taking a deep breath and holding it, Sarah opened the icebox door. Any odors of rotten food must have dispersed long ago, because the only smell was mildew. A moldy bottle was labeled *Collins Dairy, Maple Hill, Massachusetts*. Irene might know it. She set the bottle on one of the tables, so she would remember to show it to Irene.

There wasn't a sink with a faucet. Only a dry sink with a drain at the bottom where water could be poured in, then let out. Why would anyone have such a fabulous house, but no running water in the kitchen?

She didn't try the hand pump. She would need water to prime it, assuming the pipes were intact. Rust stains showed where water had dripped. If the house's pipes were rusty, Neil and Reginald had even more work ahead of them.

A search of the cupboards and drawers was fruitless. Tarnished silver and nice china were properly stored, but Sarah didn't find anything to identify who had lived in the house. She opened another door to find a large pantry. A calendar on the wall was from 1940, matching the date on one of the magazines in the children's room. Rusty spots showed where cans had been stored on the shelves, but only a few dozen tins remained. The labels were either faded or completely gone.

"Here you are." Chester looked into the pantry. "Though it was pretty easy to find you. Did you know that you left a trail in the dust behind you?"

Sarah came out of the pantry. Shutting the door behind her, she saw two sets of footsteps across the cracked linoleum. "I hadn't even noticed. I was too busy looking around."

"Did you find anything interesting?"

"I found out *I* wouldn't want to live here. There's no running water in the kitchen. I'm too used to modern conveniences."

"That's a nice stove, though," Chester said.

"Looks state-of-the-art for 1930. It probably runs on propane." She looked out a window. Near the backdoor, a pair of propane tanks were hooked to the wall. "I'm glad I didn't have to drive the truck that delivered those tanks. Have you found anything interesting?"

"Interesting, yes. There may be some valuable pieces here. Not necessarily true antiques, but items that have some real value. But answers about the family, no." He gestured back toward the direction they had come. "I thought I'd go and see what Maggie and Irene have found. After they finished in the toy room, they decided to check out the living room. They figure the family would have spent much of their time there. Want to come along?"

"I'll be there in a few minutes. I want to explore some more."

"Do you want some help?"

She heard the anticipation in his voice. She couldn't help thinking of his lingering hug and Maggie's question about whether Chester knew she and Liam were spending time together. Too many puzzles intrigued her, and she didn't want to be distracted by any attempts to divert her attention from the mystery that seemed to permeate the house.

"There are a lot of rooms to cover," Sarah said. "While I'm finishing up here, why don't you look around in another room? That way, we can cover more ground more quickly."

Chester slowly nodded. Slowly and reluctantly. "Okay. Give a shout if you find anything." He waved as he walked out of the kitchen.

Sarah continued back to the front of the house and up the stairs. The risers squeaked as if annoyed at being wakened after so many years. One about halfway up the first curve of the spiral felt spongy, and she grabbed the banister in case the tread gave way.

A long gallery stretched to the right from the top of the stairs. All the doors were closed, but two large windows allowed sunshine to wash across the wood floor, highlighting where sections had warped. She wondered if water had gotten into the house, or if the damage was due to the fact that there hadn't been any heat in the house in decades.

Sarah went to the two doors at the front of the house and opened the farthest one. Its window overlooked the porte cochere. The light coming through the glass was cut by hundreds of flies that clung to the window. The shrill sound of their wings beating against the glass was painful.

Sarah closed the door. Neil needed to get some fly strips in the room.

The other door opened to a bedroom. Two double beds were set on either side of a small table that held another oddly modern lamp. The mattresses were bare, and a trail of stuffing warned that some rodent had found a home in at least one of them. A few flies battered themselves against the room's only window.

Walking in, Sarah saw a barrel topped chest opposite the beds. She lifted the heavy top, leaning it against the wall. The pungent aroma of cedar rushed out. Hope filled her. The fragrant wood kept pests away.

A layer of tissue concealed what was in the chest. The paper was dry and unstained. She carefully took out the paper and set it on the floor.

A bright blue patchwork quilt seemed to light up the room. Taking it out, she balanced it on one arm. She didn't want to put it on the filthy floor. She stretched to place it on the tilted lid and reached in for the next quilt. This one was a glorious rose color.

She held it up to her nose. Unlike so much in the house, it didn't smell of mildew. The cedar had protected it. Were these quilts special? Was that why they had been stored like this? Or was the cedar chest simply a blanket chest?

"Oh my!" she breathed as she lifted out another quilt. A yellow one.

"Sarah!" Neil stood in the doorway. "I thought I heard footsteps up here. What have you found?" he asked as he walked in.

"Quilts." Sarah reached into the chest to take out the last quilt, a stark black-and-white one. "Four of them."

He laughed. "If there are quilts around, you always seem to find them."

"Or they find me."

Sarah scooped the quilts off the lid and asked Neil to hold out his arms. She placed the quilts on them before closing the top of the chest and placing the tissue on the lid.

"They look brand-new," he said when she took the quilts and stacked them on the tissue paper.

"The chest protected them from damp and sunshine, two big enemies of textiles." She opened the black-and-white quilt and spread it across the others. Tilting it, she ran her finger along one seam, then the next. "I'd say it's handmade, Neil, but I'd want to check it a lot more closely." She smiled at him. "I've learned my lesson about jumping to conclusions."

The quilt's center was a single large medallion. Along the border, fabrics that had been used in the medallion repeated in a complex pattern of flowers and vines.

"Are they all the same?" Neil asked.

Sarah handed him one of the folded quilts. "Handle it carefully. It's been in one position for a long time."

"So quilts are like people."

"What do you mean?"

He chuckled. "When they get old, they need more time to flex after they've been sitting for a while."

Sarah laughed too, while Neil carried the quilt to the bed and draped it on the footboard. The cedar scent strengthened as he picked up a second one and did the same, overlapping the yellow quilt with the pink one.

Opening the last one, Sarah realized they did all have the same pattern. A medallion with a border of flowering vines. She had seen variations of this pattern many times, but she knew each quilt's history was unique.

"It's a pattern often used by the Pennsylvania Dutch," Sarah said when Neil asked if she had any first impressions. "Whether it was made by an Amish woman or someone else will require a lot more research. Can I borrow one of these so I can examine it back at the house?"

"Sure. Do you want to take them all?"

"If you don't mind." She refolded the black-and-white quilt. "Then I can compare them. Maybe I'll be able to determine if they were made by the same person."

"You can tell that?" He began to fold another quilt. "That's amazing."

"Maybe," Sarah cautioned. "But it still won't give me the answer to why the family got up and left."

"That would have been too easy, wouldn't it?"

"I wouldn't mind easy when it comes to solving this mystery. It'd be a nice change."

Neil picked up the quilts. "I'll put these in your car."

"Thanks." Sarah leaned on the top of the cedar chest to make sure it latched. "Neil, you said you'd asked around Maple Hill about the house."

"Quietly. We don't want a lot of looky-loos up here."

"So there won't be a problem with any of us mentioning it?"

He stepped aside to let her lead the way out of the bedroom. "No, that's fine. We're going to have a parade of contractors coming in, so word will get around. Sorry about being secretive before, Sarah. Reginald and I wanted to see your initial reactions when you didn't have any preconceived notions of what was here."

"I guess that makes sense." She ran her hand along the dusty banister edging the gallery.

Neil closed the bedroom door. "Reginald wants to show everyone what he saw in the garage after he pried the shutters open on a couple of the windows. That's why I came looking for you. Everyone else is in the living room."

Sarah doubted there could be anything in the garage more exciting to her than the quilts, but she started down the stairs, testing each tread before she put her full weight on it. "Neil, do you think the family ran away from something or someone?"

"It's possible, but there are a lot of other reasons they could have left."

"Without all their stuff?"

"That's the kicker, isn't it?" He grimaced when he stepped on the riser that gave too much. He didn't say anything else as he went past her down the stairs and out the door.

The family's living room was almost as cluttered as the children's toy room across the wide hall. Sarah had expected the furniture to be protected by sheets, but the only thing covering it was dust. Artwork hung on the walls. Ashtrays had cigarette butts balanced on them, and books lay open, still waiting for someone to come back and finish reading. Knickknacks sat on every flat surface, including the radio that was over three feet tall. A desk had been placed at an angle in the far corner. If the shutters were open and the trees trimmed, whoever sat at that desk would have an astounding view of Maple Hill.

Sarah smiled when she saw Maggie and Chester deep in a debate over the faded marks on two small china pitchers. A third one was on the mantel. Each had a unique crest on the front. Irene held an old-fashioned camera up as if aiming it, then set it down and took a photo of it.

"Sarah!" Irene came over to her. "Could you take some better photos with your camera? I wish I'd thought to bring one. I can't get the detail I want with my cell."

In short order, Sarah was snapping pictures of the camera, a pen, the obscure marks on the bottoms of the jugs, as well as the room itself. She noticed another tapestry through her viewfinder. When she examined it, she saw it was modern. Like the tapestry in the toy room, it also had cloth squares sewn to the bottom of it. The squares were quilted. Was there a pattern to the quilting or did the stitches simply hold the fabric to the torn tapestry?

She didn't have a chance to look more closely because Reginald called, "Hate to interrupt, but let me show you what I found outside. It's pretty cool."

The air was heavy with humidity when Sarah stepped outside. She glanced up, looking for storm clouds. The sky was a hazy blue. The heat probably wouldn't break today.

Reginald led them to the garage that was connected to the house by a covered walkway. It was as big as an old-fashioned carriage house.

"It's locked up," he said, "but I rubbed some grime off the windows after I got the shutters open. You can peek inside. I've got a locksmith coming tomorrow, but I didn't think you'd want to miss seeing these."

Three windows had a thick crust of dirt, but half the bottom pane had been cleaned on two of them. Cobwebs and dust clung to the inside of the glass, obscuring the view. The bright sunshine reflected off the glass, so Sarah cupped her hands on either side of her face. She leaned close to the window and peered into the garage.

Workbenches and storage shelves lined the back wall, and stairs led up to the upper floor. Two vehicles were parked inside, but the vast space had room for at least two more. One was a dark car that resembled a Volkswagen Beetle, but the headlights were raised above a much longer hood. There was no back window, only louvers in a V-design. The other was a carriage, much lighter in color. Its roof was lowered, revealing a single bench seat.

"Does anyone know what that black one is?" asked Sarah.

"I think they both may be cars." Chester looked in the same window. "The one that looks like a carriage doesn't have anything on the front to connect it to a horse. It's probably turn of the last century. The black one has the lines of cars built in the late thirties."

"Wow!" Reginald grinned. "Really? That old?"

"Could be." Chester continued to peer through the window. "But it's hard to be sure from outside. Once we get inside, it'll be easier to tell. Let me take some photos, and I'll see what I can find on the Internet to help us later."

"But cars that old are pretty valuable, aren't they?"

"Some are, especially if they run, but don't get your hopes up until we get a closer look."

Reginald sighed, and Sarah saw his frustration. He wanted easy and quick answers, but Chester wasn't going to give him those. Chester prided himself on *accurate* answers.

They took turns putting their camera lenses against the window and snapping photos. The pictures were laced with images of dusty cobwebs, but Sarah could make out the shapes of the shadowed cars. She wasn't sure what she would do with the photos, but waited while Chester took enough pictures to be satisfied that he had gotten a good one.

They walked toward the front of the house. Sarah learned the other cars were parked on the far side of the porte cochere. When Neil pointed to the quilts piled on the passenger seat of Sarah's car, the others teased her about being a quilt magnet.

"Let's just hope they lead to some answers," Neil said. "The more history we have about this place, the better it'll be."

"And let us know if they've got historical significance or value," Reginald said. "If they do, we might be able to use them in the hotel."

"I'll let you know as soon as I have anything to share," Sarah said.

"Me too," echoed Maggie, Irene, and Chester at the same time.

That brought another laugh. Sarah got into her car while the others walked toward theirs. She had come up the mountain with a lot of questions, and she was going down with even more.

CHAPTER FOUR

Sarah was getting out of her car by the town green the next morning just past eleven when she saw Martha Maplethorpe pulling her green minivan into a parking space a few cars away. Martha wore a vivid pink blouse over her khakis, and her eyes twinkled just as brightly. She gave Sarah a hug as they met in front of The Spotted Dog. Liam's place was Sarah's favorite in the center of town.

She opened the door to the luscious smell of cinnamon and walked in to be greeted by Murphy, Liam's black-and-white corgi and the store's namesake. He wagged his tail so fast it was a blur.

"Hi, Murphy," she said, bending to pat his head.

He gazed at them with hopeful brown eyes, and Martha picked a dog treat out of the bowl on the counter. She gave it to him and left him happily crunching as they went into the café.

Liam came out of the kitchen. His eyes were as expressive as his dog's, but an emerald green. He had almost convinced a couple of Martha's grandchildren that his eyes used to be brown, but that any good Irishman takes a bit of the green with him when he leaves Ireland.

"I see Murphy conned you into giving him a snack, Martha," Liam said as he wiped his hand on his black-and-white checked apron. "He knows a soft touch when he sees one."

"And who keeps that bowl full of treats for customers to sneak to him?" Sarah asked, smiling.

He grinned back. Even though his hair had little of its original red left, he still had a boyish charm that he used liberally on his patrons.

"There's a table by the window," he said. "Good for people watching."

Sarah and Martha took his advice and crossed the cheerful café. They liked sitting where they could watch the green and the parade of traffic around it.

As soon as Sarah and Martha sat, Karen Bancroft, Liam's part-time waitress, came over with menus. She was tall and slim and as pretty as a model.

"How's school going?" Sarah asked as she took a menu.

Karen smiled and fluffed back her short black hair. "I'm spending the fall semester looking at early nineteenth-century architecture in the Berkshires. I think I may do my thesis on it."

"How much do you know about twentieth-century architecture?"

"Not much." Karen's nose wrinkled, rearranging her freckles. "I like *old* houses and buildings. What's got you interested in twentieth-century architecture?"

"I'm doing some research for a friend about a house he's bought," Sarah said.

"I'm sorry I can't help you much."

"That's okay."

"But I can get you something to drink. What would you ladies like?"

After ordering iced coffee and some of the cinnamon buns that smelled so heavenly, Sarah and Martha handed back the menus.

Martha said, "You sounded all excited when you called, Sarah. What's up?"

Sarah told her friend about Neil's call and the visit to the house on Lookout Mountain. Martha's eyes got wider and wider, but she didn't ask any questions until Karen put the coffee and two large rolls in front of them. Icing dripped onto the plate, revealing that the fragrant rolls were warm.

"I've never heard of a house up on Lookout Mountain," Martha said as she drew one plate in front of her. "What's it like?"

"Amazing," Sarah said as she passed the sugar bowl to Martha. "That's the only word I can use to describe it."

Martha put a single spoon of sugar into her coffee and reached for the milk pitcher. "Tell me about it."

"It's like nothing else you've seen around Maple Hill. On the outside, it looks English. All timbered on the upper floor like an old Tudor house. Like a place Shakespeare might have lived. But inside it has this real modern flair with big windows and chrome lighting."

"It sounds strange. You said it's filled with furniture?"

"And dishes and toys and cars and everything else a family would need. As well as four beautiful quilts that are now on my dining room table. The only thing missing is the family." Sarah looked down into her cup as she thought about the drive back from Lookout Mountain.

She'd had to fight to focus on the road because her thoughts kept returning to the question Neil had posed: Why had the family left? Sarah hoped there was some reason for their abrupt departure other than that they were frightened.

"Someone packed those quilts away carefully," Sarah said. "But everything else looks like someone was in a rush when he left. And the quilts were abandoned like everything else."

"It's a real mystery." Martha's eyes twinkled. "So what are you going to do to solve it?"

"I'm going to see if I can get any clues from the quilts. I took a bunch of photos too. Everything from furniture and knickknacks to a couple of cars. I even got pictures of two beautiful tapestries."

"Like the ones they used to hang in castles?"

"Miniatures compared to those. About two feet long." She took a sip of her coffee, then pulled off a small piece of her roll. Putting it in her mouth, she smiled. "Yum."

"Now there's what I like to hear," Liam said as he paused at their table.

"These may be better than your pies," Sarah said as she tore off another small piece.

"But Karen made *these*."

"Oops!" she said as Martha chuckled. "I guess that's because she learned from a master, Liam."

"Good save," Martha said, laughing along with Liam. "Hope you're just as quick at solving Neil's mystery."

Before Sarah could answer, Liam asked, "What clues are you chasing down now?"

Sarah quickly related the previous day's events again. "Neil doesn't mind that anyone else knows about the house now, but he sure was secretive yesterday. Imagine my surprise when I saw Maggie, Irene, and Chester there."

"That's quite a crew." Liam rubbed his hands on his apron. "I wonder why Neil decided to ask Chester *and* Maggie. They're both antique dealers."

Sarah looked down at her coffee cup. Out of all she had told him, Liam had reacted first to Chester's being there. Was he bothered that she was working with Chester? She and Chester were just friends, while Liam...but she couldn't say that in a busy café, even if she knew the right words.

Liam answered his own question by saying, "With such a big house, there are probably enough antiques to keep a dozen experts busy." He started to add more, but his name was called by another customer. He excused himself and went to another table.

Sarah was glad when Martha turned the conversation back to Neil's house. Was Liam really upset, or was Sarah reading too much into a simple question? She took a deep breath. She needed to stop being silly.

"So where will you start looking for clues, Sarah?" Martha asked, drawing her out of her uneasy thoughts.

"The problem isn't a lack of clues. It's how all the clues tie together and lead us to an answer."

Martha set down her coffee cup. "Us? I wish I could help more."

"I understand." Sarah leaned back in her chair and gazed out the window at the shimmers of heat coming off the sidewalk. She looked at her friend and smiled. "You're up to your ears with the Sunday school Round-up this Saturday."

Bridge Street Church sponsored a fun day for the town's grade school children every year in September. Games were planned along with craft projects. Hot dogs and hamburgers were served while a fun movie was shown. Maple Hill's kids, whether they attended Bridge Street Church or not, counted the days from the beginning of school to the Round-up. And every year, Martha was deeply involved in the planning. She loved being around children, whether her own ten grandchildren or other youngsters.

Martha peeled off a piece of her roll. "I haven't missed it in over thirty years. My kids enjoyed it so much."

"Mine did too. It was such a great chance for them to be with their friends without classes or homework."

Martha took another big bite of her cinnamon roll and murmured, "These really are yummy." She licked her lips and smiled broadly. "But this isn't helping you solve the mystery at Neil's house."

"The mystery at Neil's house," Sarah laughed as she sipped her coffee. "That sounds like a Nancy Drew story."

"So let's get started. I've got about an hour and a half before I need to meet with the Round-up committee."

Sarah smiled. Martha loved a mystery as much as Sarah did, and Sarah sensed her friend wished she herself had gone up to Lookout Mountain. Martha always had good ideas about how to solve a mystery, so Sarah was more than pleased to have her help.

"Okay. Let's get started." She slapped the table. "The most important mystery is the one at the center of all the questions about the house. We need to find out more about the family who lived there."

Martha didn't answer quickly as she reached for her cinnamon roll again. She took a bite, then a second one before she said, "Do you think something awful happened? Maybe one of the parents died, and the other one took the children away."

"But that doesn't explain why everything was left behind." Sarah opened her purse. Pulling out a pen and a pad of paper, she set them on the table. "The family was there at least until 1940." She explained about the calendar she had found in the kitchen. "What was going on at that time that would scare someone enough to leave everything behind?"

Martha tapped her cup. "The country was still in recovery from the Great Depression. Maybe they were about to be foreclosed on."

"The house looks like they had plenty of money."

"Don't forget that millionaires went broke during the stock market crash."

"That's true." Sarah wrote down *foreclosure*, and then put *death* beneath it. She wanted to cross out the second word, because it was sad to think of the young children who had played with those toys losing a parent and then their home. "Let's figure out what else it could be. War was looming in Europe and Asia, but the U.S. was still trying to stay neutral then."

"What about the coming war would make a family flee from Maple Hill?"

"Nothing I can think of."

Martha's voice dropped to a conspiratorial whisper. "What if they were gangsters and the feds were on to them? We're fairly close to the Canadian border. They could have been bootleggers."

Sarah laughed. "You've been watching too many reruns of old movies."

"Maybe, but write it down."

"Okay." She wrote *on the lam*, then put down the pad. "This isn't getting us anywhere. Let's research some of the items I saw up at the house." She pushed back her chair and stood. "Why don't you come over to my house, and we'll see what we can find before your meeting?"

Martha looked at her own watch. "Okay."

"I'll meet you there. I'll pay for our coffees and rolls." Sarah held up her hand to halt Martha before her friend could speak. "My treat."

"As long as you let me pay next time."

"You bet." Sarah went to the cash register at the end of the counter closer to the front door. Hot, humid air thrust into the café when Martha opened the door and walked out.

Liam came over to ring up Sarah's order. As he took her money, he said, "I'd like to take you out for dinner tonight. I thought we could drive over to the Waterview by the Cheshire reservoir. The review in the paper said the food is really good." He put her change in her hand and folded her fingers over it beneath his broader ones. "What do you say, Sarah?"

"It sounds nice," she said, startled by his holding her hand in such a public place.

"So let's go and have a nice time. Say yes, and I'll make a reservation." His warm green eyes held her gaze as his beguiling smile tipped his lips.

Sarah nodded because she suddenly seemed unable to remember a single word. She nodded again when Liam said he would call later to arrange a time to pick her up. And she nodded a third time when he told her to have a good day before he raised her knuckles to his lips and brushed them with a quick, teasing kiss. As she left, he winked.

Outside, as she hurried to her car, Sarah released the breath she had been holding... how long? Liam sure knew how to be charming, but he had never flirted with her so publicly. It made her feel as giddy as a teenager. She couldn't stop smiling.

Yet...

Was Liam acting like that because Chester was going to be working with her to solve Neil's mysteries? *Oh, Lord,* she thought while she opened her car door and got in, *don't make me look for trouble where there isn't any. I know you want me to be happy, so help me remember to be grateful for the people you bring into my life instead of questioning what they do or say.*

Vowing not to make everything in her life a mystery, Sarah started her car so she could go home and get to work unraveling the puzzles in Neil's house.

CHAPTER FIVE

Not a breath of air moved through Sarah's house when she opened the door and ushered Martha in. She switched on the oscillating fan on the hall table, but the heat was so thick that the air barely moved.

"We need a good thunderstorm," Martha said, "one of those ear-crackling, house-shaking storms." She paused. "Are you okay? You look flustered."

Sarah considered telling Martha about Liam's invitation and how he had acted by the cash register, but she didn't. She had promised herself that she would focus on the mysteries at Neil's house.

"Must be the heat," she said, and that was at least partly the truth. "Let's get to work."

"Where do you want to start?"

"The pattern used for the quilts."

"That's no surprise."

Sarah unfolded the black-and-white quilt to show Martha its striking pattern, then led the way to the sewing room at the back of the house. "This should be quick. I know where to look to learn more about the pattern. Finding information about the tapestries may take a lot longer."

"Then let's get going." Martha linked her arm through Sarah's.

The sewing room held most of Sarah's quilting tools as well as her computer and printer. On a warm fall day like this one, the sun shone into the room, making it bright and welcoming. She closed the door behind them and turned on the air conditioning unit she'd had her son Jason put in the window. The room would cool quickly. Sarah loved working in the room. The ever-changing colors outside the window inspired her. She could see flowers and vegetables in her garden. The brilliant orange from ripening pumpkins reflected into the room, and soon the colors would change to reds and golds before becoming the eye-searing blue of a winter sky reflected off freshly fallen snow.

Martha drew up another chair by the desk. While the computer booted, Martha viewed the photos from Neil's house on Sarah's camera. She said, "Wow!" over and over.

"I told you. It's amazing."

"You weren't kidding."

It didn't take Sarah long to open her favorite quilting site and find the pattern on the four quilts. It confirmed what she had guessed. The medallion pattern was popular with the Pennsylvania Dutch. What could the connection be between an Amish-style quilt and Neil's house? She began to search the Amish and their quilting history.

Martha leaned over to read the screen. "You know the Pennsylvania Dutch are really German, don't you? Ernie and I went down to Lancaster, Pennsylvania, six or seven years ago, and we learned a lot about their history."

"And they had a lot of quilt shops there, didn't they?"

"Everywhere we went, quilts were for sale. Beautiful quilts. Now that you mention it, I remember seeing some with a similar pattern."

Sarah clicked on a couple more sites. There was a ton of information about Amish quilts on the Internet. She had a lot of reading ahead of her. She sent several articles to the printer, so she could go through them later.

Martha held up the camera so Sarah could see the screen. "Let's see what we can find out about these tapestries. They're definitely old."

"I think so too." She typed in *tapestries* and then clicked on the image links. Leaning in, she scanned through the thumbnails. She didn't see either St. George or a unicorn. She went to the next page.

"There!" Martha pointed at the screen. "About halfway down. It's a unicorn."

Sarah scrolled down and double-clicked the picture. It opened a site with a larger copy of the same photo. It wasn't quite the same image as the tapestry she had seen. The unicorn was inside a slatted fence, but how the unicorn was rendered was similar.

She squinted at the caption. "Hmmm...It says it was made in Germany in the thirteenth century. Look! Here's another tapestry with a unicorn. That one was made in France around the same time."

"Do you think it could really be that old?" Martha asked.

"It's possible. Maggie and Chester were bowled over by what's in the house." She folded her arms in front of her and relaxed against her chair. "I never knew Chester loved cars so much. He was salivating over the two vehicles in the garage."

"He does drive a fancy car."

Sarah laughed as she took the camera from Martha and set it on the desk. "You should have seen him. He was like a kid in a candy shop."

The phone rang. Sarah got up to get it. "Oh…hi, Chester," she said.

Martha chuckled.

Sarah wished she could too. Just because she had accepted an invitation for dinner with Liam wasn't any reason to feel guilty about talking to Chester. He was her friend, and she was being silly again. Focus on the mystery, she reminded herself.

"Yes," she said, "Martha and I are beginning to track down information on the textiles."

"Anything to share yet?" Chester asked.

"The quilts are definitely an Amish pattern, and the style of the unicorn tapestry could be either German or French." Talking about the textiles pushed all other thoughts away.

"That's interesting," Chester said. "I've been doing some research on the cars. I can't resist antique European cars. I think the car that looks like a Volkswagen Beetle is an early prototype made in the thirties in Germany."

"What about the other car? The horseless carriage car?" She idly clicked on the slide show icon on her camera and let her pictures from Neil's house begin cycling. She wondered what they should research next. The rocking horse? The magazines?

"Unfortunately I couldn't get a good look or a good picture of it. When we get back up there, I'll look at it more closely. Some of its lines resemble very early cars made by Mercedes or Bugatti."

Sarah sat straighter in her chair, forgetting about the photos. "So it could be German or Italian."

"Both are German."

"Isn't Bugatti an Italian name?"

"He was Italian, but he founded his factory in Alsace in the early twentieth century."

"Alsace is part of France, so the car could be German or French then."

She could almost see him shake his head as he said, "Nope, whether it's a Mercedes or a Bugatti, it's a German car. Alsace was part of Germany until the end of World War One, and it was annexed by Germany in 1940."

"But it was French in between."

"And now." His laugh boomed through the phone. "Of course, it might not be either model. I won't know until I get back up there and into the garage for a closer look. That's all

I've found out so far. I'm going to e-mail Neil the links for the sites I've been reading. I'll copy you."

Sarah thanked him and hung up the phone. Three different articles from the house, and each one could have a connection to Germany. The quilt connection was the most tenuous, and the tapestry could be French. She needed more information before she drew any conclusions.

When she told Martha what Chester had found out, her friend said, "You don't seem surprised."

"I am...and I'm not."

Martha smiled. "Now there's a straightforward answer."

Sarah went to the computer and zoomed in on the thumbnail of the unicorn tapestry. "It does look similar. Let's see if there's an image like the St. George and the dragon tapestry."

Martha pushed back her chair and stood. "I've got to get over to church. Okay if I call you later to find out what you've discovered?"

"Definitely."

Suddenly a loud squeak rang through the house. Martha gave a startled "What's that?"

"The front door," Sarah said. "It needs oiling, but I never think of it unless it squeaks when I'm opening or closing it. It's probably Lucie."

"Lucie?"

"Lucie Meadows. My newest boarder. She's doing half of her student teaching at Maple Hill High. She's in town for about a month. Next month, she transfers to Pittsfield for the other half of her student teaching session. She's working with special needs children, focusing on children with speech issues."

"She must have been thrilled to discover that she could board here for only a month," Martha said.

"Apparently she's already spread the word, because I've gotten a couple of calls from other college seniors who plan to student teach in Maple Hill."

"Sarah," came a cheerful voice from the front hall, "are you around?"

"Back here in the sewing room."

A young woman opened the door, a bright red backpack slung over one shoulder. Her curly blond hair caught the light from the window and glistened. Her retro plaid skirt and simple white blouse made her look no older than her students. Though she wore black ballerina flats, the top of her head almost touched the door's frame.

After Sarah introduced her and Martha, Lucie's eyes focused on the camera. "Whose house is that?"

Sarah looked over her shoulder. "It belongs to a friend." Martha smiled, knowing that Neil didn't want too many people to know about the house yet.

"I love those windows." Lucie came over to look more closely. "Sorry to intrude, but I forgot some of my project materials, so I decided to get them between students." Her eyes flicked toward the screen as the slide show began to repeat. "Those big windows are wonderful. Bauhaus, right?"

"I don't know," Sarah said.

"What's Bauhaus?" asked Martha at the same time.

Lucie pointed to the screen. "Can you get that picture back?"

Sarah stopped the slide show and flipped to the photo of the windows in the formal foyer. She handed Lucie the camera. "Here it is."

"Yeah, they look like Bauhaus. Was your friend's house built in the thirties?"

"We think so." Excitement began to rise through Sarah. "How did you know?"

"My mother is an interior designer," Lucie said, "and she used to take me with her on her jobs when she couldn't get a babysitter. She usually did colonial homes. Whenever she got a chance to work on a modern or postmodern house, she was really excited. Bauhaus was her favorite, because the founder of the Bauhaus style settled in Massachusetts before World War Two."

"Do you know where he came from?" Sarah asked.

"Germany."

Sarah looked at the picture of the windows. Maybe they were going about this the wrong way. Instead of what was inside the house, maybe they needed to find out more about the house itself.

As soon as she had seen Martha out and promised to tell her everything she found, Sarah returned to her computer. She typed in *property records Massachusetts* and hit the search button. She opened the first site listed, but it required a payment to search records. She knew property records should be available free online. The second site she opened was the one she needed.

She selected Northern Berkshire County. That took her to a page where she found a link to property records. She wasn't sure of the street address for Neil's property, so she typed in *Lookout Mountain* for the street name and put in Maple Hill for the town. She pushed the search button and held her breath.

A new page opened with two properties listed. One would have to be the Morrisseys' farm, the other Neil's house. Various documents were listed for each address, the most current ones first. Mortgages and liens and discharged liens and deeds.

Which property was which?

Sarah clicked on the first deed listed. It was for the Morrisseys' place, and it listed the current owner and the previous one. She read through the survey information and found a listing of owners back into the early twentieth century because each one had been granted an easement and access for the road.

Sarah got excited as she clicked back to the page listing the documents. She looked for a deed listing for the other property. The most recent one had been filed earlier in the year before Reginald and Neil bought the house. She wondered how long it took for the site to be updated. It listed the current owner as Berkshire Properties Management, and the previous one as Meadowlands Family Trust.

If she learned more about them, she might gain more information about the people who had owned the house previously.

She found a Web site for Berkshire Properties Management, but it didn't have a lot of information. The Internet gave her no information on the Meadowlands Family Trust, so she went back to the most recent deed. She read the property description. The specific numbers referred to a survey map, but judging by the long list of directions and distances from the survey, she was certain this was the deed she had been looking for. Unlike the Morrisseys' deed, there was no listing of a grant for access, so she couldn't see the names of previous owners who had agreed to access each time the property changed hands.

Sarah went back to the documents page. The oldest listed documents were from the mideighties. To test the date limit, she searched for her address and Jason and Maggie's. The same result. Online records for Maple Hill didn't go back beyond that date.

She needed to go downtown to the Registry of Deeds and look at the materials that hadn't been put online yet. Then she paused and glanced at the clock. It was past one, and the twins would be arriving midafternoon. She also needed to get ready for dinner with Liam tonight. The search would have to wait until tomorrow.

She hoped it would be worth the wait.

CHAPTER SIX

L iam called to let Sarah know he would be picking her up shortly after four thirty. The only reservations still available had been very early or very late. She was glad he had picked the very early one. She would have to dress quickly after the twins went home, but she wanted to be up good and early in the morning to be at the Registry of Deeds when it opened.

While Sarah waited for the twins to arrive from school, she spread the black-and-white quilt across her dining room table. She had already gathered the tools she needed. She picked up a small handheld black light and turned it on. She aimed at a corner of the black-and-white quilt. If the white fabric had been made before or during World War II, it wouldn't have a bleaching chemical that was later used to keep white fabrics from yellowing. If the chemical was present, it would glow under the black light. She had used the black light before and found, when thread shone brightly, that an antique top had been quilted with modern thread.

There was no glow in either the white fabric or the thread. She switched off the black light and put it aside so she could unfold the other three quilts and examine the quilting lines. All the stitches were neat and almost identical in length and tension against the fabric of the four quilts. She examined the ties around the centers of the medallions. Each had been knotted with three knots. Those two aspects were enough for her to believe that the same person had sewn all four quilts.

She was reaching for her magnifying glass to check the thread when she heard the front door open.

"Grandma?" she heard one of the twins call.

"I'm in the dining room. Come on in." Sarah was especially pleased to see her granddaughters in the middle of such a busy season for them. Amy was busy every afternoon after school with field hockey practice or a game. And Audrey was already working on the middle school's autumn play, a musical she was thrilled about.

Amy shrugged off her backpack as the two girls came into the dining room. She put it on a chair while Audrey put hers on the floor before walking over to the table. Both girls wore jeans. Audrey had on a bright green T-shirt, and Amy a red one. Clasping her hands behind her back, Audrey leaned forward to examine the quilt.

"Did you make it?" Audrey asked.

"No, I think it's from the 1930s. Back before I was born," she added with a smile because she could see both girls trying to figure out if Sarah had been alive then. She showed her granddaughters the experiment she had done.

"That's cool, Grandma," Audrey said. "Whose quilt is it?"

"It belongs to Mr. Lawton and his business partner. They asked me to find out more about it." She smiled at Amy, who was quieter, as usual. "What do you think, Amy?"

"It's nice," she said absently, and Sarah knew her granddaughter wasn't interested in the quilt. Something else must be on Amy's mind.

Sarah smiled. Jason and his family had moved back to Maple Hill not much more than a year ago, but in that time, the twins had changed a lot. Last year, they had been kids. Now they were only part-time kids. The rest of the time, they were becoming teenagers, equal parts thoughtful and thoughtless. Wanting to be just like everyone else while learning about being a unique individual.

It had been a fascinating, frustrating time when Jason and Jenna were teens. Sarah had feared she and Gerry would never survive those years. She and her late husband had prayed a lot, never forgetting that God was a parent, too, of plenty of exasperating children. Every time she or Gerry would remind the other of that, they would laugh, and the anxiety would lessen. She and Gerry had been a good team. She was grateful every day that they had succeeded.

"How about some cider?" Sarah asked.

"Sure!" Audrey said. "Can we have it hot with cinnamon?"

"In this weather?" Sarah shook her head with a laugh. "Aren't you hot enough already?"

"But it tastes better hot. Doesn't it, Amy?"

Her twin nodded but didn't say anything as they walked toward the cheerful kitchen. Audrey chattered about the play and the practices and the lines she had flubbed. Sarah poured cider into three mugs and put two of them in the microwave.

When Audrey excused herself to go to the bathroom, Sarah asked, "Amy, are you okay?"

Amy traced a random pattern on the kitchen tablecloth. "Sure, Grandma. Everything's fine."

"You don't act like it."

Rolling her eyes as only a teenager could, Amy asked, "Did Mom tell you to talk to me?"

"Nope." Sarah opened the spice cupboard and took out a box of cinnamon sticks. "You just seem kind of down."

"I've been slammed with school and field hockey." Amy looked at Sarah for the first time. "They're giving us a lot more homework this year, and coach is making us do a ton of drills."

"Sounds exhausting."

"It is, not to mention everything else."

Sarah put three cinnamon sticks on the table and gave Amy's shoulders a squeeze. "I don't know how you do it. You're a sports star and your grades are good and you've made so many good friends since you moved here. I'm very proud of you, Amy."

Tears welled in Amy's eyes, but she stared at the table again as her sister returned. Sarah knew better than to push. The important thing was that Amy understood her grandmother was there to listen whenever she was ready.

The microwave beeped. Sarah carefully took out the mugs and carried them to the table. Putting one in front of each granddaughter, she sat between them.

Amy seemed to let the warm cider melt away her troubles. Soon she was laughing along with Audrey about their friends at school and a joke they had played on their father.

Too soon, Sarah heard Maggie call a greeting as she came into the house. Was that a second set of footsteps with her?

Irene smiled as she walked with Maggie into the kitchen. They both carried thick books. "Hi, Sarah, girls. I hope you don't mind me hitching a ride over here with Maggie. We couldn't wait to show you what we've found."

Sarah had Audrey pull a couple more chairs up to the table, while Amy poured cider for everyone and asked if they wanted it warm.

"No, thanks, sweetie," Maggie said. "Cool is perfect for today." She wiped her brow as she sat. Opening one of the old books, she flipped to a page with a sticky note on it. "Thanks, Amy," she said as Amy put a cup in front of her. "Sarah, look here."

The upper half of the open pages were filled with odd symbols. The numbers next to them referred to the lower half of the pages, which listed European cities where porcelain was made.

"Chester and I disagreed on where that small jug might have been made," Maggie said. "The porcelain mark was barely visible, but we think it was either this one or that one."

She pointed to two marks that resembled crossed swords. There were only tiny differences between them. "I thought it was the one on the left, and Chester believes it's the other one."

"Tell her which cities they belong to," said Irene, picking up her cup and taking a sip.

"If I'm right," Maggie said, "the jug is from Berlin. If Chester's right, it's from Volkstedt."

"Both are in Germany?" asked Sarah, even though she was already sure of the answer. When Maggie nodded, Sarah looked at Irene. "I bet that camera you found is from Germany too."

"Yes. It's a Leica. It was made in—"

"The 1930s." Sarah and Irene finished in unison, then Sarah quickly explained what she and Chester had discovered along with what her boarder had told her about the founder of the Bauhaus style settling in Massachusetts.

Irene twirled her charm bracelet around her wrist. "Lucie had to be talking about Walter Gropius. He fled Nazi Germany and came to Massachusetts in 1937." She laughed when Sarah looked at her in surprise. "When I worked at the JFK Library in Boston, we often had questions about the architecture. It was designed by I. M. Pei, who was influenced by Gropius. So we were given a crash course in modern architecture. That way, we were ready to answer questions."

"Wow!" said Sarah. "Remind me never to play trivia games against you. I looked up the deed for the house on Lookout Mountain." She explained what she had and hadn't found. "I'm going to the courthouse first thing tomorrow to check out the older records. With all these items pointing to Germany, I want to find out if whoever had it built was German."

"Great idea." Maggie closed the book. "But if the house was built by a German, why does it have that English Tudor façade?"

"Maybe they have timbered houses in Germany too."

Irene said, "You know who would know about that? Karen Bancroft. I'll give her a call tonight."

"Okay," Maggie said, "I'll keep checking on some of the other items."

Sarah offered to send Neil an e-mail, but Maggie held up her hand.

"No, you get ready for your date with Liam, and I'll send the e-mail," she said.

"How do you know about that?" Sarah asked.

"I can't tell you. I promised." Maggie's grin widened, and Irene's eyes sparkled with amusement. "Just suffice it to say that I'll send Neil an update. Why don't we meet at Liam's around eleven tomorrow and share what we've found?"

Sarah and Irene agreed.

When the cider was finished, she showed her daughter-in-law and Irene the quilts she had found at the house. They admired the intricate needlework and wished her luck with finding out more about them.

The twins collected their backpacks. Audrey walked out with Irene and Maggie, but Amy paused and faced Sarah.

"Grandma, are *you* okay?" she asked.

Sarah didn't pretend not to understand. She and Amy had often gone together to Bradford Manor to visit her father. Amy had even followed the Los Angeles Angels baseball team so she could tease her great-grandfather when they won a game against his beloved Boston Red Sox.

"I miss Grandpa," Sarah said, cupping her granddaughter's chin. "And I know you do too. If you need to talk about that, I'm here."

"And I'm here, if *you* need to talk." She gave Sarah a big hug, then ran down the porch steps and out to the car at the curb.

Sarah waved as the red Tahoe pulled away. It blurred as tears filled her eyes. Even though Amy was upset about something she wouldn't discuss, she took the time to worry about her grandmother.

Sarah closed the door as she whispered a prayer of gratitude for her family. It was heartfelt, but swift, because she needed to get ready before Liam arrived. She hurried to the stairs and rushed up to find something nice to wear for their visit to the Waterview restaurant. She couldn't wait.

CHAPTER SEVEN

The restaurant was every bit as beautiful as Sarah had imagined. The ceiling was laced with thick rafters, and the furniture shone with the patina of age and excellent care. While they were led by the hostess to a table with a view of the reservoir and, past it, the mountains, Sarah admired the soft glow of candlelight from the tables and wall sconces.

Liam, handsome in a dark suit, had presented her with pink roses when he picked her up. He told her that he had stopped at Magpie's Antiques to ask Maggie if Sarah liked roses, solving the mystery of how Maggie knew about Sarah's date with Liam tonight.

The food was excellent, and she found Liam's company equally so. The topics of their conversation roamed far and wide, though no matter the subject, Liam kept Sarah entertained with his stories and witty comments. She learned more about a man she had considered a friend for years in one dinner than in weeks of casual conversation. She hadn't known that he once belonged to a Celtic band that had taught old folk songs to a new generation.

"We tooled around the countryside in my old pickup—you know, the one I got when I first got here. People knew the music was coming when they saw that old red and blue truck with the one headlight. I doubt there's a song from the auld sod that we didn't sing at least once," he said as he added more sour cream to his baked potato. "Though everyone wanted us to sing the one about the unicorn, which isn't even an Irish song, but written by an American poet."

"Which were your favorites?" She watched as some ducks landed on the reservoir's choppy waters. Soon they would be heading south for the winter.

"We liked singing "Bonnie Kellswater" and "Green Grow the Lilacs." Our listeners always asked for "Danny Boy" and "The German Clockwinder."

German…It seemed as though every conversation led back to that country. She took another bite of her delicious chicken parmesan while Liam reminisced about his time with the folk band.

"Sarah," Liam said, "you've got that sleuthing look."

"Sleuthing look?" She wasn't always sure when Liam was serious and when he was teasing.

"Sure enough. You're staring across the room, but you don't seem to see anything. That tells me you're thinking deeply about something that's puzzling you. Is it Neil Lawton's house?"

Sarah laughed. "Good guess."

"Neil stopped by this afternoon for some coffee, and he was excited about his dream team helping him get to the bottom of some mysteries about his new house."

"Yes, we're trying to figure out what happened to the family who lived there."

"What have you found so far?"

Sarah outlined what each member of the team had learned and how much they still had to check into. "I know I'm not the only one who can't wait for another invitation to go back up there."

"Neil said that he'd heard from Chester that the old cars in the garage might have some value."

Sarah tried not to read too much into Liam's comment. She knew she shouldn't. Chester was her friend, and he had been helpful when she had solved previous mysteries. And Liam hadn't ever acted as if he saw Chester as competition, but Liam had been really romantic tonight. The elegant restaurant and the flowers. Sarah shook her head slightly to dislodge her silly thoughts.

Focus on the mystery.

"There are a lot of puzzles at that house," she said. "It's going to take a while to appraise all the antiques. Maggie and Chester are determined to get answers, so they'll be swamped with work."

"As determined as you are, I would say. I've always admired that about you, Sarah. You're like Murphy with a bone. You don't give up until you get right down to the marrow."

Her nose wrinkled. "Is that supposed to be a compliment or should I just dismiss it as your usual blarney?"

He put his hand to his heart, and his Irish brogue deepened. "M'fair *cailín*, ye wound me to the heart."

Sarah couldn't help giggling, glad to be able to enjoy the evening before she dug into the mystery once again tomorrow.

Registry of Deeds was painted in block gold letters on the glass of the office door that Sarah opened first thing the next morning. Her thoughts were going a million miles an hour.

The tapestries could be German.

The jug and the camera were made in Germany.

The cars could be German.

The quilts had been made with an Amish pattern, and the Amish in Pennsylvania were descended from immigrants from Germany.

Even the style of the house had been developed by a German immigrant.

Everything seemed to connect to Germany, but why and how? She hoped the answer was in the oldest deed recorded for the Lookout Mountain house.

Going to the counter, Sarah took a deep breath, girding herself for the battle that was about to come. No one was behind the counter, so she folded her arms on it and waited. She didn't look forward to another war of words with Tim Barclay, the less-than-helpful Register of Deeds. He preferred to spend the day immersed in role-playing games on the computer rather than helping residents.

But if he wasn't sitting at his computer, where was he?

Sarah looked at the bell on the counter. If she tapped it to get Tim's attention, he might be annoyed and even less cooperative. If that were possible.

A door behind the counter opened, and a woman Sarah recognized came out. Denise Amberson had been Maple Hill's town clerk for decades. She had gray hair and twinkling blue eyes. A bit chubby, her look and personality were the opposite of Tim's. She took pride in helping people maneuver through town and state bureaucracy.

"Sarah," she said as she came to the counter, "I haven't seen you in ages. I was so sorry to hear about your father's passing."

"Thank you." That familiar pang of sorrow pinched her, but she was able to say, "He had a long and wonderful life, and now he's with my mother. I know that's what he wanted."

Denise smiled. "What can I help you with today?"

"I was hoping to look at some of the old deeds books."

"I'll try to help. Tim's not in today."

Sarah kept her sigh of relief silent. She was glad she didn't have to spend half an hour trying to convince the unhelpful young man to give her access to the records.

"He's at a training class in Boston," Denise said. "I'm just watching over the office and answering the phones, but maybe I can get you what you need."

"I'm looking for deed books from the 1920s and thirties." She wasn't sure when the property had been purchased and the house built.

"I can handle that. Which district are you looking for?"

"Lookout Mountain."

Denise chuckled. "Well, that should make your search quick. Not too many properties up there. The places along Hillside Road at the foot of the mountain and the Morrisseys'." She opened a swinging door in the half wall. "C'mon in. Go into the other room, and I'll bring the books in to you."

Sarah thanked her, but Denise rushed off so fast that Sarah wasn't sure she had heard.

The other room was lined with bookcases. Tall, thick volumes filled the shelves. Sarah drew in a deep breath. The room smelled almost as dusty and abandoned as the house up on Lookout Mountain, though the tables in the middle of the room were polished to a sheen, and the marble floor was spotless.

Footsteps could be heard upstairs and going past in the adjacent hallway. The building was positively alive with the hustle and bustle of work being done.

Denise came in with three ungainly volumes. They weren't very thick, but so tall that they wobbled in Denise's arms. Sarah helped her place them on the table. A puff of dust erupted from the books.

"I guess," Denise said, "nobody's looked at these for a long, long time." She turned when the phone rang in the other room. She rushed away, calling over her shoulder, "Let me know if you need anything else."

Sarah sat at the table and took the top book off the stack. The dates on the spine were from the Roaring Twenties. The book creaked as she opened it and put on her reading glasses. She ran her finger along the map until she found Lookout Mountain Road.

She hadn't been sure if it would have had a name at that time, but now she could search more quickly by scanning through each document and looking for that name. She struck out with the first book, but partway through the second, she saw a deed that listed the Morrissey property to the southwest. That would be in the right direction for Neil's house.

The property was unimproved, so she knew the house hadn't yet been built. She turned the page to see the date and the signature.

The deed was dated 1935, and it was signed by Walter Ackermann.

She tapped the page as she stared at the name. It could be English or German. Just like the house.

But she had a name. Now she had to match it to the man who had bought the land.

After returning the books to Denise and thanking her for her help, Sarah left the courthouse and headed toward the village green. She glanced at her watch. She was going to be about fifteen minutes early meeting Maggie and Irene at Liam's, but she could pass the time looking around the bookstore or sipping a chai while she waited for them to arrive. She couldn't wait to share what she had found.

Liam smiled at Sarah when she walked into the café. "Just one?" he asked.

"I'm meeting Maggie and Irene. They should be here in ten or fifteen minutes."

He led her to her favorite table and handed her a menu. As he bent toward her, he said, "I had a lovely time last night."

"Me too." She smiled, grateful for Liam's kindness. It warmed a part of her that had become so cold with grief since Gerry's death and now her father's passing.

"We'll have to do it again soon."

She nodded and guessed her eyes were twinkling as brightly as his.

A bell dinged from the direction of the kitchen. Liam winked before hurrying in to get something out of the oven.

Sarah sat and put her purse by her feet, then gazed out the window, wondering when she or one of the others would find the keystone clue. The clue that held everything together perfectly. What they had found so far seemed to be leading in the same direction, but she wasn't sure what would be at the end of the road.

A few minutes later, Liam came over with a steaming cup. The aroma of spices told her that it was her favorite chai.

He set the cup in front of her, but didn't have time to say anything before he was called to another table.

Maggie and Irene walked in and joined Sarah. When Karen came over, Irene said, "Thanks again for your help last night, Karen. I found just what I needed on that Web site you gave me."

"Glad to help." She gave them one of her scintillating smiles. "It's fun to put what I'm learning at school to work. Now what can I get for you?"

They each ordered the special. Fruit and yogurt drizzled with honey and a whole wheat roll. Karen told them she would bring over their coffee with the rest of their order.

Irene handed Sarah some pages. "This is what I got from the German tourist site that Karen sent me to. As you can see, there are plenty of timbered structures—or half-timbered, as they call them—in Germany. They have a whole tourist route where you can drive through towns with these buildings."

Sarah scanned through them, then handed them to Maggie. "Then our assumption that the house was built in an English style could be wrong."

Karen returned with two steaming cups and three plates. She didn't stay to chat more because a tour bus had just stopped in front of the café. She rushed to the counter for the tourists who were already coming in and browsing the bookshelves.

Maggie put down the pages and took a bite of the sliced apples. "Did you find the original deed, Sarah?"

"The property was bought by Walter Ackermann in 1935."

"At least we have a name now," Irene said. "If you want, Sarah, I can look up the 1940 census records and see if he was still in Maple Hill by then."

"He could have been, because the calendar I saw in the kitchen was from 1940."

Maggie's forehead threaded with concentration. "A calendar?"

"Yes, in the pantry. I thought I mentioned it."

"Goodness, now I don't remember," Maggie said.

Irene spread butter on her warm roll, then handed the butter to Sarah. "We need a central clearinghouse for this info."

"Why don't you send everything to me?" Sarah asked. "I've got a file set up with your e-mail addresses already. I'll make sure I get the information to everyone else. That way nobody gets left in the dark."

"That's a great idea," Irene said. "What about Reginald and Neil?"

"I do need Reginald's e-mail. I'll ask Neil for it." She swirled an orange slice in the yogurt. "After this, I'm going to the tax office. Then I want to see what more those quilts can tell me."

Maggie dipped her knife in the butter. "You always say quilts have a story to tell. I hope this one has a happy ending."

"For us *and* the family."

CHAPTER EIGHT

The tax office was busy when Sarah walked in that afternoon. She took a number slip. Number 56. The lit sign announced number 47 was being served. At least the line wasn't as long as it was at the Registry of Motor Vehicles. She had waited for over an hour at the RMV the last time she'd had to renew her license.

She found an empty seat and settled her purse on her lap to wait. Every few minutes, the number would change on the lighted board, and someone would call out the new number.

Half an hour passed before Sarah's number was announced. She got up and went to the counter where a harried young woman gave her a forced smile and asked how she could help.

"I'd like to look at the tax records for this property." She pushed forward the slip of paper that had the number of the deed recorded with Walter Ackermann's name.

The young woman glanced at it, then handed it back. "Ma'am, the quickest way to view our tax records is on your computer."

"I didn't see tax records when I went to the property records site online."

"You probably went to the state property records site." She didn't wait for Sarah's reply. "Go to the Maple Hill municipal site and click on the tax record link on the left. Then you can put in this information and see all the tax records for that property."

"Thank you."

The woman was already looking past her and calling to the next customer.

Sarah drove straight home and switched on her computer. After pouring herself some iced tea against the heat of the midday sun, she carried the glass back into her cooled sewing room.

With a few keystrokes, she got onto the town site. She wished she had tried it earlier, but she had been focused on finding the deed and hadn't thought to look elsewhere. The link for tax records was where the young woman had said it would be.

The site was much more user-friendly than the state one had been. She typed in the address for the house exactly as she had copied it off the deed. She clicked the button to have the records show up in reverse chronological order, so she could see the oldest ones first.

The screen blinked, and then a list for both properties on Lookout Mountain Road appeared. She clicked on the link for Neil's house.

A new list appeared, showing the appraised value of the property and the tax rate for each year. She looked to the right side where the name and address of the taxpayer was listed.

Johnson, Carl and Edith were the names in the first block.

Johnson?

There must be a mistake.

Sarah returned to the search page and put the information in again. She got the same result. She looked at her notes, then back at the screen. The earliest record was for the Johnsons, and it was dated 1938. Had the Johnsons purchased the house from Walter Ackermann? If so, why weren't there any tax records with his name for 1935?

The Johnsons were listed as owners for 1938 and until the 1940 tax year. The rest of the entries had the address of a tax accountant in Maryland. Harold Lehrer. She copied his name and address, though there wasn't a telephone number. She hoped the firm was still in business.

Sarah opened another screen and typed in the address. A map popped up with the name of the businesses situated there. One was Lehrer and Sons. It had to be the same firm.

She switched back to the screen with the tax information. She paged down to the most recent year. The name was still listed as Harold Lehrer, so either Berkshire Properties

Management hadn't owned the house long before selling it to Neil and Reginald or they had continued to have Lehrer and Sons handle the taxes. Neil would take care of paying the property taxes from this point forward, but she might get some information from the previous accountants. Probably not the Harold Lehrer who had handled the taxes for the Johnsons, because he would be in his nineties. Maybe his son or grandson.

Sarah got her phone and dialed the number for the firm. It rang once, then a second time before it was answered in a pleasant female voice, "Lehrer and Sons. To whom may I direct your call?"

"May I speak with Mr. Lehrer, the tax accountant?" Sarah asked.

"Ma'am, which Mr. Lehrer do you wish to speak to?" The voice grew cooler as if she'd had to explain this too many times already that morning. "There are three who work here."

"May I speak to Mr. Harold Lehrer?"

"Who may I say is calling?"

"Sarah Hart."

The receptionist seemed to wait for Sarah to say more. When Sarah remained silent, the woman asked her to hold while she checked with Harold Lehrer.

Sarah listened to classical music until a man said, "Harold Lehrer. How may I help you?"

It took only a few seconds to explain why she had called, but Mr. Lehrer interrupted before she finished.

"I am sorry, Mrs. Hart, but I can't discuss my clients' business without their express permission."

"I was hoping you could just confirm that you were the accountants for either Walter Ackermann or Carl and Edith Johnson." She knew she was being pushy, but she didn't want to let this clue lead to a dead end.

"I don't recognize either of those names as either present or former clients of this company." His voice became less rigid as he added, "I'm sorry, Mrs. Hart, that I can't help you, but we've never had clients by that name. Are you sure you've got the right accounting firm?"

"Your company is listed on the tax records for a property on Lookout Mountain Road in Maple Hill, Massachusetts, but you've never had any of those people as your clients?"

"That's right."

"About the property—"

"That's all I can say without violating my clients' privacy. Have a nice day."

Sarah put the phone on her desk and opened her e-mail to send a message to the others about what she had found. Two messages waited for her. One from Neil said he would get Reginald's e-mail address to her as soon as he heard back from his business partner. Reginald was away from his Albany office, but Neil had left him a voice mail message and expected to hear from him soon.

The other message was from Irene. She had gone through the Maple Hill census from 1940 and hadn't found any entry for Walter Ackermann.

"No kidding," muttered Sarah as she typed her message to Neil and the rest of his team. She added that maybe the Johnsons could be found in the 1940 census.

She pushed back from the computer. There was one other place she could check where she might find something to help them. She glanced at her watch. The library was open for another hour. She didn't have time to waste.

Sarah remembered warm summer days from her childhood when she had come to the library and sat with her back against the shelves while she read a favorite book for the third or fifth or tenth time. The library had smelled of heat and books then, just as it did now.

"Hi, Sarah." Spencer Hewitt, the librarian, greeted her from where he was putting books on the new titles display. "Can I help you find anything today?"

"Okay if I go up and check something in the newspaper archives?"

"Sure." He wiped his sweaty brow on his sleeve as he walked over to the desk. "Even with the air on, it's warm. I'm ready for fall."

"You know New England weather. It's never what you expect it to be."

"That's the truth. Let me know if I can help." He opened the desk's top drawer and drew out a key ring. He handed it to her. "The library's closing in forty-five minutes, but if you need a little extra time, I've got some paperwork I need to do. It'll take me about an hour."

"I should be done long before then, but thanks, Spencer."

He gave her a smile and wished her good luck in her search.

Sarah climbed the stairs to the library's upper level. The door to the archives was at the back beyond the DVDs and current magazines. Nobody was upstairs, and she walked directly to the door and into the room where shelves held so much of Maple Hill's history. The only sounds were the buzz of a lone fly and the muted rumble of traffic around the town green.

Sarah surveyed the shelves. The older magazine she had found at the house was dated early 1938. Why not start the year before?

Sarah walked along the shelves, running her finger across the spines of the bound newspapers. There were two volumes for each year in the 1930s. She carried the first volume for 1937 to a table and sat.

The newspaper pages were much wider than modern ones, so the open book covered almost the whole table. There were fewer pictures and longer articles than in the current *Maple Hill Monitor*.

Page after fascinating page, she was tempted to read articles about the issues of the day that seemed quaint over seventy years later. The ads drew her eyes. She didn't recognize many of the products or the shops around Maple Hill. A few products, like laundry detergents, were still sold at the local supermarket.

Her back grew cramped, but she forgot the discomfort when she came to the issue for September 20, 1937. A large picture was at the top of the second page. It was the house up on Lookout Mountain.

In front of it stood a tall, straight-backed man who appeared to be in his early forties. He wore a dark suit and a fedora that shadowed his face. *The woman beside him must be his wife.* She was dressed in a thinly knit sweater and skirt that dropped to midcalf. The sweater was belted at her narrow waist, and she wore a jaunty, small-brimmed hat. Sarah remembered Myrna Loy wearing something similar in *The Thin Man* movies.

Four children posed in front of them. All four had light hair. The two girls wore Shirley Temple curls and high-waisted print dresses. The boys looked uncomfortable in sailor suits. One of the boys was making a face at the camera.

Sarah laughed in spite of herself. The boy was doing what kids had done since the beginning of photography.

She squinted to make out the tiny, faded words beneath the picture. Her heart skipped when she read, "Carl and Edith Johnson and family at their recently completed house on Lookout Mountain."

Sarah returned the books to the proper places on the shelf, then locked the door behind her. She returned the key to Spencer.

"That was quick," he said.

"Fortunately, yes. Do you mind if I use one of the computers? I won't be long." She didn't want to admit that her curiosity wouldn't let her wait until she got home.

"Go ahead." He motioned toward the three computers at one side of the room.

Sarah sat at the first one. She typed in Walter Ackermann. Several sites appeared on the list. She glanced through them. Several blogs and a few business pages. She added Maple Hill to the search. Again there were results, but not a single one was connected to Maple Hill, Massachusetts.

She did the same for the Johnsons, and she got the same outcome. Typing in Lehrer and Sons brought her right back to the business site.

Other than the accountants, she couldn't find anything that connected either Mr. Ackermann or the Johnsons to Maple Hill. She needed to find another way to get to the truth.

Maybe it was in the quilts ...

Sarah took off her glasses and set them and her Bible on the living room table by her rocking chair. Her nightly reading brought her calm at the end of a hectic day. Tonight, she had read the parables of how those who were lost were found. The shepherd hadn't given up looking for his sheep, and she couldn't give up until she found out what had happened to the missing family.

She had examined the quilts after supper, but she hadn't discovered much more. The quilter had been an expert, because each stitch was almost identical to the others in the quilting lines. Making four identical quilts would have bored Sarah, but she wondered if the seamstress had made one for each of the towheaded children in the newspaper photo.

Sarah reached to turn off the living room lamp, but paused. Footsteps sounded on her front porch just before there was a firm knock on the front door.

Who was at her door at this hour? It must be past nine, and fog had clamped down completely on the street. She went out into the front hall. Lucie looked down the stairs and shrugged when Sarah glanced at her.

Sarah opened the door. "Neil!" Her surprise burst out of her along with his name.

"I'm sorry it's so late, Sarah, but do you have a few minutes?"

"Sure. Come in." She stepped aside to let him enter. Tendrils of fog danced around the newel posts on the porch, and the streetlights were dim within the mist. She closed the creaking door, but it resisted, the wood swollen. She was so ready for cooler weather.

Neil sat on the living room sofa and clasped his hands on his knees. His eyes followed her when she walked past him, but he didn't speak until she sat again in her rocker.

"I got your e-mail about the tax records," he said. "I didn't mean for you to spend so much time satisfying our curiosity about the house."

"It's less about the house and more about the family who lived there." Sarah slid her hands down the rocking chair's smooth arms. Gerry had made it for her, and she found it both comforting and inspiring.

Her late husband had shared her faith, her love of family, and her need to help others. He would have understood how, now that she had begun to look for the truth about what had become of the family who had lived on Lookout Mountain seventy years ago, she couldn't stop.

"I figured," Neil said, "that you would help us clear up the mysteries at the house by tracking down the origins of a few pieces. I didn't have any idea that you'd be going through tax records and contacting tax firms."

Sarah frowned. He stared at the unlit fireplace as if it were the most fascinating thing he had ever seen. Was he avoiding looking at her?

"I'm happy to do it, Neil, but if you want me to stop..." She didn't want to say that she would give up the search, because she was too curious to walk away with unanswered questions.

"It's not me." His eyes flicked from her to the hearth. "It's Reginald. He's concerned that we might be needlessly stirring up a hornets' nest."

"Really? How?"

"Reginald is upset that you contacted the tax firm without consulting us first." Neil sighed, then looked her squarely in the eye. "Sarah, you and I have known each other for more years than either of us is willing to admit, but Reginald doesn't know you. He's wondering why you've gone to such lengths, probably thinking you have an ulterior motive."

"If you know me, Neil, then you already know the answer."

He chuckled. "I do. You love puzzles, and once you begin trying to solve one, you don't give up until you have the answer." Balancing one leg on his other knee, he relaxed for the first time since he had come into the house. "And, Sarah, even though I told Reginald I'd speak with you, if you want to keep looking for the reason those people left, I'm fine with that. I really want answers too. I don't like mysteries."

Sarah began rocking slowly. Neil was a man of integrity, so she wasn't surprised that he had chosen to tell her what his business partner had said. On the other hand, he was an accountant, and he liked to have everything neatly arranged. Owning a house with so many mysteries wouldn't sit well with him.

"Will Reginald be okay if we keep looking?" she asked.

He considered her question for a moment, then nodded. "There's more bark than bite to him. When we were in college, he always talked about doing some huge project to show our professors he should get a higher grade. I'm not sure he ever did."

"So you were good friends in college?"

"Yes, and roommates for a couple of years. He's an intense guy, but I'm not Mr. Laid-back either. We had a good time at school, but we'd kind of lost touch other than Christmas cards. Then he called and asked if I wanted to go in with him on this investment in Maple Hill."

Sarah digested that fact. She couldn't imagine calling someone out of the blue and asking him to invest so much money.

"I'm not crazy," Neil said as if Sarah had spoken her thoughts. "Reginald has had some flops with his investments, but overall he's done very well through the years. Even with those few missteps, he's such a shrewd businessman, he was able to bounce back quickly. He's asked me several times to work on one project or another with him."

"And you said yes this time."

"Yes, because it was in Maple Hill. I like the idea of doing something good for both the town and myself at the same time. Who would have guessed that the house would turn out to be the epicenter for a mystery?"

Sarah couldn't help smiling at Neil's question, though it was filled with his frustration. He had probably expected to fix up the house and turn a profit quickly.

"What do you know about the previous owners?" she asked when she realized he was waiting for her to say something. "Berkshire Properties Management?"

"I don't have a copy of the deed yet, because it's got to be filed at the courthouse. Once I get it back, you're welcome to look at it."

"Shouldn't that be soon?"

"Probably early next week, but you know how bureaucracy is. It could take a couple of extra days, if not weeks."

Sarah swallowed her impatience. Getting riled over something that couldn't be changed was silly.

"Berkshire Properties," Neil went on, "is where Harriet Richards, the Realtor, works. Reginald contacted them several months ago and asked them to keep an eye out for an appropriate property." He pushed himself to his feet. "The rest will have to wait until we get the deed back. I'll call you when it arrives."

"I appreciate that, Neil." She got up too.

Sarah walked to the front door with him. He reached for the knob, but didn't turn it. He started to speak a couple of times, then halted himself as if he were searching for different words.

At last, he said, "I hope you won't let Reginald's comments bother you."

"I won't, and I won't contact anyone else without clearing it with you first."

"That'll probably make him feel better." Twisting the knob, he opened the door and stepped into the foggy night. "By the way, I've hired a cleaning team. A husband and wife with excellent recommendations and references. The next time we go up to the house, we won't have to wade through layers of dust." His smile wavered before he said, "I'm hoping to get everyone together for another visit in a few days."

"Just let me know, and I'll try to make it. I'd like to have another chance to examine those tapestries with the blocks sewn along the bottom."

"In the whole mess, I didn't even notice them." He waved good night before walking down the porch steps and toward the street.

Sarah closed the door and locked it. Maybe by the next time she went up to the house, she would have some answers. Or at least she would know the right questions to ask so she could see the truth amid the family's abandoned possessions.

CHAPTER NINE

Cheers erupted through the warm Saturday afternoon air as Amy's team ran toward their goal and intercepted the ball, sticks clacking. One girl emerged from the jumble.

Sarah cheered as Amy, in her red plaid skirt, rushed the other way down the field. The ball seemed to dance along her hockey stick. She controlled it and sent it through the other team's goal. The rest of her team encircled her, hugging and bouncing as if they were standing on pogo sticks. They broke apart when a whistle blew to start the next play.

Time was called, and water was taken to the girls. It was only a little past noon on Saturday, but the heat was building. The girls drank greedily, then lined up in ragged lines in the middle of the field.

No clouds over the mountains to the west offered the promise of a storm to break the heat. The unrelenting sun continued to burn down on them.

"Want more sunscreen?" Jason asked from where he sat one row below Sarah.

She took the bottle and rubbed some on her arms and face as well as the back of her neck. She handed the bottle to him, taking care not to knock over her iced tea.

"Who'd ever guess we'd be sweltering in September?" He spread the lotion on his neck. "It used to be hot like this in California, and I'd hoped we'd put those heat waves behind us when we came here."

Audrey walked past the bleachers with three friends. All of them were talking at the same time and giggling, and two were sharing one set of ear buds connected to Audrey's MP3 player. A boy walked behind them, not part of the group, but looking like he wanted to be.

Jason called to Audrey and held up the bottle. She glanced at him, but just shook her head and followed her friends to the far end of the bleachers. She didn't seem aware of the boy trailing her like a disconnected shadow.

Jason sighed.

"It can't be as bad as that sounds," Sarah said.

"I know it's tough being a teenager, and I wish I could make it easier for them. But it's rough when they're embarrassed by their old man."

Sarah patted his shoulder. "Don't you remember the time you begged your father and me to stay away from where you were going with your friends?"

"I didn't!" He looked back at her.

"You did."

When he rolled his eyes and smiled, Sarah could see both his father and his daughters in his expression. She also saw his sadness that the little girls who, only a year ago, had come running to hug him when he got home from work were growing more independent.

"Maybe it'd be easier if they were boys," Jason said as he turned back around to watch the game. "I don't think boys are as moody. Amy almost bit everyone's head off this morning."

"Trust me. Boys aren't any easier than girls." Sarah kept glancing at the boy who now sat behind Audrey, his gaze fixed on her face. Audrey was busy with her friends and seemed oblivious to him.

Jason put two fingers in his mouth and whistled shrilly. Amy's team was celebrating again, but Sarah hadn't seen which girl had sent the ball into the goal.

Amy glanced toward her father and waved. Jason's grin grew even wider.

Sarah continued to glance toward Audrey as the Pittsfield team took control of the ball and rushed down the field to score. Groans sounded around her, while the bleachers on the other side of the field erupted in cheers.

"Defense isn't exactly the strong suit of either team," Sarah said. "But at least they're having a good time."

"How's your part of the mystery going?" Jason asked beneath the cheers and shouts.

"Slowly." She took a sip of iced tea. "It's bizarre, Jason. Everything that's caught our eyes seems to have come from

Germany. Did Maggie tell you that we've got two different names for the family who supposedly lived there at the same time? I can't find when Mr. Ackermann sold the property to the Johnsons."

"The sale might not have been recorded properly. It may have been a handshake deal." He leaned his elbows on his knees and propped his chin on his hand. "Do you think the family could have gone back to Germany? They might have left everything behind because it was too expensive to ship."

Sarah cheered as Amy's team prevented Pittsfield from scoring a goal, then said, "That's a real possibility. Maybe I've gotten so used to seeing a mystery everywhere that I overlooked a simple explanation like that." Then she shook her head. "But why would anyone take their family across the Atlantic at the beginning of the war? I don't know if civilian passengers were allowed to travel on ships at that time."

"True. Most of the ships were transporting troops and supplies."

"And there were U-boats prowling the shores here and in Europe. I wouldn't take children into a war zone unless I had no other choice."

"Maybe they didn't."

As Sarah continued to watch the games, her son's words resonated in her mind. She thought of the list she had made up with Martha and then tossed away. The events on the list had been catastrophic. Had one of them compelled a family to risk being sunk in the icy waters of the North Atlantic?

She couldn't help imagining the Johnsons waking their four small children in the middle of the night and sneaking out. Maybe they had told the children that they were going for a short ride, so they didn't need to take anything with them. Or perhaps the children had taken one special toy with them to comfort them when they realized they weren't coming home.

However, neither of those scenarios explained the lack of photographs. Had there never been any in the house, or had they been destroyed? If the Johnsons had been the family who fled, they must have forgotten about the picture in the Maple Hill newspaper. Or they didn't have a way to destroy archived copies.

"Mom?" Jason said, interrupting her thoughts. "The game is over."

Sarah smiled and apologized for her drifting thoughts.

"How are you doing?" he asked as he climbed up and sat beside her. "It feels like so long since Grandpa died and yet... If I can do anything..."

"I'll let you know." She patted his hand. "I find myself thinking that I haven't stopped by Bradford Manor lately and that I should go over today. Then I remember."

"I'm going out to the cemetery tomorrow. Would you like to go with me?"

"Yes. I'd like that. Very much."

"Good." Jason stood and shoved his hands in his pockets. The motion instantly brought both her late father and Gerry to mind. She wondered if her son had picked the habit up from his father or his grandfather. "It seems right to visit them on Sunday. We went to Grandma and Grandpa's house so many Sundays after church. I've been thinking about that a lot since Grandpa passed."

"Are you thinking, too, about the times we had to practically drag you out the door? Back when *you* were a moody teenager?" She smiled and squeezed his arm.

He laughed before he hugged her. "Thanks, Mom. See you tomorrow morning."

She gave him a kiss on the cheek.

Sarah remained in the bleachers as the two teams and the spectators began to disperse. She wondered what her father might have been able to tell her about the Johnsons and Mr. Ackermann and the house on Lookout Mountain. He had become a part of her mystery solving, and she missed the small role he often played.

She reminded herself she wasn't on her own solving this puzzle. What she needed was Martha's clear-eyed perspective. She glanced at her watch. One thirty. The Bridge Church Round-up must already be underway.

Sarah stepped down off the bleachers and saw Amy walking toward her with another player. She was about to call congratulations, but paused when a boy intercepted the girls. Amy's cheeks became a brighter pink, and she stared at him as he chatted with the other girl. Amy didn't seem to be talking. Just listening.

Amy glanced toward her, and Sarah gave her a bolstering smile. Her granddaughter ducked her head. Parents and grandmothers were in the way at times like this.

Sarah took the hint and walked in the other direction before her granddaughter could see her smile.

An hour later at Bridge Street Church, Sarah still hadn't had time to talk to Martha. Sarah was put to work in the kitchen as soon as she arrived at the church. She mixed gallons of fruit juice before starting to frost what looked like an acre of cupcakes. Paper plates and cups were unpacked and carried out to the room where the movie would be shown.

Martha was outside, supervising the games. She peeked into the kitchen once, but didn't have time to talk. Sarah knew her friend would be too exhausted to talk tonight. Maybe tomorrow at Sunday services...

Sarah's shoulders were aching from hunching over the table as she moved the last tray of cupcakes next to a bowl of chocolate frosting. Two dozen more to go, and then she would be done.

"Hi, Grandma." Amy walked into the kitchen. She still wore her field hockey skirt. Its pleats looked tired, and so did she. "What are you doing?"

"I'm frosting these cupcakes. Do you want to help? It'll be nice to have the company." Sarah handed her the other spatula and turned the tray so the other end was close to her granddaughter.

Amy picked up one cupcake, but accidentally put her finger through the paper cup. Tears welled in her eyes.

Sarah took the cupcake and set it back on the tray. She hated seeing her usually vivacious granddaughter downtrodden. "Why don't you get a stool and come over and supervise? Every job needs a supervisor, doesn't it?"

Amy gave her a small smile before turning to get the stool that had been left by the sink. She set it beside the table as Sarah spread chocolate icing on the ruined cupcake.

"Are you hungry?" Sarah asked.

"Starving. I could eat a horse."

"I don't have a horse, but how about doing a little quality control for me?" Sarah handed the punctured cupcake to her granddaughter. "Why don't you make sure these cupcakes are good enough for the little kids?"

Amy didn't need to be asked twice. She peeled off the yellow paper and took a huge bite. "It's good!"

"There's nothing that chocolate can't help." Sarah held out the extra spatula. Amy took it and ran a finger along it and popped her frosting-laden finger in her mouth.

Sarah pulled up another stool and sat facing her granddaughter. "Your great-grandmother taught me about the healing properties of chocolate. Somehow, she always had brownies around when I needed comfort food, especially when I was your age."

"I hate being thirteen."

"I did too. It was as if all the rules had changed."

Amy sat straighter. "That's it! It's like everyone but me changed over the summer. If I even as much as say hi to a boy, everyone thinks I'm in love with him."

"At least you can speak to a boy. I remember being so tongue-tied I couldn't say two words in a row."

"You?" She reached for another cupcake and peeled back the paper. "You can talk to anyone any time, Grandma."

"Maybe now, but not back then. The worst was when I had science class with the best-looking guy in school. Every day I dreamed about the next time I'd see him and how eloquent I'd be. Then I'd see him and be completely mute. I was so afraid of saying the wrong thing that I couldn't speak at all."

Amy stared at her in disbelief. "Did you ever talk to him?"

"Not for a long time, but eventually I did. And you know what I found out? He was just as nervous around me as I was around him."

"How did you get up the guts to talk to him?"

"I didn't. I was friends with his cousin, and I spent a lot of time talking to her. When he joined us, I just kept talking to her and eventually we both were talking to her and finally talking to each other. Building a relationship can take time, but it's worth it in the long run."

Amy nodded. "I know, Grandma. When we first moved to Maple Hill, it took a long time to make real friends. But it was wicked worth it. See ya, Gram."

Blowing Sarah a kiss, she ran out of the kitchen and wound her way through the crowd of younger children who had come into the church for the movie and treats.

Sarah smiled as her granddaughter disappeared around a corner. Had Amy guessed that Sarah was talking about Gerry? Whether she had or not, maybe the story would help her with whatever was bothering her.

The church no longer echoed with the excited shouts and laughter of children by the time Sarah returned to the kitchen to get her purse. The dishes had been washed and the trash cans emptied. It had been a wildly successful Round-up. She had seen Martha beam with pride when parents thanked her for her hard work. Martha had asked Sarah what she wanted to talk about, but instead of explaining, Sarah had asked Pastor John to drive Martha home because she was half-asleep on her feet.

The sun was casting long shadows across the parking lot when Sarah walked to her car. Heat rose from the asphalt, but the air seemed to have a touch of fall in it. Or was it just the crunch of the leaves that had started to fall?

She pulled out her keys and opened her car door. A shadow fell over her.

"Sarah?"

She nearly jumped at the voice, though a look over her shoulder had her letting her breath out in an unsteady laugh. "Liam, I didn't expect to see you here."

"I had a brainstorm, and I tried calling you."

"With all the noise from the kids, I couldn't hear myself think, let alone hear my phone ring."

"Sounds like it was a fun day."

She tossed her purse in on her car's passenger seat, then closed the door. "They had a blast. So let's hear about this brainstorm."

"Have you tried looking in old phone books?" Liam leaned against the car, his easy smile returning. Yet his eyes were intense while he told her about his idea. "If they had a phone up at Neil's new house, the number and their names would be listed in the Maple Hill phone book."

"What a great idea!" It really was, and it was simple too. Old phone books must be available somewhere. Online? At the historical society? Or were they upstairs in the library and she had walked right past without noticing?

He winked at her. "I only have great ideas, Sarah. I thought you knew that."

"I do now."

"Let me tell you about my other great idea. Me taking you out for dinner tonight."

Sarah looked down at herself. "It'll have to be some place where they don't mind chocolate stains on my shirt."

He chuckled. "Let's go out to Ella's diner."

Sarah agreed and decided that while she enjoyed dinner with Liam she would put aside the mystery. Monday morning would be time enough to begin again, and she would hit the ground running with chasing down Maple Hill's old phone books.

CHAPTER TEN

The historical society was filled with third graders when Sarah walked in on Monday morning. Irene had them sitting in a circle in front of the empty hearth. All the windows were open, but the main room of the historical society was as hot as if a roaring fire burned in the fireplace.

Irene gave a furtive wave to Sarah, but didn't pause in her lesson about how the first settlers in Maple Hill cooked their meals.

Sarah went around the curved counter and sat on a folding chair to wait for Irene to finish. After a Sunday spent with her family at church and the cemetery, Sarah was ready to get back on the trail of the truth.

She had seen Martha at church, but hadn't mentioned anything about the mystery. Her friend was so pumped from the successful Round-up, though dark circles ringed her eyes. They had talked about their favorite activities and who should chair the committee next year. Sarah suspected her friend had found that supervising the plans and dealing with her husband's Parkinson's was too much.

The kids clapped politely when Irene finished. Sarah listened, smiling, as they asked questions. The third graders had a very interesting perspective on life three hundred years before.

Irene took each question seriously. She didn't laugh until the door closed behind the last child and teacher.

"Talking to grade-schoolers is one of my favorite parts of this job," she said, carrying her leftover handouts to the counter. "Thanks for being patient. You look like a woman with a mission."

"Liam gave me a good idea about finding information about our elusive family." Sarah stood as she explained Liam's suggestion about old phone books. "Do you have any here?"

Irene shook her head. "You'd think that we would, because the telephone has become such a vital part of life. But we don't. I guess nobody ever considered that something so throwaway would ever be valuable. Have you tried the library?"

"Going there was my Plan B."

Irene straightened her stack of handouts and put them on a shelf under the counter. "I wonder how much longer phone books will be printed. The Internet is great for looking something up, but its information is fleeting. In the future, anyone looking for facts about the here and now is going to be out of luck."

"True." Sarah walked around the counter. "Let me see what they've got at the library."

"Just remember that it's a long shot. Less than half of the homes in Maple Hill would have had a phone in the 1930s. The phone only stopped being a luxury after the war."

Sarah sighed. Every good idea seemed to lead nowhere. Telling herself not to be pessimistic, she said, "I remember when we had party lines, and every phone on the line had a different number of rings. And," she said, to prop up her hopes, "anyone who had all that nice furniture surely had a phone."

"Let's hope so." Irene glanced at her watch. "I've got a few minutes before the other third grade class arrives. While you go to the library, I'll get on the computer here and check the 1940 census and see if I can find the Johnson family. It's quick with this census because it's online."

"Much better than having to go through line by line as we've had to before." Sarah opened the door and grimaced as hot air struck her. "This weather's got to break soon."

"There were a couple of rumbles of thunder last night, and I saw some heat lightning too. Eventually a storm will come, and I bet it'll be a doozy."

Sarah said good-bye and closed the door behind her. It wasn't a long walk, but she was drenched with sweat by the time she entered the library.

Fans oscillated on Spencer's desk and on the three ta-bles in the center of the main room, but the air stubbornly refused to move. It was too heavy. Books were piled in three towers on the table by the librarian's desk.

"I'll put them away when it cools down," Spencer said when Sarah glanced at the stacks. "The air conditioner's having a hard time keeping up with this heat. It's worse than July! Maybe because we expect it in the summer. What happened to that New England adage?"

"Which one?"

He smiled as he carried several more books to the table. "The one that says if you don't like New England weather, wait five minutes, and it'll change."

"But one thing hasn't changed."

"What's that?"

Sarah leaned her purse on Spencer's desk and chuckled. "How we New Englanders like to complain about the weather."

He came back to the desk. Shifting the fan so its air blew toward Sarah, he asked, "What can I do for you today? More newspaper articles?"

"No. Today I'm looking for phone books. Old ones from the 1940s. Do you have any of those?"

Spencer opened the top drawer in his desk. "I'm surprised you haven't noticed them before. They're upstairs. Look just past the newspaper archives."

Sarah shook her head in disbelief. "I need to notice what else is around when I'm up there," she said.

"Hey, then there wouldn't be any need for a librarian." He grinned as he handed her the key.

Thanking him, Sarah went upstairs. The phone books were right where Spencer had said. She looked at the dates on their spines. She couldn't remember the last time she had opened one at her house. Irene was right. They had left the low-tech phone book behind.

Sarah found the 1940 phone book. The cover art was an American flag fluttering in the breeze. Flipping through the thin volume, she searched for Walter Ackermann and the Johnsons. No Ackermanns were listed at all. There were several Johnsons, but none named Carl or Edith or any other Johnsons on Lookout Mountain Road.

It was possible that the house hadn't had a phone, but she was surprised that they would have had a state-of-the art stove in the kitchen and not had a phone. Could they have had an unlisted number? Did unlisted numbers even exist back then? She would have to look for a phone the next time she went to the house. Neil had said they would be going back. She hoped it would be soon.

Sarah's cell rang as she walked out of the library. It was Maggie, wondering if Sarah could come over to the store. Irene was there too, which surprised Sarah because Irene had just been at the historical society.

Irene explained as soon as Sarah came into the antiques store. She'd had a second field trip scheduled, but the teacher had decided it was too hot for her kids to walk from the school, so the outing had been rescheduled for next week.

"I just hung a 'Back in 10' sign and hustled over here for a minute. Any luck with the phone books?" Irene asked.

Sarah put her purse on a nearby table and grimaced at the line of perspiration beneath the strap. "The library has them, but I didn't find any phone number listed for the house in 1940."

"And I found nothing in the census for Carl or Edith Johnson." Irene turned to Maggie. "How about you? Have you made any progress?"

Maggie shook her head, and her ponytail danced above her light blue sleeveless shirt. "I'm spinning my wheels too. It's pretty clear that we need to pay another visit to the house."

"So let's go." Sarah picked up her purse.

"Now?" asked Irene as she hefted the straps of her large cloth bag to her shoulder.

"Why not?" asked Maggie. "Neil wants answers too. He keeps saying he doesn't like mysteries. Let's have him let us back in the house."

Sarah asked, "Can you come now?"

Maggie reached for her cell. "Let's see if I can get someone to watch the store. My assistants have been bugging me to let them handle the store on their own. Maybe one can come in."

"With this heat, nobody's interested in the historical society," Irene said. "I'll leave a note on the door to call me if anyone needs something right away."

Sarah talked with Irene by the door while Maggie made her calls. Irene wanted to get a better look at the books and magazines in the house because she had checked only a few on the first floor. Maybe there were some on the upper floors that had been overlooked, and they would get the clue they needed. She would bring a notebook and a camera and her laptop with her … just in case they would be useful.

"I've learned it's better to be overprepared," Irene said with a grin. "What are you going to look at first?"

"My top priority," Sarah said, "will be the tapestries. Not just the antique ones, but the newer ones that were oddly repaired with patchwork blocks. I want to get a closer look."

When Maggie announced that her assistant would be over in five minutes, Sarah's heart began to thump with excitement. She couldn't wait to get back up to the house on Lookout Mountain. The answer *had* to be there.

Neil's secretary, Nancy Armstrong, looked up with a smile while Irene held the door for Sarah and Maggie. "Hi, ladies," she said cheerfully. "Come in and close the door, so the cool air doesn't slip out. It's hard to believe in a couple of months we'll be complaining about the cold."

"Never happy, are we?" Sarah went over to the desk. "Do you think Neil could see us?"

"He's got someone in the office. Let me check how long he's going to be." She clicked a button on the phone, then picked it up. "Mr. Lawton, Sarah and Maggie Hart and Irene

Stuart are here to see you." She paused, listening. "All right." She put down the phone. "Go right in."

"Thanks," all three said in unison, then smiled.

Sarah opened the door and waited for Maggie and Irene to precede her.

Neil's office was spare and modern. Abstract paintings decorated the white walls, and the furniture looked like it had been made to discourage anyone from sitting on it, though that was only an illusion. Sarah had discovered the curious furniture was as comfortable as an old, overstuffed sofa.

A young man sat in front of the desk, and Neil was behind it. The young man came to his feet as Neil did. When he turned, Sarah saw he was good-looking, though his dark hair was thinning. His eyes were bright blue. He wore a suit and tie with the discomfort of a man who was used to being more casual. In his hand was a leather notebook with letters in gold on the cover.

"Ladies, this is Don Monroe," Neil said. "He's working on his master's degree in history at UMass Amherst. Don, these lovely ladies are helping me find answers about the house." He introduced each of them, then said, "Don's thesis focuses on German families from Alsace who emigrated to America after being expelled when the region became French after World War One. His research has brought him to Maple Hill to find out more about Walter Ackermann."

Sarah glanced at Maggie and Irene. Nobody in Maple Hill had heard of Mr. Ackermann a week ago, and now Don was here asking about him. That seemed too coincidental for comfort.

Neil must have sensed their disquiet because he said, "Don has shared his notes with me, and I'm very impressed with how he's followed the paths of a couple of families from their departure from Germany to where they—or their descendants—live now. He thinks he may be able to help us learn more about who lived in the house."

Sarah nodded, realizing that Neil believed that Don was a legitimate student whose arrival in Maple Hill was a windfall. She relaxed, because Neil was usually an astute judge of character.

"Mrs. Hart," Don said with a shy smile, "Mr. Lawton tells me that you were the first to make a connection between the house he bought on Lookout Mountain and Walter Ackermann."

"I found Mr. Ackermann's name on an old deed," Sarah said.

"Do you mind if I ask you a few questions and take notes?"

"Not at all, but I'll warn you right up front that we've got a lot fewer answers than questions."

Don sat again and balanced the notebook on his knees. He flipped to a section about halfway through the stack of pages. The page was filled with handwriting.

"I learned early on to keep my notes together," he said, scanning down the page. He turned to the next which was only half-filled. "Everything I have for my thesis is in this book as well as on my laptop." He turned another page.

"Okay, here we go." His finger paused two-thirds of the way down the page.

Sarah couldn't read his scrawling handwriting, especially not when it was upside down. Not that she should be trying.

"You said, Mrs. Hart," Don said, "that you found a deed with Walter Ackermann's name on it. Do you remember which year it was recorded?"

"I think it was nineteen thirty-five, but let me check." Sarah opened her purse and brought out the page where she had taken notes. "Yes, it was nineteen thirty-five."

Don wrote that down. "Mr. Lawton mentioned you checked the tax records as well, but found no mention of Walter Ackermann."

"The names listed were Carl and Edith Johnson. Have you come across those names in your research?"

"No, I don't have anything about anybody named Johnson. Would you mind telling me what else you've discovered about Walter Ackermann?"

"That's pretty much it."

Don tried to hide his disappointment, but failed. "You don't know anything about what Mr. Ackermann did while he was in Maple Hill?"

"No. I scanned issues of the local newspapers published around that time, and I didn't see him mentioned at all." She looked at Irene.

"He doesn't seem," Irene said, "to have spent much time here. He owned the property up on Lookout Mountain, but Sarah discovered the Johnsons built the house."

Don sighed. "I'd hate to think this was a dead end." He closed the leather notebook and drew the stretch strap around it to keep it from opening by mistake. "As for the Johnsons, I don't have the slightest idea how they might be connected with Walter Ackermann."

"It was a long shot," Sarah said when she saw Irene's and Maggie's disappointment.

"No," Neil said, "I don't think so. Just because Don hasn't found anything yet doesn't mean it doesn't exist. Look how much you've found out in the past week."

Maggie sat on the white sofa. "But we're running into stone walls everywhere. We need to visit the house again. Would you mind if we went up today? Sarah said you've got a cleaning team there, but we'll stay out of their way."

"That's a good idea. Such a good idea, I'll go with you." Neil came around his desk and offered his hand to Don. "Feel free to call me if there's anything else I can do to help you."

Don raised his hand to shake Neil's, then lowered it. "Can I come with you? I'd really like to see the house and its contents." He talked fast, not pausing to take a breath, clearly afraid to give Neil a chance to say no. "Walter Ackermann may never have lived in the house, but walking around the grounds could give me some insight into where to look for him next."

Neil looked at Sarah, then the others. "Another set of eyes couldn't hurt."

"Definitely," Sarah said and was rewarded with a big smile from Don.

"Will you call Chester, Sarah," Neil said, "while I see if I can get Reginald?"

Sarah pulled her cell from her purse. It didn't have a very strong signal, so telling the others she would be right back, she went out onto the sidewalk.

Again the heat seemed to press down on her like her iron on a quilt seam. The sunlight had dimmed, and Sarah saw a thick wall of sharply white clouds rising above the mountains. She stepped into the shade beneath a store's awning. The air was a little less oppressive there. She looked up Chester's number and pushed the button to call it.

Chester answered on the second ring. "Hi, Sarah, do you have some exciting news about Neil and Reginald's house?"

"Yes, but not the kind you're asking about. We're heading up to the house to look around some more. Do you want to come?"

"I'll meet you there!" His eager chuckle stayed in her ear after he hung up.

Sarah put her phone in her purse and smiled. This should be fun, and she hoped, by the time they returned to Maple Hill, they would have solved the puzzle of the house on Lookout Mountain.

CHAPTER ELEVEN

The drive up Lookout Mountain in Neil's black Mercedes was more white-knuckle than when Sarah had driven herself. She gripped the door handle when Neil took the sharp corners without braking. He didn't lose control of the car, but she hoped he wasn't getting overconfident because he had driven the road often since he and Reginald had bought the house.

Looking away from the road, Sarah saw the clouds were climbing fast. They should get to the house before it began storming. The lightning would be doubly dangerous high on the mountain.

She heard Maggie murmur a soft prayer of relief when Neil edged through the stone gate and down the dirt road leading to the house. The Mercedes bounced hard, and the crunch of metal near the tires was a warning Neil couldn't ignore. He slowed the car.

From the back seat, Irene said, "I think we've lost Don."

The young man was driving his own car up the mountain, and Sarah was glad that he had decided to take the steep road more slowly than Neil had.

"He'll be along," Neil said, glancing into the rearview mirror. "The road doesn't go anywhere but here. There aren't any real side roads, just those slightly wider areas where two cars can pass. If his car can't get up the mountainside, Reginald should be along soon and will bring him up."

"It's great we could get together again on such short notice," Maggie said.

"Reginald wanted us to wait until next week because he's got a big project going on at work," Neil said, steering the car around a huge pothole. "I told him that he didn't need to come, but he decided he'd join us." Good humor returned to his voice. "The bushes look better than the last time you were here, don't they?"

The thick briars by the side of the road had been cut back. Sarah saw some of the trimmed bushes were roses. It must have been beautiful when those dual rows of bushes were properly cared for and filled with colorful, fragrant blossoms.

A precious memory slipped into her mind of the time when she wasn't even old enough for school. She had watched her parents working in the yard and their garden. Her father's green thumb helped him grow flowers that were his pride and joy, but that year the flowers hadn't bloomed because Sarah had decided to show her father how she could "help." After seeing him transplant some rosebushes, she had decided to transplant the rest of the flowers by cutting off the stems and sticking them in the ground far from their roots and bulbs. Her father must have been very upset, but he had been patient as he taught her about the parts beneath the ground. She had gained her love of gardens that day as well as an understanding of how hard gardeners work, but best of all, she had spent time laughing with her father.

"I don't know if they'll survive the winter," Neil said, and she realized he had noticed her admiring the roses. "The gardeners who chopped the bushes back said that roses are resilient, especially when the roots are as well established as these are. It'll depend on how cold the winter is."

"Do the gardeners think the roses are as old as the house?" asked Irene.

"Their best estimation was that the roses were probably planted within a year or two of the house being built, so they've had a long time to put down roots." Neil looked toward the house. "I wonder if the people who built this house ever put down roots somewhere else."

No one replied. The air of sadness and abandonment surrounding the house reached out to them.

Then Sarah said, "We have to trust that the good Lord had a plan for them just as he does for us."

Maggie smiled. "Good reminder. Just because we can't see the whole pattern of the past doesn't mean that God can't."

Neil slowed the car in front of the house. Two other cars were already parked not far from the front door. Sarah recognized Chester's silver BMW. The other car, a red one, had seen better days. The back bumper was dented and repainted black.

When Sarah got out of the car, she saw Chester and two other people on the porch. He waved to them as they walked to the front steps. The first riser creaked a warning as Neil put his foot on it.

Chester smiled as if he were the host. Shaking Neil's hand when they had climbed onto the porch, he said, "Sounds like you're going to need to get some new steps put on this porch."

Sarah paid no attention to Neil's answer that set Chester to laughing. She looked at the other man and the woman Chester had been talking to. Sarah guessed they must be at least five years older than she was. The man was large, but bent around the shoulders like someone who had worked hard his whole life. The woman's hair was as gray as his, and she was almost as tall as he was. She was slender, and her face had wrinkles that suggested she smiled often. Both of them wore stained jeans and dark brown chamois shirts. They had rolled up their sleeves, and Sarah noticed foam on the man's lower arms. He must have stuck his hands into a bucket of soapy water.

Her guess was confirmed when Neil greeted the couple and said, "Ethan and Agatha Kramer are the brave souls who agreed to clean the house. I half-expected them to turn tail and run after one look inside." Neil introduced everyone else, then said, "We'll try to stay out of your way. Where are you working today?"

"In the kitchen now," Ethan said in a deep voice.

Sarah noticed how Agatha looked at her husband before saying, "After that, we'll be cleaning the pantries. We hope to move on to the big dining room soon." Her voice was soft and feminine, the complete opposite of her burly husband's. She must be shy because she never met anyone else's eyes other than her husband's.

"If you'll excuse us..." Ethan took his wife by the elbow and walked around the corner toward the back of the house.

"They don't talk a lot," Neil said, "but they've got a reputation for doing a good job."

"I hope you don't mind that I made myself at home before you got here," Chester said. "I've been puttering around the dining room, looking at the dishes, silver, and the furniture. There's so much that I didn't want to waste a minute."

"You're welcome anytime." Neil smiled at each of them. "Anyone who can help clear up this mystery is more than welcome here."

"Did you get the garage door unlocked? I can't wait to poke around in there."

Neil's forehead threaded as he searched his memory. "I honestly can't remember if Reginald was able to get a locksmith up here or not. Check with him when he gets here."

"I'll do that." Chester gave them a Cheshire cat grin. "While I was waiting for you to arrive, I found a few pieces that may be valuable."

"Really?" asked Maggie. "What did you find?"

Before Chester could explain, Neil said, "I bet that trail of dust is Don's car."

It was. As soon as Don parked his dust-covered black car beside the others, introductions were made again. Neil led the way into the house, eager to show Don all they had discovered. The door creaked a welcome.

Sarah thought she would be less awed on her second visit, but the stunning staircase and wall of windows were as impressive as the first time she saw them. The windows gave a view of the darkening clouds still rising above the mountaintops.

The formal parlor looked very different without the thick layer of dust. It was as if everything had regained its natural color. The furniture and the fabrics had shaken off their sleepiness and now seemed vital and alive. The richness of the wood floors glowed in the sunshine.

Chester urged them to go into the smaller dining room to see what he had found. Soon he and Maggie were sitting on the floor with a stack of plates and pieces of blackened silver between them. Don wandered around the room, looking at the furnishings and out the windows. He wrote in his notebook and, with Neil's permission, began to take pictures. Irene excused herself to explore the kitchen. She unpacked her camera and her laptop so she could document any interesting items she found.

Sarah considered going with Irene, but the Kramers were working in the kitchen, and they didn't need a parade of people walking through. She stayed in the dining room and listened as Chester and Maggie examined the silver.

"This mark is definitely French," Chester said as he tilted a teapot on its side. "The boar's head and the lark on a stone. That's Auguste LeRoy & Cie."

"From the 1930s?" asked Sarah.

He nodded. "Like so much else in the house, except that it's French instead of German."

Don turned from the window where he had been looking out into the ruined garden. "Don't let the fact it's French influence you." He walked around a bucket filled with cleaning supplies. "There's always been a lot of trade between the two countries, especially because the Rhine has often been the border. Rivers provide an easy way for merchants to take their wares to market."

"Mr. Lawton," Ethan said, knocking on the door frame, "sorry to interrupt, but I forgot to tell you that a few of the shutters were so rotted that they fell apart when I opened them. I gathered up the pieces, but they can't be repaired. Too much dry rot and too many insects got in them."

"Don't worry," Neil said. "We're going to have to do a full upgrade of the exterior. Paint and repairs. I saw some wasps' nests up near the eaves. We'll have to get them knocked down." He waved aside the matter as if it were of the least importance.

But was it? Sarah noticed how his jaw worked and his gaze turned inward. He probably was calculating the costs of the repairs needed before the house could be opened as a hotel. It had to be a ton of money because even the best preserved rooms like this dining room still must have wallpaper stripped and replaced. The plaster was loose in one corner, and everything needed a fresh coat of paint.

She didn't say anything. Neil trusted his friend. She hoped he hadn't trusted him blindly.

As if they had spoken his name aloud, Reginald came into the room. Again he was enveloped in a cloud of ritzy cologne. He must have used half a bottle. He called greetings to everyone and gave Ethan a smile and a nod before Ethan went to rejoin his wife in the kitchen. He shook Don's hand, then rubbed his own together.

"So what have you found?" he asked. "I spent the whole trip from Albany wondering what new treasure we'd discover this time." He gave Sarah a big smile. "And what new facts our top-notch sleuth would uncover."

If Reginald wanted to act like he had never been upset with her, Sarah would be equally gracious. "Two of our sleuths are already at work." She gestured to Chester and Maggie.

Reginald didn't need a further invitation. He squatted beside the dishes and began asking questions. Neil moved closer to hear the answers.

Don remained by the window, and Sarah walked over to stand beside him.

Beyond the window, the garden was a ruin. Weathered statues were covered with lichen, and several small ponds were green with duckweed. Roses grew wild, climbing up the stone wall that was topped with parapets. Somewhere under the weeds, there must have been flower beds. The rickety half of an arbor had lost its battle against blackberry bushes.

"It must have been amazing once," Don said, not taking his gaze from the garden. "The formal gardens and the less formal ones around the stables and carriage house."

Sarah looked at him questioningly. "I thought this was your first trip up here." The stables and carriage house were not visible.

"Neil's so excited about the place. He's been telling me a lot about it."

She wanted to ask him more, but that would be too pushy. It wasn't any of her business what Neil told anyone. Don was right. Neil *was* really excited about his investment.

"Why don't we sit down and make a plan to go through the house?" Neil asked from behind her. "I think we need to have a better plan of attack this time. Last time, we sort of wandered around without any definite purpose."

"That sounds like a good idea." Chester helped Maggie to her feet. "We were too awed to do much other than point and say, 'Look at that!' Not that it's any different this time. Did any of you notice the plates hanging above the windows? I can't tell from here, but they look like early Dresden china to me." He chuckled. "I'll check later."

"I'll get Irene," Neil said, "and meet you in the living room."

Reginald frowned. "Why not here?"

"The chairs are more comfortable in the living room." He hurried out, leaving Reginald muttering something.

Maggie glanced at Sarah and shrugged. "Coming?"

"I want to look at one more thing here," Sarah said.

"Okay." Her daughter-in-law grinned. "Don't get so caught up in your investigation that you forget to join us."

Sarah laughed, grateful for the comment that cleared the tension in the room. "You know me too well. I want to look at the tapestry by the window. It'll take only a sec, then I'll head straight for the living room."

The others left, and Sarah went to the other side of the room. One of the modern tapestries hung there. It had faded in the sunshine that slipped through the shutters. The colors were pale shadows of their original shades, and the patch-work blocks used to repair the bottom had suffered the most. At first she thought they had been stitched with white thread, then she saw hints of pink. The thread might once have been a bright red.

Why would anyone put patchwork squares on a tapestry? Each one was about three inches square. Looking closer, she saw some of the blocks were appliquéd instead of quilted. The appliqués seemed to be random designs. One looked like a circle and another could have been a cow or a horse. It wasn't easy to see when the thread and the cloth were both now close to the same shade. She couldn't guess their purpose, but it seemed like a ridiculous waste of fabric and time.

She shouldn't linger. As Sarah turned to leave, a shadow crossed the doorway. A masked face peeked in, and Sarah gasped. Then she realized Agatha was coming into the room.

"Sorry to startle you, Mrs. Hart." Agatha lifted off the dust mask. "I'll come back later."

"No," Sarah said. "I'm the one who needs to get out of your way. I was just admiring some of the items in this room."

"You should see the main dining room. It looks like something out of a castle."

"Where is it?"

"On the other side of the kitchen, but Ethan's mopping the floors." She crossed the room and picked up the bucket. "I didn't do more than peek in."

"You've done an astounding job with this room," Sarah said. "I never thought anyone would be able to get this house back in shape so quickly."

Agatha smiled shyly. "It's a lovely house."

"I bet you've learned a lot of tricks and shortcuts to getting a room clean."

"Yes." She looped the dust mask around her wrist with a couple of easy flicks. "I'm going to miss this work when we retire."

"You'll find things to do."

"Maybe, but I like the people I meet on our jobs." She spread out her fingers to encompass the whole house. "And if we'd retired last year as my husband had hoped to, we'd never have seen this house and met you nice folks."

Sarah liked Agatha whose face was as open as her words. "I can't believe you managed to get everything so clean when you had only rusty water to work with."

"After we pumped it for a while, the water became cleaner." Agatha caressed the long table. "I don't know why anyone in their right mind would leave such beautiful things behind."

"Neither do we. Have you found anything with a person's name on it? An envelope? A book? A canceled check?"

Agatha shook her head. "Mr. Lawton told us to keep an eye out for those things, but so far we haven't found anything."

Agatha would be a good ally in the search. "Have you seen a phone in the house?"

Agatha gave the question some thought, then said, "I haven't noticed one. Would you like me to keep an eye out for one?"

"That would be great." Sarah didn't have much hope there would be a phone, and she wasn't sure that it mattered any longer, but she never knew what might help in the future.

Agatha gestured with the bucket toward the door. "I'd better get back before Ethan wonders what's happened to me."

Sarah hurried along the hallway, not pausing to look at anything. She heard voices from the children's toy room, and she discovered the others there. The rocking horse seemed to fascinate Don, and he was peppering Chester and Maggie with questions about it.

"Sarah's here," Neil said, "so let's go on to the living room. If we keep getting distracted, we'll never see half of what we should."

Sarah went across the corridor. Her nose wrinkled at a faint lemony smell as she entered the living room.

"What's that?" she asked.

"What is what?" Neil asked.

"Do you smell anything different?"

He glanced at his business partner and chuckled. "Just Reginald's new cologne."

Everyone laughed, and Sarah did too. The lemon scent must be from a cleanser the Kramers were using. She didn't recall its odor in the dining room, but the veteran cleaners would probably use something special for the wood.

"Watch out," Reginald said, pointing at some water that had gathered in low spots on the hardwood floor. "It looks like the Kramers have been working in here. Why don't we go back to the dining room? It might not be as comfortable, but I don't want to step in puddles." He glanced down at his loafers that looked brand-new.

"All right." Neil went to the front windows. "Let me open the windows to get some circulation in here."

The shutters were down, so when he opened them, the heavy, humid air oozed in. A distant rumble of thunder hinted that relief from the unseasonable heat was on its way.

As she turned to go, Sarah looked at the mantel. Where were the porcelain jugs that Maggie and Chester had examined? There had been three, all of them cream colored. Each had a different crest on the front.

Had they been moved somewhere?

She glanced around the room. The jugs weren't the only items missing. Going to the shelves, she saw two spots where someone had tried to brush the dust so it wasn't obvious that items had been removed. She couldn't remember what had been there, but she might be able to tell from her photos. She was glad she hadn't erased the images from her previous trip.

Taking out her camera, she snapped several quick pictures, then hurried after the others, already heading into the dining room.

Sarah quickly looked through her photos, comparing the old ones with the new ones. The old camera and the silver pen that Irene had admired were no longer on the desk. Other than that, she wasn't sure if anything else was missing.

Sarah knew she should tell Neil and Reginald about the missing items, but she hesitated. She didn't want to get everyone upset needlessly. Maybe the Kramers had moved them while cleaning. She would check with Agatha.

She hurried along the hall, but stopped when she passed where the two medieval tapestries had hung. They were gone. In their place were identical pale spots on the wall.

A shiver slid through her. Had they simply been moved? Each missing item had been examined by one of them the last time they were here. Was there something about those antiques that might point to the truth about the missing family? Or was there another reason they had vanished... just like the family?

CHAPTER TWELVE

hen Sarah went into the dining room, she motioned to Maggie to join her by the large window. Her daughter-in-law hurried over, and Sarah guessed Maggie knew something was up. Everyone else was busy making plans about where they would look next in the house, so Sarah quietly told Maggie about the missing items.

"We'll be right back," Maggie said, linking her arm with Sarah's.

Neil nodded, but turned to listen to Reginald's opinion about important rooms they must visit first.

In the living room, Sarah skirted the puddles on the floor and pointed to where the jugs had been. Maggie looked around the room and found some empty spaces on the bookshelves. Neither of them could remember what had been there, so Sarah turned on her camera and showed Maggie the pictures she had taken on their first visit.

"There should be a leather-bound book with a gold-tooled title here," Maggie said, tapping the second shelf. She scanned the bookcase. "I don't see it anywhere."

"So the jugs, the silver pen, the old camera, and at least one book are missing." Sarah switched off her camera to preserve its batteries. "Or possibly just moved."

"All small things," Maggie said, walking with Sarah toward the door. "The kind of things that could easily have been hidden in a coat pocket or a purse."

"If anyone wore a coat in this heat, that would call more attention to him or her than if someone just tried to walk out with an item."

"I honestly don't think anyone would have to *sneak* anything out of here. There's nobody around to notice."

"Except us." Sarah bit back her next words when Neil stuck his head around the door.

"Here you are!" His eyes were bright with excitement, but he flinched when thunder cracked sharply overhead. "We're going to look around the outbuildings before the storm gets here." Lightning flashed again. "Or maybe we'll wait." He gave a shaky laugh.

"We should head home before the storm gets bad." Maggie tensed as the house trembled when the rising wind hit it.

"Nonsense. This house has withstood a lot of storms much worse than this one." He patted the wall. "They don't build them like this any more." He looked past them. "Ah, the water is drying in here. I've got to say the Kramers are turning out to be a real find."

Sarah took advantage of Neil's changing the subject. "When did they start?"

"On Saturday. Can you believe how much they've done already?" He motioned for them to follow him to the dining room.

Sarah slid her camera into her purse as she walked beside him. "How did you find them?"

"Through an employment agency. They offered excellent references. Every person I spoke with said they trusted the Kramers implicitly."

As Neil went into the dining room, Sarah hung back to whisper to Maggie, "Why don't we talk to Agatha and Ethan? We're making assumptions while they may have just moved the objects somewhere safe while they cleaned."

"You're right," Maggie whispered back. "We're getting ahead of ourselves."

Sarah entered the dining room just as lightning flashed. She flinched when, only a few moments later, thunder rumbled in the distance. In the garden, trees whipped back and forth in the wild wind.

"Maybe we should head back to Maple Hill," she said.

"It's just a thunderstorm. It'll pass quickly." Reginald motioned to Neil. "Let's look around the front staircase. I saw what looks like a door under it." He walked out with the others following, chattering eagerly about what they might find.

Sarah went over to the tall windows and looked at the dark sky. It churned like a pot of fudge, thick and roiling.

A hand settled on her shoulder, and Maggie said, "I hope they don't wait too long. This storm looks big, and I don't like leaving the girls home alone in it."

"I'm sure they'll be fine. The school won't let the kids out in a thunderstorm."

"I know, but I still worry." Maggie took a step back when a bolt hit another mountaintop, then laughed at her own skittishness. "It's a mom's prerogative. By the way, thanks."

"For what?" Sarah edged away from the window too. This visit wasn't going as she had hoped. She had looked forward to poking around through the rooms and finding the clue that would clear up the mysteries about the house.

Maggie walked along the table with Sarah. "Amy told me that you gave her some good advice on Saturday."

"I'm glad she got something out of my tale of my own teenage trials." She smiled at her daughter-in-law.

The overhead lights flickered.

Sarah wrapped her arms around herself. As a little girl, she had been terrified of thunderstorms until she sat on her father's lap during a loud one and he had explained that the thunder was the sound of angels having a good time bowling. She wondered if he might be watching a few frames in heaven today.

"Do you think we should talk to Ethan and Agatha now?" Maggie asked.

Sarah nodded. "I hope they'll have a simple explanation to clear up the whole thing."

"Me too."

Agatha was scrubbing the stove top when Sarah and Maggie walked into the kitchen. Ethan stood on a step stool and was emptying out the cupboards. Dust surrounded him, and motes sparked when lightning flashed. They both looked up and smiled a greeting.

"Do you need something?" asked Agatha, wringing out the paper towel she was using. "We've got some coffee on."

Sarah declined the offer, but thanked her. "Can we ask you about a few items that were in the living room on our last visit?" She listed the missing items. "We didn't see them today, and we're wondering if you moved them."

Ethan slowly stepped down off the stool and leaned his hands on a table. "No, we haven't even cleaned that room yet."

Sarah frowned and asked about the smell of the lemon cleanser and the puddles on the floor.

"Pools of water?" asked Ethan. "How did those get in there?"

Agatha grabbed the roll of paper towels. "I'd better mop them up before the floor is ruined."

"No." Ethan snatched the roll from her. "I'll do it. You don't need to go in there." He gave her a stern frown.

His wife quickly acquiesced, and Sarah wondered if Agatha was always so meek.

Before Ethan could leave, Sarah asked, "Have you seen those items?"

"Are you accusing us of stealing them?" he asked, his voice as sharp as the snap of a whip.

"Of course not!" But she couldn't help thinking that they were acting oddly. Agatha had mentioned that Ethan had hoped to retire last year. Maybe they had delayed retirement for financial reasons. If the missing items were valuable, selling them might provide the money the Kramers needed to retire.

Agatha said softly, "Ethan, these nice ladies—"

He wasn't ready to be placated. "Before you convict us for something we didn't do, you should know that we weren't the first ones to arrive today."

Agatha twisted the paper towel that was now little more than shreds. Pieces of it fell onto the floor. Her breathing was sharp and irregular, like she was gasping.

"Isn't that right, honey?" Ethan asked.

"Yes." Agatha's voice was strained. "We don't want to accuse anyone else—"

"But," he said, "we saw a car we hadn't seen before when we pulled up, and we were concerned until he introduced himself."

"Who's he?" Maggie asked.

"Mr. Winslow. He was *in* the house," explained Ethan.

Lightning flashed in the kitchen, and the lamps overhead flickered even more wildly. Thunder thudded against the house, shaking it. Rain wasn't falling yet, but Sarah looked at Maggie. Her daughter-in-law was right. They should leave. If the road turned to mud, it would be a dangerous drive down the mountain.

"How did he get in here?" Ethan asked. "We always lock up. Always."

Sarah wasn't sure what she could say that wouldn't muddle the situation more. Items were missing. The Kramers said that they hadn't seen them and that Chester had been in the house before they got here. She didn't have all the pieces of the puzzle, and nothing made sense.

"We saw his car and then the door was unlocked," Ethan said when Sarah remained silent. "We almost called nine-one-one. Mr. Winslow must have heard us, because he came out and told us that he was working for Mr. Lawton and Mr. Carruthers. We kept him talking while we decided if he was legit or not. We were never so glad to see anyone than we were you ladies and Mr. Lawton. Maybe you should be speaking to Mr. Winslow." Ethan folded his arms in front of him. "He's the one who was inside all by himself."

Sarah blinked as almost constant lightning laced through the sky. "Did you see any sign of forced entry?"

Ethan's bluster faded as quickly as it had erupted. He put his arm around Agatha's trembling shoulders. "We haven't seen anything unusual."

"I'm sorry if you thought we were accusing you," Sarah said. "We weren't. We hoped that you'd simply moved the missing items. I'm sure someone else did. All we wanted to do was make sure the things are okay."

Agatha wagged a finger at her husband. "I told you they were nice ladies."

Ethan took a deep breath, then nodded. "I'm sorry. I overreacted. Thunderstorms put me on edge. We'll keep an eye out for those things while we're cleaning, but you should keep an eye on Mr. Winslow."

"Let me know if you find the missing things." Sarah left the kitchen with Maggie. As soon as they were out of the Kramers' earshot, she said, "I think they're telling the truth."

"But that still leaves the question of where the items are."

She recoiled at a particularly stunning strike of lightning. She really wanted to find out what had happened to the family who had lived here, but the storm was about to break around them. Beside her, Maggie gave a soft gasp as thunder made the house shudder again.

"I think it's time for us to go," Sarah said. "The others were headed toward the front hall. If Neil won't take us back down the mountain, I'm sure Chester will."

"I can't imagine he'd tell you no, Sarah." Maggie winked.

Sarah just rolled her eyes, feeling more and more like Audrey and Amy with every inclination of romantic feelings. Maggie saw the expression and put her arm around Sarah's shoulders.

"I'm just teasing." Maggie said. "I know you're just friends."

Sarah hoped Chester knew too. Not to mention Liam.

She shook the silly thoughts away and walked down the hall.

When Sarah and Maggie reached the front entry, they saw the others clumped around Neil. He had one end of a crowbar against a gap in the paneling under the stairs, and he was pressing on it.

Everyone looked up when Sarah said, "Sorry to interrupt, but I think we should head down to Maple Hill before the storm gets worse. Maggie wants to make sure her girls are okay."

Again the house shook in the wind, as if seconding her request.

Neil shifted his grip on the crowbar. "We'll head back after we see what's under the stairs."

"Neil, if you want to stay longer, I'm sure Chester can give us a ride back to Maple Hill."

Chester nodded. "Be glad to."

"Are you," came Ethan's voice, "just going to let him leave without explaining why he was inside when we got here today?"

Everyone froze as their gazes shifted from Ethan to Chester and back.

Chester spoke into the silence. His voice was calm, but it held the power of the thunder crashing overhead. "When I got here, the door was ajar. I came in to see if anyone else was here. Then I heard the Kramers' car arrive. I went out to let them know the door had been open when I got here."

Sarah heard a sharp intake of breath, then realized it was her own. Why hadn't Ethan and Agatha told them Chester's excuse?

Lightning flashed through the wall of windows, and Ethan just told Neil that he and Agatha were moving on to working in another room and walked back down the hallway.

"Chester, you didn't mention that the door was open when you got here," Neil said.

"Sure I did. I told you I was here before the Kramers were."

"We all misunderstood," Sarah said before another conversation could get out of control. She wasn't sure why Ethan had come out to stir everyone up. "Now, I think we should go."

Neil reached into his pocket and pulled out his car keys. "If you insist on leaving, I'll take you to Maple Hill. I know this road better than Chester does."

"Thank you," Sarah said. She was eager to know what had happened to the family who once lived here. But solving the mystery today wasn't worth making Maggie worry more.

As she walked to the front door, Sarah looked back toward where Ethan had gone. Why hadn't the Kramers been honest about Chester telling them the door was ajar? Were they afraid they would be fired for being careless and leaving the door open? Again she wondered what she was overlooking.

CHAPTER THIRTEEN

Neil opened the front door for them, holding it tight so the wind didn't tear it out of his grip. As they stepped out on the porch, he put his hand on Sarah's arm to keep her on the porch instead of following Maggie and Irene, who had decided to go with them, down the steps where wind flung dirt and leaves in minicyclones.

"How well do you know Chester?" Neil asked beneath the steady growl of thunder.

"He's a good friend."

He released his breath and smiled weakly. "I'm glad to hear that. I wish he'd told us that he'd found the door ajar."

Sarah wished Chester had too. She didn't like having a friend on a list of suspects. Yet she couldn't forget how interested he had been in the jugs and other antiques.

"I wonder who left the door open," she said. "The Kramers were adamant that they always lock the door."

"Someone left it open."

"How about the guys who cut down the briars?"

"Reginald was here the whole time they were working because he wanted to make sure they did the job right. He told me that nobody, not even he, went inside the house." Neil shook his head. "Another mystery."

He said *mystery* like it was a bad word. Neil didn't try to hide how much he hated anything that didn't solve itself like an equation. Sarah hid her smile as she rushed down the steps and out to where Maggie and Irene were waiting by Neil's car. They looked anxiously at the angry sky. Lightning crackled overhead, and the pungent odor of ozone surrounded them.

"The storm's getting closer," Maggie said needlessly. "I'll be glad when we're off this mountain."

Sarah scrambled into the car and looked at the formidable house. Were the missing items connected to the disappearance of the family? She sighed as Neil got behind the wheel. She might never know.

Neil started the car as large drops of rain splattered on the windshield. He reached for the wipers, setting them to intermittent.

"Maybe we've still got a chance to beat it down the mountain," he said with false cheerfulness.

Nobody answered as a gust struck the car. He held tight to the wheel to keep the wind from sending them into the briars. The storm released its full fury as Neil drove through the gate. Wind rocked the car, and Neil had to fight the wheel so they weren't swept off the road. Rain battered the windows. The wipers at top speed couldn't keep up.

Sarah peered through the windshield, praying that they wouldn't slide off the narrow road. She couldn't see more than a couple of feet in front of them. Neil must not have been able to either, because he slowed the car to a crawl on the windward horseshoe turns. He regained a little speed when the walls of rock sheltered them from the storm's worst winds.

Suddenly he braked. The car slid forward in the mud, then stopped. Branches broke on the front bumper. Sarah gasped when she saw a shadowed hulk in the road.

Neil opened his door. Wind shrieked into the car, pelting him and the seat with rain. He got out and was instantly swallowed by the storm. Before Sarah could even ask if Maggie and Irene were okay, he returned.

He climbed in. When he slammed the door, the scream of the wind muted to a roar. "There's a tree across the road." Lightning gave Sarah a quick view of massive branches. "We don't have any choice but to turn around and go back while we can."

"Can we can turn around?" asked Irene.

"Not here. We'll have to back up to the gate."

"There's no way!" Sarah said. "Even on a clear day, it'd be almost impossible to back up that far safely."

Maggie leaned forward. "The road widens about twenty feet back. One of those spots where two cars can pass. I'll get behind the car to guide you."

"I can't let you take that risk!" Neil said. "I barely saw the tree. How do you think I'll see you? If I skid, I could hit you, or you could slip under the car. And the lightning is dangerous."

"Do you think you'll be able to find the pull-off with only back-up and brake lights?"

Neil didn't answer as another blast of wind rocked the car. Reluctantly he said, "Okay, but be careful."

"I will." Maggie opened the backdoor.

Sarah reached for her own door. "I'll help too. You can be in the back, and I'll stand next to the window to relay your signals to Neil."

"If you're all going to get soaked, we might as well walk back," Neil said.

"It shouldn't be far to a place where you can turn around." Irene got out too, before he could argue more.

When the wind tried to sweep Sarah off her feet, she almost wished she had listened to Neil and stayed in the car. Bolts struck mountaintops to the west, and she realized the storm's center was still miles away. She held on to the side of the car and prayed for everyone's safety while Maggie headed farther up the road. When Maggie was at the edge of where Sarah could see through the storm, Sarah tapped on the window and gestured for Neil to begin backing up straight.

He lowered the window and gave the car a bit of gas. It leaped back, then moved more smoothly and slowly. Sarah and Irene took turns passing along Maggie's directions. Irene climbed in when they reached a place where Neil could turn the car toward her. With short, sharp turns of the wheel and dozens of maneuvers guided by Maggie and Sarah, Neil got the car headed up the mountain.

Sarah and Maggie got in the car. They laughed at how drenched they were, but everyone was uneasy until they reached the gate. Irene cheered and applauded as they turned onto the narrow road. Sarah bowed her head and held Maggie's hand as they thanked God for bringing them safely through the storm.

When Neil guided his car close to the house and parked it, Sarah reached forward and patted his arm. "Nicely done, Neil."

"Thanks to you ladies helping me." He unclenched his fingers on the wheel and flexed them. "I'm sorry you got soaked."

Sarah waved aside his apology as they rushed into the house. If they hadn't been wet before, they would have been before they reached the porch. The wind had turned frigid as the storm swept away the unseasonable heat.

Chester was coming down the staircase when they entered, bringing pools of water with them.

"What are you doing back here?" he asked.

Neil explained about the toppled tree just as Ethan and Agatha walked in from the kitchen. Behind them, the door rattled as the wind tried to get in. No one spoke after Neil was finished, the only sound besides the storm was a steady drip of water off their clothes.

"That means we're all stuck here," Chester said at last.

"Until the tree is moved." Neil pulled out his phone. "I'll call the roads department. That way they can get someone up here as soon as the storm is past."

Sarah saw Maggie shivering. "We need to get some dry clothes. Let's go upstairs. There may be some clothes that fit us in one of the closets."

Maggie wrapped her arms around herself as more lightning flashed through the windows. Rain ran in sheets over the uneven glass. Overhead, the lights flickered. "We'd better hurry. I don't know how much longer we're going to have power."

"I'm surprised we still have it if there's a tree down," Ethan said. "It must have missed the wires." He didn't look at Chester or Neil.

Agatha offered to make some coffee to help warm them up. "We brought it to keep us going on long days. Sorry there isn't anything else."

"Coffee sounds wonderful," Sarah said. "Thanks. Why don't you bring it to the living room? We'll meet you there."

Agatha stiffened, then shook her head. "I'll bring it here. It's no problem."

"The living room would be better," Neil said. "Then we can sit and recover from that harrowing trip."

Sarah frowned when Agatha suggested serving it in the fancy parlor instead. Was Agatha avoiding the living room? If she was, why? Did it have anything to do with the antiques that weren't there any longer? Agatha had seemed grateful when Ethan offered to take the paper towels in to clean up the puddles. Really grateful.

And where were Reginald and Don? From the way Maggie and Irene glanced around, she wondered if they were asking themselves the same question. Nobody mentioned either man.

Stop being so suspicious, Sarah chided herself. She needed to concentrate on the reason they had come up to the house: to learn more about the family.

"I'll bring you some towels and a couple of flashlights," Agatha said. "You'll need them upstairs." She rushed toward the kitchen, and Sarah couldn't help thinking that Agatha was glad for the excuse to leave.

"In case the lights go out?" asked Irene.

"There isn't any electricity on the upper floors." Chester paused as thunder cracked. Or was it another tree falling in the high wind?

"There are a lot of closets on the second and third floors. They shouldn't need to go all the way up to the attics," Neil said.

"No, there isn't any electricity on any floor save the first floor. I didn't see any outlets or switches or lamps on the second floor," Chester said.

Neil groped for the banister, his face as green as it had been in the lights from the dashboard. "None?"

"None that we've found," said Agatha as she returned with three towels and two flashlights. She handed the towels to Maggie and gave the flashlights to Sarah and Irene.

"I didn't know that." Neil's voice was unsteady. "I wonder if Reginald did."

Sarah put a comforting hand on his shoulder before she climbed the beautiful staircase to the second floor. Maggie paused about halfway and held up her cell. She cautiously turned one way and then in the opposite direction.

"No signal," she said as she caught up with Sarah. "Maybe I'll get something on the second floor."

"Or you can borrow Neil's phone."

"I don't think he's having any better luck getting a signal."

Sarah looked over the banister to where both Neil and Chester were hoisting their phones and staring at the screens. Neil began pacing. Sarah had never seen him so on edge.

She sighed. "They're going to have to get a cell tower here, because hotel guests are going to want reception."

"Do you think they can really turn this into a hotel?" Maggie asked.

"I've got doubts." She switched on her flashlight and hurried to catch up with Irene who was heading along the hall.

They went into each bedroom and opened the closets and wardrobes. Some were filled with musty-smelling linens. Children's clothes were in others.

In the fourth room they checked, Irene opened a closet door and said, "Here we go." She pulled out a coat, and her nose wrinkled. "The wool is ruined. Moth holes." She closed the door. "Do you think there's another closet with summery clothes? They might be wearable." She began opening other doors in the room.

Sarah brushed her hair out of her eyes, sending more water cascading down her back. "Any luck getting through on your cell, Maggie?"

"I've got one bar, and I don't know if that's enough to get a text through to the girls and Jason." She raised her eyes. "The twins check their phones more often than he does, so I've got a better chance of having them see a message, if I can get one through." She tapped on the keys for several seconds, then put the phone in her pocket. "Once we find something to wear, I'll try from the other side of the hall. Maybe there's a cell tower in that direction."

Sarah opened her own phone. "The storm isn't helping. I can't even get one bar."

"Me neither," Irene said. "Maggie, next time you try, will you ask Jason to call Chris and let him know that I'm okay?"

"I asked him to contact your hubby as well as Sarah's house in the one I just sent. That way, Lucie can let anyone who calls know you're safe, Sarah."

"Thanks." Sarah went to the next room.

The bed was mussed as if someone had just gotten up. A large wardrobe was set on one side, and there were two other doors. Sarah opened one and found a flight of stairs. Curiosity urged her to go up, but she closed the door. First she needed to get some dry clothes. She went to the wardrobe.

Irene opened the other door. "Jackpot! Here are some dresses. Look! There's still a Montgomery Ward tag on this one." She chuckled as she lifted a blue print dress from the closet. It had a sweetheart neckline and four velvet bows on the bodice. The skirt flared out beneath a belt of the same fabric. "It cost the princely sum of $1.98. Maggie, it looks like it'll fit you."

Maggie draped it over her arm. "It's really nice in a retro sort of way, and it'll look great with my muddy sneakers."

"There are shoes in here too, but I don't think they'll fit you." Irene pulled out another dress. It was dark green velveteen. "This one is wild. Its collar looks like something a Pilgrim would have worn to the first Thanksgiving."

Sarah turned from the wardrobe. She put a light blue sweater set and a simple A-line skirt of black wool on the bed. A pungent odor surrounded them. "If you can endure me smelling like mothballs, I'll use these."

"The smell will dissipate, and you won't catch cold," Irene said as she began to change out of her soaked clothes. She looked out the window that was streaked with rivers of rain. "I hope I didn't leave windows open at home."

Sarah hurried to pull on the sweater and skirt. She hated putting her feet back in her drenched shoes, but she didn't want to go barefoot.

"Anything?" Sarah asked when she saw Maggie checking her phone again.

"No." Worry etched her forehead.

"It looks like we're going to be stuck here for a while. What do you say we get back to solving our puzzles?" Sarah asked.

That brought a smile from both Irene and Maggie as they hurried down to the first floor, ready to figure out what had caused a family to vanish.

CHAPTER FOURTEEN

Sarah led the way into the kitchen. Chester and Reginald were there with Ethan, sipping coffee out of brightly colored cups. Agatha stood on the opposite side of the room and held her cup close to her mouth. She stared over the top of it, watching Reginald closely. When she noticed Sarah looking at her, Agatha averted her eyes, raising the cup even more so it concealed most of her face. She coughed a couple of times, then gulped her coffee.

Chester poured three more mugs and gave them to Sarah, Maggie, and Irene. Sarah put her flashlight on the table, then reached for a cup. Wind threw itself madly against the windows, rattling the panes like an earthquake. Lightning flashed, and the overhead lights blinked out, then came on dimmer than they had been.

"Where's Don?" Sarah asked.

"He said he needed to find something," Chester said.

"What?"

"I don't know. I hope he doesn't find a leak in the roof." He tried to smile, but nobody was in the mood for a joke.

"At least, the rain will fill up the cistern," Ethan said as he started another pot of coffee.

Neil poked his head out from the laundry room where he was hanging his dripping clothes over a drying rack. He now wore a simple cotton shirt and dark work trousers held up by black suspenders. "Cistern? What about the well?"

"There's no well up here." Ethan looked at him as if Neil had lost his mind.

"No well?" His gaze focused on his business partner.

Reginald rubbed his nape. "I told you about that."

"No, you didn't." Neil came into the kitchen. He glanced at the rattling panes that sounded ready to jump out of their frames with the next gust.

Reginald didn't seem bothered by the noise. He emptied the last of the old pot of coffee into his cup and mixed in creamer and sugar. "You must have seen it in the report from the house inspector."

"Not in the one you sent me."

Sarah saw Chester and Irene glance at each other with raised brows. Ethan and Agatha slipped out of the kitchen to return to work, and Sarah wished she could go with them. Listening to Neil's and Reginald's private business made her uncomfortable.

Reginald shrugged. "I told the inspector to send you the findings he sent me."

"I never got anything from him. Just the pages you forwarded to me with your concerns." Neil's face grew gray. "What else don't I know about this house?"

Sarah took Neil by the arm and guided him to the closest chair. She was afraid he was going to keel over right there.

"I don't know what you don't know," Reginald said, his voice indifferent to Neil's shock. "The mountain is solid granite. There's no way anyone could drill a well into it."

"How do you think we'll put a spa in here?"

"Where there's a will, there's a way. We can pipe water up."

Neil's gaze turned inward, and Sarah guessed he was trying to figure out who to hire for such a job and how much it would cost. "The pipes will have to be heavily insulated. Otherwise, they'll freeze in the winter."

"That can be done."

"Not cheaply."

Again Reginald shrugged. "You've got to spend money to make money."

The lights flickered faster, then went out. This time they didn't come back on. Lightning dashed through the room, and the house quivered with the power of the thunder.

"Don't move," Neil said. "There are some candles and old-fashioned lanterns in the pantry. I'll get them."

Irene clicked on the flashlight Agatha had given her. "We're set, Neil."

"We don't know how long the power will be off." His voice was grim. "We should conserve the flashlights. Just in case."

Neil went into the pantry and returned with a handful of candles and four lanterns. He set them on the table. With Chester's assistance, because Neil's hands were shaking badly, he lit the candles and put one in each lantern. He set them in the middle of the table.

"There are more candles and lanterns in the pantry, so help yourselves if you need more. I guess having the power go off wasn't unusual here."

Reginald picked up Sarah's flashlight. "Let's look around like we'd planned. There wasn't anything but dust in the closet under the stairs. I want to see what treasures this house holds."

Sarah bit back her retort. Reginald was acting as if the storm had hit just so he could have fun. How could he be oblivious to the tension?

Agatha came into the kitchen to get more sponges from a bag under the sink. She tiptoed around like she hoped nobody would notice her, staying far away from where Reginald and Neil had begun arguing again.

"Where are you and Ethan working now?" asked Chester with a smile. "I want to make sure I don't walk across your freshly mopped floors. My mother always scolded us kids for that."

He meant his words kindly, but Agatha's voice was barely above a whisper when she replied. She and Ethan were working in the front rooms upstairs. She hurried out of the kitchen, and Sarah heard her coughing again.

Raised voices came from where Neil and Reginald stood, arms crossed. Sarah glanced at the others, then picked up a lantern and left the kitchen. She didn't want to listen to the quarrel. When nobody followed her, she was relieved. She needed some peace and quiet to sort through the tangle of facts and clues.

Thunder boomed overhead, reminding her there wasn't any quiet place on Lookout Mountain now.

"Sarah, wait up!" Maggie rushed along the hall. "Where are you headed?"

"Somewhere else."

Maggie chuckled. "I don't blame you. Neil and Reginald need to stop bickering."

"Poor Neil's acting like he's been blindsided. He's not a fan of any mystery, let alone the dozens of twists and turns with this house. I wish we could find some good solid facts to help the mystery along."

"I have one you don't." Maggie's voice grew teasing.

"What's that?" Sarah stopped.

Maggie did too. She folded her arms in front of her and leaned one shoulder against the wall behind her. "Chester was asking me about you and Liam."

"What?"

"He's curious about how serious you are about Liam."

Sarah stared at her, then laughed wryly. "We're stuck on top of a mountain with a fascinating puzzle, and *that* is what's on Chester's mind?"

"Actually he asked me before we tried to get back to Maple Hill." Maggie arched her brows. "I figured I'd tell you once we were away from here and everyone else. Now that we're stuck up here, I thought I should let you know."

"All of a sudden, I feel like I'm in high school again and we're whispering by the lockers."

Maggie laughed. "Yeah, I guess I'm being ridiculous, but I wanted to let you know that Chester was asking."

Sarah considered going back to the kitchen and talking to Chester, but she didn't want to embarrass her friend that way. She decided to stick to her resolution and spend her time finding out why the family who lived here had disappeared without a trace.

Sarah started walking, and Maggie matched her steps. They reached another hallway, and Sarah held up her lantern. Lightning glowed through a window to the left, so she turned right.

"How much longer can this storm go on?" Maggie asked.

Sarah didn't bother to answer the unanswerable. Instead, she said, "We know a family left without their possessions. We know Walter Ackermann purchased the property and so did a couple named Carl and Edith Johnson. We know some of the items I photographed on our first visit are no longer where they were. Maybe they were moved, but we haven't seen them. Ethan and Agatha said they haven't either."

"So where does that leave us?"

That was a good question, and Sarah wished she had an equally good answer. Had someone taken the antiques? If a door had been left open by mistake, anyone could have snuck up to the house and taken anything. Despite that fact, she eliminated Maggie and Irene from the list; she had been with them off and on since the last time they had been up to the house.

That left too long a list of suspects: the Kramers, Don, Neil, Reginald...and Chester. She didn't want to add Chester's name to the list, but she knew how much he loved antiques. And she couldn't forget that he had been alone in the house before the Kramers arrived.

She seemed to be missing a vital clue that would tie everything together. Her head felt ready to explode.

"I wonder," Sarah said as they went along the dark corridor, "if Nancy Drew or Miss Marple felt this buzz of anticipation when they had only a lantern and didn't know what lurked around the next corner."

"Odd you should ask. I've been feeling like the heroine of a gothic novel who needs to discover if it's the wind or the tormented owner of the castle who's moaning in the night." Maggie laughed again, the light sound dispelling the gloom.

"At least we know it's a storm," Sarah said as she heard hail strike windows and shutters with a staccato beat.

Sarah and Maggie stepped through an arched door, and thoughts of the others in the house fell out of Sarah's mind. The space in front of them was huge. It was as cold and damp as a cellar. The candlelight didn't reach the far wall or the ceiling. The nearby windows were shuttered, though one shutter was so rotted that the rain and hail were getting through to hit the glass.

"Wow!" Maggie said.

The patter of falling rain came from overhead. How high up was the ceiling? Holding the lantern higher, Sarah was astonished to see a vaulted ceiling and thick rafters. They crisscrossed above her head, then were set parallel to each other as far as she could see.

"Wow is right!" Sarah said. "What do you think this room is?"

"I have no idea. Let's look around."

Sarah turned the lantern and saw something on the wall. It could have been a life-size portrait or a huge tapestry. She couldn't tell because it was lost in the shadows.

A thick rug on the stone floor was so filled with dust and dirt that puffs exploded up around her legs with each step. She sneezed once, then a second time. Much harder.

"This must be the larger dining room," Sarah said. "We must be at the end opposite the door to the kitchen. Agatha warned me that it was filthy and that we should stay out until she and Ethan had a chance to get it cleaned."

"Now that we're here, let's take a quick look."

Sarah held up the lantern as she slowly spun. She still couldn't tell what hung on the wall, but the light washed over a sideboard. A pair of china pugs, one black and one fawn colored, stood next to a platter with a gravy boat set on it. The style was modern with a bright red orange stripe painted about an inch from the edge. She focused her light on it and saw a single small orange cornflower painted on the gravy boat. At the other end of the sideboard, an ultra-modern lamp craned its neck to illuminate the pugs.

"What an odd collection!" she said.

Maggie picked up one of the pugs and examined it. "I can't see well enough to read the printing on the bottom."

Sarah shifted the lantern and saw a long table that disappeared into the darkness. Thick chairs were pulled up to it. She heard a skittering and guessed she had disturbed some mice.

The rug didn't reach to the wall on her right. Telling Maggie where she was going, she stepped onto the stone floor. It was dirty and cold even through her shoes, but dust didn't rise with each step. She placed her feet, one cautiously in front of the other as if she walked a tightrope.

Water glistened on the floor in front of her, and she heard a steady drip, drip, drip. There must be a hole in the roof. Another repair for Neil and Reginald. Not just one hole, because she heard more water dripping to her left.

Sarah edged around the puddle and went to the wall hanging. "It's another tapestry, Maggie. Look at it. It's got to be more than eight feet long and half that wide. Look at this. It's a castle being stormed by an army."

On the tapestry, soldiers stood on the parapets gazing down at the approaching army. Overhead, angels flew, which struck Sarah as odd until she noticed a beam of light coming down to earth around two mounted men who held out their hands toward each other in a gesture of peace.

Moth holes pocked the tapestry. She bent to see if it had been further damaged by mice chewing on it. Her brow furrowed when she discovered more cotton squares sewn onto the bottom. She peered at them, but the lantern's light wasn't strong enough for her to make out what design had been sewn onto each square. Her fingers ran along them, and she could tell that no two squares were identical. She needed to come back here when the shutters were open and the sun was shining.

Maggie crossed the room. Sarah heard a splash and turned to see Maggie shaking her right foot.

"I'm going to have to borrow a pair of shoes from upstairs," Maggie said, grimacing. "Watch out. These puddles are deeper than they look."

"Do you want me to go back with you?"

"I'll find my way. There's enough light. You keep on exploring." With a wave, Maggie left.

Picking her way carefully across the filthy, wet floor, Sarah was glad to leave the gloomy room behind her. She went along a hallway that ended in a flight of stairs. She went up. Lightning flashed through a large window at the top, but the thunder didn't come instantly. She counted to three. The storm must be going past. Not that it mattered. They couldn't get back down the mountain until the tree was moved off the road.

No one else would even know the tree had fallen unless Maggie's texts had gotten through. Sarah thought fondly of her cozy home. If she had been home, she would have been sitting on her porch watching the storm approach, moving inside to sit in the rocker Gerry had made for her while the storm raged and rain wove through the spindles on the porch.

Something moved in the shadows, and Sarah froze. She laughed shakily when a light bounced along the hall. It was Don. He carried a flashlight.

"We were wondering where you were," Sarah said as he stopped in front of her. "Have you found anything interesting?"

His mouth twisted. "To be honest, for the past hour, all I've been doing is looking for my notebook. I've misplaced it." He grimaced and shook his head. "I can't remember where I left it, so I'm retracing the route I took through the house after you left. But you're back." His eyes narrowed as he looked her up and down. "What are you wearing?"

Sarah explained about the tree on the road. "So we're stuck here for now."

"I can't say I'm sorry." Don smiled. "I won't leave until I find my notebook. I've put too much time into my research. I've already noted several items in the house that may support my thesis about Germans fleeing from France and Nazi Germany. Reginald tells me there are a couple of interesting German cars in the garage, but one look outside was enough to convince me to wait until the storm goes by."

"Smart decision." When she continued along the hall, she was surprised that he joined her. She wondered why he was interrupting his search for his notebook.

"You'll be interested to know, Sarah, that I've recognized several things from Alsace."

Maybe he just wanted to share his excitement over what he had discovered. "France, right?"

"It is now, but back in the early part of the twentieth century, it was part of Germany."

Sarah nodded. "I remember Chester mentioning that."

"After World War I, when France took control of Alsace, many Germans were expelled. The Nazis reclaimed it in 1940, because they believed Alsace was rightfully part of Germany. Have you noticed the tapestries in some of the rooms?"

"Yes, particularly the patchwork blocks sewn onto them."

"Look at the tapestries themselves. Several have Alsatian scenes on them. Castles from the west of the Rhine as well as mountains and villages. Oh, and I saw something you'd be interested in up here. In one of the bedrooms, I noticed a couple of quilts in an Amish style, which connects to Alsace too."

"How?" Sarah asked.

"Many of the Amish who settled in Pennsylvania were from Alsace."

Sarah pondered that information. Everything in the house was either German or from that one small region of modern-day France. That had to be a very important clue, but she didn't see how it answered any questions about the family's fleeing from Lookout Mountain.

Sarah promised to look at the quilts, and Don went back the way he had been walking. She looked for the room with the quilts, but didn't find it. She paused when she reached the large bedroom where she had found the staircase behind the door.

Holding her lantern high, she went up the stairs, testing each step before she put her weight on it. Chewed acorns and droppings warned that squirrels had wintered there. The steps went on and on, and she guessed she had passed the third floor. Did these stairs lead to the attic?

Not the attic, she discovered when she reached the top. The castle tower.

Windows encircled a room that looked like it belonged in a classical turret. Ragged curtains were pulled back from each window. A set of shutters banged, but didn't hit the glass. Rain swirled outside the tower room, and thick, black clouds were so low they seemed ready to swallow her.

Sarah turned away from the windows and looked at the room itself. The space wasn't large, probably no more than ten feet in any direction, and she realized it wasn't round. It was hexagonal, which allowed for a table to be pushed up against the one wall without windows.

She went to the table to look at what was piled on it. Her eyes widened when she realized it was a radio. Not an AM/FM radio, but a ham radio used for sending and receiving messages. It must be decades old. She could see tubes in an open section. The lettering on the dials was yellowed, and the dust on the largest unit was thicker than on other articles in the house.

She put her lantern on the table so she could examine the collection of dials and controls. They were as complex as an airplane cockpit's. She couldn't even guess how the radio turned off or on.

Sarah scanned the table to see if there was some sort of manual to tell her exactly what type of radio it was and maybe offer a clue as to why it was here. A long narrow book was pushed halfway under a stack of blank pages.

She picked it up and brushed off layers of dust. With care, she opened it. The pages slid easily on the spiral binding, even though the paper was thicker than modern paper.

It was some sort of accounting book with numbers and words. No, it was a logbook. Some of the handwritten numbers were dates and times. The first was in January 1938. The word and number mixtures must identify other radio operators and locations, but she wasn't sure what any meant. Where was Köln? Other words, written next to them, she couldn't read because they weren't in English.

She flipped to the last entry. It was dated December 11, 1941. The week Pearl Harbor was bombed and the Americans entered the war against Japan and Germany.

Sarah took the book and hurried down the stairs to the first floor. She saw Agatha wiping down the baseboards in the entry.

When Sarah spoke, Agatha jumped. She laughed when she saw Sarah, but her laughter sounded forced.

"I'm sorry if I startled you." Sarah wanted to ask Agatha why she flinched so often, but she didn't want to make her even more self-conscious. "I'm looking for Irene. Have you seen her?"

"In the pantry?"

"Thanks, Agatha."

"You're welcome." Was it Sarah's imagination, or did Agatha emphasize the "you're"?

Giving Agatha a smile, Sarah hurried to the kitchen. She found Irene on her knees in the pantry.

Irene was making a list of the boxes and canned goods she had found. She examined what old labels were left, noting which products had been produced in the area. She wondered aloud if Neil and Reginald would let her have some for the historical society.

Sarah broke in when Irene took a breath. "What do you make of this, Irene?" She handed the book to Irene.

Irene stood and began to flip through it. "I can tell you that the thick paper feels like what was used before World War Two." She tilted the book so she could read what was written on the pages. "Where did you get this?"

"Upstairs. In a room with what looks like a ham radio set."

Irene turned a few more pages. "I think you need to show this to Don. He must be able to read German. He stopped by here a few minutes ago, then went toward the living room."

Sarah took the book and thanked Irene, who happily returned to her search while Sarah left the kitchen.

Fifteen minutes later, Sarah was about to give up on finding anyone else in the large house when she heard voices ahead of her in another wing of the house. She walked into a room she hadn't seen before. Chester and Don were discussing the carving on the legs of a fancy billiards table. They looked up when Sarah walked in.

"Don," she asked, "did you find your notebook?"

"Not yet." He gave her a sheepish grin. "Chester sidetracked me with this table."

"I'm assuming you read German."

"Yes. What did you find?"

Sarah held out the logbook.

Don opened it and began paging through it as Irene had. "Where did you find this?"

"Upstairs. There's a staircase that goes up from one of the bedrooms to a room in a tower at the top of the house. I found a radio up there."

"Show us." Don held onto the book while Sarah led the way to the stairs. He kept scanning through it until they climbed to the hexagonal room. Looking around, he whistled. "This is higher than the roof."

"Perfect for a radio operator." Chester walked over to the radio and examined the dials without touching them.

"That makes sense," Don said. "All the messages logged in here are aimed at cities in western Germany. Here are a couple of locations in France too. All places that could be reached from here by a ham radio operator."

"Even Köln?" asked Sarah.

Don frowned. "What?"

"Köln. I'm probably mispronouncing it."

"Show me." He handed her the book, and she turned to the first page. "Ah, Köln." His pronunciation was very different from hers, because he squashed the letters together. "That's what Germans call their city of Cologne."

"What about the numbers with the quotation marks and apostrophes between them?"

Chester looked over Don's shoulder and said, "I'd wager a guess that those are map coordinates using latitudes or longitudes. Maybe both. Two sets of the numbers could belong together, but I have no idea what the coordinates would mean."

"We can check on a map when we get back to Maple Hill," Sarah said. She turned to the last page with writing. "I wanted you to see this because it's interesting. The last entry is for December 11, 1941."

"Right after Pearl Harbor, huh?" Chester rubbed his chin, then said, "As I recall from high school, the U.S. declared war on Japan the next day. December eighth. It was only a couple of days later that Germany and Italy declared war on us. We returned the favor by going to war with them the next day."

"Do you remember which day Germany declared war?" she asked.

"It may have been the twelfth or thirteenth."

"It was December eleventh." Don looked up from the logbook. "All those dates are branded on my brain. Whoever was using this radio must have been here until at least that day."

Sarah looked at the radio, wishing she could decipher what the setting on the dials meant. "One thing bothers me. How do we know the dates in the logbook are accurate?"

"We don't," Chester said, "but why wouldn't they be accurate?"

"Because the calendar I found in the pantry was dated 1940."

"They wouldn't be the first family to put up a calendar and then forget to take it down."

Sarah smiled wryly. "That's true." Her smile fell away as she said, "But if the Johnsons were here until 1941, why weren't they listed in the 1940 town census?"

"There could be any number of reasons," Chester said. "Maybe they were away when the census taker came to the house. Maybe they weren't contacted because they were so high up here on the mountain. Think how hard it was for us to get up here in modern cars. Imagine what it would have been like in an old car back then."

"Maybe." She wasn't convinced.

Don put the logbook on the table by the radio. "Maybe the reason they weren't in the census has something to do with why they vanished." He looked from Chester to Sarah, his forehead threaded with frustration. "December 11, 1941. Don't you find the date a bit obvious?"

"In what way?" Sarah asked.

"A few days after Pearl Harbor, a family with obvious interest in German things—who may be German themselves—vanishes. It might have gotten too dangerous for them to stay here, especially with all these messages to Germany."

"Are you suggesting that someone here was communicating with the Nazi government?" asked Chester.

"That would explain why there isn't any listing for Walter Ackermann or the Johnsons in the 1940" census Don said. They were hiding out. They wouldn't want their names on any government lists."

"But I saw a photo of the family in the local paper," Sarah said.

"The only sign they ever existed." Don leaned toward her, his eyes glittering with excitement. "Don't you see, Sarah? Someone here—either Ackermann or one of the Johnsons— may have been an enemy spy."

Sarah's breath caught. Could there have been a German spy in Maple Hill in the days leading up to World War II? Her late father had volunteered to fight in the war, signing up as soon as he could. Was it possible that even as he was holding up his hand to risk his life, someone had been in this house sending secrets to Germany in hopes of defeating the Americans? Maple Hill wasn't that far from Westover Air Base, and someone could have been monitoring flights there or gathering intelligence on the base and coming back to Lookout Mountain to send the information to Germany. Of course, it was possible, but it was an appalling thought.

Her father had been proud of his service to his country, and she had been proud of him. Every Memorial Day, she had cheered for him when he had marched past with the other vets. He had always worn a serious expression but winked at her when he passed by.

She took a steadying breath. Even if a spy had lived here, nothing that person did could taint her beloved memories of her father.

"Let's not assume anything until we've got a few more facts," Sarah said, as much to herself as to Chester and Don. "We're not even sure what the messages logged in that book are."

"I can translate them for you," Don said. "It's going to take some time because there are a bunch of entries, but maybe a pattern will emerge, and I won't need to translate all of them before we figure out why someone here was communicating with Germany as war was breaking out." His smile returned. "And it'll take my mind off my search for my notebook. Sometimes doing something else helps me remember what I've forgotten."

Chester squatted to look at the snarl of wires beneath the table. "While you're doing that, I can see if I can unsnarl this rat's nest. I used to fix up old radios when I was a kid. I may be able to put this back together, but I'm going to need power."

"I didn't think there was any electricity on the upper floors," Sarah said.

"Not in the bedrooms, but there's an outlet here. They must have run wires up here specifically for the radio."

"Do you think you can alert the police that we're stuck here?"

"Don't get your hopes up. There have to be enough tubes still working, and the wiring has to be intact. But without electricity, getting this radio started may be impossible. We may be on our own for a rescue for longer than any of us wants."

CHAPTER FIFTEEN

An hour later, while Sarah was showing Neil and Reginald the photos she had taken of the radio set, Ethan came into the dining room.

"Do you want me to try to get the generator started?" Ethan asked. Both men looked at him, baffled. "You know there's a generator out back by the garden shed, don't you?"

Neil and Reginald gave each other accusing looks, then chuckled.

"Obviously we didn't," Neil said.

"It needs gasoline." Ethan wiped an oily cloth between his hands. "I just checked it over. It looks fairly new."

Reginald nodded. "Now that you mention it, I remember Harriet saying something about a new generator."

"The fuel tank is as dry as a bone," Ethan said. "We need a couple of gallons of gas. One to get it going, and the second to get us through the night if we're stuck here that long."

Neil frowned. "The only place we've got any gas is in our cars."

"If you bring one into the garage," said Chester as he came into the dining room, "I can siphon enough to get the generator running. Then maybe I can get that radio juiced up and call for help."

"Let me change back into my wet clothes, then I'll bring my car in. No sense anyone else getting wet." Neil aimed a frown at his business partner, but Reginald didn't seem to notice as he began asking Chester about the radio.

Sarah put down her camera and turned to Chester. "You can fix radios and siphon gas. You're a real Renaissance man."

"Let's see if I can actually make the radio work before you sing my praises."

"If we're going out to the garage," she said, "we should find Don and ask him if he wants to come along. He's interested in seeing the cars."

Chester paused as he was leaving the dining room. "There's plenty of time later to see the vehicles. Right now, what's in that logbook may be the vital clue we've been searching for."

"True," Neil said. "Having Don translate is the best use of his time. After that's done, I'll give him a tour of the garage myself."

When Neil went to change his clothes, Chester said he wanted to go and examine the generator himself. He walked toward the kitchen.

Wind and rain whipped through the covered walkway as Sarah rushed after Chester toward the garage's side door. He opened the door, and they went in, shutting out the storm. The garage reeked of oil and damp. The odors seemed even stronger in the dark.

Chester pulled out a flashlight and swept the interior of the garage. The two cars appeared, then vanished as the light played over them. Sarah saw tools hanging on the walls and the workbench, which was set between two windows opposite the garage doors. Now that she was inside, she could see the staircase leaned precariously into the wall beside it. Lightning flashed, turning everything into a negative of itself.

Sarah's damp shoes made strange squishing sounds as she stepped aside while Chester flung up one of the garage doors. It rattled along its track. Wind whipped in, driving rain ahead of it. Lightning continued to light the sky over the valley.

Sarah wrapped her arms around herself as Neil drove his car into an empty space next to the Volkswagen. Chester pulled the door down before too much rain could come in.

Neil got out and panned his flashlight around the garage. It alighted on the strange vehicle that Chester believed was a horseless carriage. "Is this storm ever going to end?"

Pointing out a window, Chester said, "It's getting a bit lighter to the west, so the storm may be past soon."

"I hope so," Neil and Sarah said at the same time.

Neil handed Sarah the flashlight, then unscrewed his gas tank cap. He set it on the top of the car. "I filled up this morning, so there should be plenty for you to get out. Just leave me enough to get back to Maple Hill."

"Ethan's right," Chester said. "We'll need only a couple of gallons. At least for now. Let me see if we can find what I need without having to go outside."

"What do you need?" Sarah asked.

"A hose. Something long like a garden hose, and I'll need some containers to put the gas in."

Sarah joined in the search. Staying longer on the mountain wasn't a good idea.

Her thoughts were interrupted when Neil edged between the cars with a couple of clanking buckets. Chester carried a bright green hose over his shoulder. Sarah found two more buckets under the workbench. She set them down beside Neil's buckets as Chester pulled scissors out of his back pocket.

He cut the hose to about four feet long. While he worked, Neil went over to the horseless carriage vehicle. He whistled low.

"What is it?" Chester asked.

"What do you make of this?"

Sarah followed Chester. For the first time, she noticed both the hood and what would have been the trunk were open. Neil was staring at the floor beside it.

Her eyes widened when she saw a trio of batteries stacked next to it. A modern battery charger sat on top of them.

"I wonder who was trying to start the cars," Neil said as he walked around the horseless carriage. "Maybe Harriet tried to get them going before she put the house on the market."

Chester squatted next to the battery charger to examine it. "These aren't regular car batteries. These look like what would be used in an electric car." He grinned. "I'm a car guy in my nonantiques life." Slowly he stood and aimed the flashlight's beam at the horseless carriage. "There's a slot for the batteries in here."

"This has got to be really old," Sarah said. "Turn of the century. I didn't know they had electric cars then."

Chester ran his hand lovingly along the leather upholstery on the topless car, then gasped. "This really is a Bugatti!" He pointed to a small nameplate.

"Did they make electric cars?" Sarah asked.

"Not that I know of," Neil said. "They make superexpensive sports cars now."

"They obviously were experimenting with electric cars when they built this model." Chester stood and wiped his hands on his trousers. He left a black mark, but didn't seem bothered. "Shall we plug the batteries in and see if they'll take a charge?"

"Step back," Neil cautioned. "Just in case something explodes."

Sarah didn't have to be told twice. She was leery of jumper cables, and that was with two regular car batteries. Maybe she should leave the boys with their toys. But she was too curious to go back into the house without seeing if they could get the car started.

Bugatti. She didn't know much about the company that had clearly impressed both men. When she got home, she would look up information on the car company.

Chester urged her to go around to the far side of the cars. She hurried over and crouched down, keeping a couple of tons of steel between her and the batteries.

"Here goes," said Neil.

Sarah held her breath.

Nothing exploded, and she looked past the rear bumper on Neil's car's to see Neil and Chester smiling like two excited kids.

"They're charging." Neil peered down at the modern charger. "Or so this says. Whether they'll stay charged is the next hurdle."

"Don't expect too much," Chester said. "The car's sat here a long time."

While Neil continued to examine the Bugatti, Chester walked over to Neil's black Mercedes. He sliced the metal end off the hose and set it on a nearby shelf.

"Shine the light right here, Sarah," he said, pointing at the gas tank. "I'm going to stick one end of this hose into the tank slowly. When I can blow on it and hear bubbles, I'll know it's reached the gasoline."

It didn't take long, because, as Neil had said, the tank was full. As soon as he heard bubbles in the gas, Chester had Sarah put a pail next to the rear tire. He took the other end of the hose and began to suck the air out of it. He paused and crimped the hose about two inches from the end. Holding it tight, he lowered it into the bucket and let go. Gas flowed into it.

"How do you know how to do that?" Sarah asked.

"Oh, I know a lot of things." He winked. "I learned when I was a little kid. My older brother loved cars, and I loved him, so whatever he liked, I liked. Whatever he did, I wanted to do too, even if it meant learning how to borrow gas from our father's car for a joy ride." He drew up the hose carefully as the bucket filled. Pinching the end of the hose again, he said, "Bring another bucket over here."

As soon as all four pails were filled, Chester clamped his fingers around the hose and raised it so the remaining gas would run back into Neil's tank. Neil twisted the lock on the garage doors and told them to make sure the side door was securely closed when they left. Taking two of the buckets, he headed toward the house. Chester put the gas cap back on and closed the small door to the tank. He left the hose on the garage floor in case they needed it later.

He picked up the other two buckets. When Sarah offered to carry one, he laughed. "Let me be the he-man, Sarah."

"But the wind's blowing pretty hard out there."

"All the more reason for the fair lady to get out of the foul weather."

Sarah gave him a grimace, which made him laugh harder. Deciding she was better off quitting while she was behind, especially since Maggie had told her that Chester was asking about her and Liam, she closed the garage door after him. She tugged on it to check that it was locked before hurrying past him to open the door to the house. The wind was really gusting and knocked her sideways into one of the pillars holding up the roof. She pushed away from it and rushed to get to the door. Needle-sharp rain struck her face, and she turned so her back was to the wind.

"Thanks," Chester said as he stepped into the house.

She closed the door behind them, making sure it was well latched so the wind didn't blow it open.

"So, tell me. Do you think there was a spy living here before World War II?" Chester asked as they went toward the kitchen.

"I was going to ask you the same thing. It sounds too much like something from a novel. Things like that don't happen in Maple Hill."

"They have to happen somewhere."

Sarah was surprised at his reply. "You sound like you believe there really was a spy."

"The house is really elevated above the valley, and a good ham radio operator should be able to reach Europe." He slowed and steadied the buckets as gas began to slosh in the pails. "I'm sure our government kept an ear out for messages to and from Germany, but who would think of looking for a spy here? Especially if they'd been living here and sending messages all along. That could explain why the family disappeared."

"You think someone found out what they were doing, and they fled?" She stopped herself and shook her head. "Never mind. If anyone in Maple Hill had known about a spy living up here, the story would still be talked about."

"People might have kept their mouths shut because of national security. Loose lips sinking ships and all that."

Sarah turned down the hall toward the kitchen. She smiled as Irene and Maggie stepped hastily aside to let Chester and the buckets pass, then fell in step behind Sarah.

"Maybe during the war," Sarah said, "but the second it was over, the story would have been repeated through town. That couldn't have been kept a secret all these years."

"Unless..."

"Unless what?"

"The feds found out and slipped in and removed the family without anyone in town knowing."

Maggie gasped at the same time Sarah shuddered. "Chester, that's horrible!"

"The government may have discovered a German citizen had a radio and wanted to be certain it wasn't used to pass along information, no matter how innocently." He stepped aside to let Sarah open the kitchen's backdoor. "Don't forget that plenty of Japanese citizens were moved out of their homes on the West Coast in the months after Pearl Harbor. The people here could have been deported to Germany, which would explain why their possessions were left behind."

The hypothesis did fit. Sarah couldn't deny that, but she still didn't know whether it was the truth. There were several facts that hadn't been explained, like why the house had remained empty for so long and forgotten. And why the same accountant had paid the taxes on the property before and after the family disappeared.

"Just in time," Neil greeted them on the back porch with a smile.

Rain slashed at the grass and trees, but they were protected by the house and the porch roof. Even so, Sarah couldn't keep from flinching when a lightning bolt threaded like a basting needle through the clouds. Thunder echoed off the mountains.

The generator's shed was set beneath a porch roof, so Neil and Ethan could stay out of the rain. She looked around for Reginald, but didn't see him. It took longer than she expected for the generator to start, but on the fourth try, Neil got it going.

Everyone cheered when the lights came on behind them. They began flickering almost as badly as the candles had, but Sarah didn't care. Now she wouldn't have to worry about a lamp tipping over and setting the whole place on fire.

Going into the house, they laughed uneasily when the wind began howling around the windows again. Rain hit the glass even harder. They had put the lull in the storm to good use.

Chester asked Sarah to go up to the tower room with him while he worked on the radio. Maybe she could find something else in the room that would help solve some of their puzzles. All the way up, he talked excitedly about the cars.

"What I wouldn't give to have that Bugatti," he said with a broad grin, "so I could take it out on cruise nights. I'd have my best girl with me, and everyone would turn to look. We'd be the talk of the town."

"If it even runs."

With a playful frown, he wagged a finger at her. "Don't douse my fantasy with reality."

She laughed along with him as they entered the room where Don was reading through the logbook. He didn't even look up when Sarah asked him what he had found.

"Not much so far," he said as he turned another page.

Sarah glanced at Chester and smiled. Don clearly didn't want to be interrupted.

Chester went to the radio and began examining it as intently as Don was examining the logbook.

Sarah explored the rest of the small room, but didn't find anything but some boxes of parts for the radio. Chester took those with a smile and thanks. He didn't add more as he bent over the radio again.

Both men were so intent on their tasks that Sarah doubted they noticed when she left to go back downstairs. She needed to get back to exploring, but first she went to the kitchen and poured herself another cup of coffee. The idea of drinking tepid coffee made her stomach turn, but she was hungry and it would help. She wished she had thought to throw a couple of energy bars or even a few candy bars in her purse before she had gone to Neil's office.

Her thoughts went to her purse and she tried to remember where she had left it. The dining room. She had been showing photos of the radio to Neil and Reginald. She retraced her steps to retrieve her purse and camera. Usually she wouldn't worry, but if the missing antiques had been stolen, that meant other things might go missing as well.

Sarah's taut shoulders eased when she saw her purse on the table with her camera beside it, just as she had left it earlier. She picked up her camera to review the photos of the radio on the chance she would see something that might help Chester.

"Sarah!" she heard Maggie call. "Come and see what Irene and I found!"

Sarah clicked off her camera and put it in her purse. She gave the dining room lights a wary glance when they dimmed again.

"Where are you, Maggie?" she called back.

"In the toy room."

The faint lemon smell still hung in the air by the living room door, but Sarah forgot about it when she walked into the toy room and saw Maggie and Irene holding two large quilts. Sarah helped Irene push the toys toward the walls to clear a space on the floor.

Once there was enough room, Sarah spread the two quilts out. Like the ones at her house, these were made with a medallion pattern. These two, however, had a variety of designs around their borders. She saw what looked like a dog or a cat and people and cars. Next to each image was a letter of the alphabet. She was confused until she realized the letters might match the word in German for the picture.

"It's a teaching quilt," Sarah said. "Like a picture book with pictures and letters."

"Turn them like this." Maggie laid them end to end rather than side by side. "Look how the letters go in order around the quilts now."

"And the two quilts are just the right size for four young children to sit on," Irene said. "Didn't you say there were four kids in the newspaper picture, Sarah?"

Sarah nodded as she knelt to examine the quilts. She put on her reading glasses so she could see the small stitches more clearly.

"The stitching looks identical to the stitching on the quilts I took to my house," she said. "My guess is that they were made by the same seamstress. I'd have to check more closely to be certain—"

Irene laughed. "Sarah, your guesses are good enough for me."

Sarah smiled as she stood and removed her glasses. "I'm not sure what else I can tell you about them." She stepped back to look at the quilts from a distance. Quilts weren't meant to be viewed close-up, but to be enjoyed from across the room while wrapped around a person or hung over a piece of furniture.

"Are the patterns in the center the same?" asked Maggie. She walked around the quilts, pointing out each letter as she went and trying to guess what the appliquéd pictures were. Some, like a tree or a flower, were simple. The animal shapes were tougher, because they looked similar.

Sarah took another step back. These medallions weren't perfectly round. Odd projections came out of the centers at unexpected angles.

She asked Irene to arrange the quilts as she'd had them first. Maggie helped, and Sarah waited until they moved aside. Then she walked around them as Maggie had. She was three-quarters of the way around when a distinct pattern caught her eye.

"Oh my!" Sarah gasped as she saw that the two medallions, from this angle, created images of mountains. She pointed them out to Maggie and Irene. "We need to get Don in here to look at these. If anyone knows whether they're supposed to represent a specific place in Germany, he will."

Irene offered to get him. While Sarah waited with Maggie, she continued to examine the quilts from other angles and by rearranging them. Only from one side and when they were set side by side could she see the mountains image. These quilts had been made by a skilled seamstress with an incredible eye for detail.

"Here he is," Irene said as she returned with Don.

He listened to Sarah's hypothesis, then bent over the quilts. Sarah urged him to stand beside her to get a good view.

When he did, he whistled a single note like Neil had in the garage. "That sure looks like the Rhine River and the disputed valley."

"Was the valley in Alsace?" asked Sarah.

"Yes." He knelt and ran his fingers along the raised fabric. "I think these little houses are supposed to represent towns and cities. They're in the right places."

Sarah hadn't noticed any little houses and was about to ask what he meant. Then she realized he meant the fabric itself. She hadn't paid attention to the pattern. Now she realized that some of the houses had been outlined with embroidery.

"It's a map!" she said.

"That's my guess, but I don't know why it's on a quilt. Where did you find it?"

Maggie stepped aside to let Don look at the quilts from another angle. "Right here. We thought it might be a teaching tool because of the alphabet along the borders."

"You could be right. Someone might have used the map to teach about Alsace too. Probably a parent teaching a child." His eyes grew dim, and he looked away. "Unless it was stashed here so nobody could find it. If I were a spy in enemy territory, I wouldn't want anyone finding a map of any kind in my possession."

Sarah didn't reply, and Maggie and Irene were silent too. Every instinct told Sarah there couldn't have been a spy here, that such a fact would have been uncovered in the past seventy years. But what if *they* were the ones making that discovery?

Chester walked in, grinning. "Well, do you want the good news or the better news first?"

"Did you get the radio started?" Sarah asked.

"That's the good news. It didn't take long to get it up and running once I'd replaced some of the tubes. I fired it up and put out a call for help. Someone directed me to an emergency frequency. The better news is that they already knew we're stuck up here, and they've got a road crew on its way up. It'll take some time. Apparently a bunch of trees are down, but they're clearing the roads as fast as they can."

Sarah clapped her hands with glee. "One of your texts must have gotten through, Maggie! Praise the Lord!"

"I'm so glad they know we're safe," Irene said.

"Now tell me," Chester said, his smile broadening even farther. "Why are you staring at these quilts?"

CHAPTER SIXTEEN

S arah glanced at her watch and tried not to yawn as she walked with Maggie through another section of the house. It had been almost two hours since Chester had gotten a message through on the radio. How many times had she glanced out a window, hoping to see someone coming through the rain? How many times had she seen the others doing the same?

Too many. So she had decided to continue exploring the house. Maggie had asked to come along, and Sarah guessed her daughter-in-law was struggling to stay awake too. The fiercest part of the storm had passed, leaving a steady downpour in its wake. She carried a flashlight in case the lights went out again, but though they dimmed often, each time they came back on. Neil was keeping a close eye on the generator, soothing it like a colicky baby.

"Let's go up to the second floor," Maggie said. "I haven't been in this section of the house before. Have you?"

"No. I wonder what we'll find." Sarah smiled at Maggie. When Maggie didn't smile back, Sarah added, "I'm sure the girls are fine."

"I'm sure they've pestered Jason to let them stay up until we get home. On a school night. They'll be exhausted tomorrow."

Sarah looked into the rooms they passed. Just as in the other wing, most of the rooms were bedrooms, with the occasional bathroom. "If they miss a day, it's no big deal."

Maggie shook her head. "It actually is. Missing practice—either hockey or the play—is *verboten*." She laughed. "Listen to me. All the German things in this house must be rubbing off on me."

Sarah halted. "Do you smell that?"

"What?"

"Lemon. Just a hint of it."

Maggie nodded. "Yes. Where's it coming from?"

Sarah went to where the corridor intersected with one leading to their left. She stopped and sniffed the air in each direction.

Before she could decide which way to go, she heard sharp coughing. It was in the corridor to the left. The coughing had a desperate edge to it. There was a loud thud. Something had fallen.

Sarah exchanged a fearful glance with Maggie, then ran toward the coughing. The lemon smell grew stronger. She looked in each room they passed, but most of the rooms were empty.

She skidded to a stop when she saw Agatha on the floor, gasping for breath.

Sarah dropped to her knees beside Agatha. Maggie knelt on Agatha's other side and drew down the dust mask she wore.

"What's wrong?" Maggie asked. "Did you fall?"

"Can...can't b-b-breathe." Agatha's voice was a whispered rasp. Each word sounded as if she had to use every bit of her strength to force it past her lips. "Inhaler!"

Sarah understood instantly. Agatha was having an asthma attack, and she wanted her rescue inhaler. "Where is it?"

"Pocket." She began wheezing harder.

Sarah found the inhaler in Agatha's apron. She shook it and held it to Agatha's lips which were an alarming blue. Agatha's hands flailed. Was she trying to grab it? Sarah didn't wait. She pressed the top, sending the spray into Agatha's mouth.

Agatha tried to speak, but couldn't. She twirled her hand, and Sarah hoped she was reading the signal correctly. Sarah put the inhaler to Agatha's mouth a second time and pushed down on the dispenser again. When Agatha groped for the inhaler, Sarah folded the older woman's fingers around it. Touching it seemed to give Agatha comfort.

"Out...of here," Agatha whispered. "Help me. Please."

Reaching under Agatha's shoulders, Sarah got her to her feet with Maggie's help. Agatha draped an arm around each of them, leaning heavily. They stumbled out of the room and along the hall.

Sarah and Maggie steered Agatha into a bedroom down the other corridor. She started toward the bed, then had second thoughts when she saw droppings on the floor. Some sort of rodent had made a home in the mattress.

"What happened?" asked Maggie.

"It's that smell." Agatha's voice grew stronger with each word. "I'm allergic to many scents. But I didn't expect I'd need to worry. Ethan went through the house before I came here the first time, just to make sure. The scent was so faint that it wiped me out before I even realized I was breathing it. What was it?"

"Some sort of cleanser," Sarah said. "I've smelled it in a couple of rooms. We assumed it was something you were using."

Agatha shook her head. "I'd never use anything like that. It would kill me. I've been avoiding any room with scents."

"Like the living room?" Sarah hadn't considered that Agatha might have another reason to stay away from the room where the missing items had been. It wasn't guilt, but that lemony odor.

"Yes." She wheezed on the single word, so she took shallow breaths. When she could speak again, she said, "I've had a tough time with Mr. Carruthers's strong cologne. I know Ethan plans to talk to him about it so Mr. Carruthers won't wear it next time he comes here, but I didn't want to complain when there's nothing he can do about it today."

"Other than run around in the rain," Maggie said, lifting the dust mask over Agatha's head and putting it on a nearby windowsill.

A hint of a smile tugged at Agatha's lips. "I don't think he'd take it well if I suggested he jump in a puddle."

Sarah guided Agatha to an overstuffed chair beside the window. Agatha trembled as she lowered herself into it. Dust billowed from the cushions, and Sarah waved it away.

"Dust doesn't bother me," Agatha said. "Just scents and really cold air."

"So, just to be clear," Sarah said, "you didn't bring any lemon cleanser with you. Could Ethan have diluted a cleanser, assuming it wouldn't bother you?"

Agatha shook her head, then put her hand to her forehead. Lines of pain were carved into her brow. She must have a bad headache. "Even a hint of some scents is too much for me. We use natural and scent-free supplies."

"Do Neil and Reginald know this?"

"I assume so. It's in the information we gave them."

Sarah grimaced. From what she had heard so far, it didn't sound like Reginald and Neil were sharing information freely. She suspected they had gotten caught up in the idea of a luxury hotel and let things slide half read. As for Reginald, she wasn't sure what to think about him any longer.

So who was using the lemon-scented cleanser? Its smell didn't dissipate quickly: Agatha had been sidestepping the living room like it was radioactive for hours.

Was that what the person using the cleanser wanted? To keep the Kramers out of certain places? So they wouldn't notice that things were missing?

No, that didn't add up, because the small tapestries had been in the hallway. Of course, the person might not have had time to spread the cleanser around before she and Maggie and Irene had arrived with Neil.

Or was Sarah going down the wrong track? There could be another reason why someone would use that cleanser: To wipe away any fingerprints that could betray the thief. As Sarah watched Agatha trying to breathe normally, she wondered if the thief had any idea that Agatha was so sensitive to the scent.

"How are you doing?" Sarah asked.

"Is there anything I can get for you?" Maggie asked at the same time.

"I'll be okay if I sit and catch my breath." A faint smile eased the strain on Agatha's face. Her eyes dimmed. "I know you've been wondering about why I refused to go into the living room. Now you understand that I couldn't have gone in there to take those things."

"I know." Sarah didn't add that she wasn't as sure about Ethan. She couldn't imagine him, however, putting his wife's health at risk, even if he *was* trying to secure their retirement.

Sarah leaned against the wall and looked at the rain steadily hitting the windows. Water seeped around the sill of one and was dripping onto the floor, another spot that needed repairing. She shifted her gaze back to Agatha and was glad to see that the older woman's face had regained a healthier color.

"I'm sorry, that I didn't explain before," Agatha said.

"You don't need to apologize," Sarah said.

"We've all been on edge with the storm," Maggie said as she opened a closet door and looked inside. "It's like we're living in an Agatha Christie novel."

"It's more than that." Agatha rolled the corner of her apron up, then released it before starting to roll it again. "I've been through this before. I was the victim of a theft. When you said some things had been stolen, I couldn't help but remember the time I was mugged. Things like this bring it back as if it's happening all over again." New tears filled Agatha's eyes. "When you asked if we'd seen those things, I panicked. On top of that, even a suggestion that we're unreliable could ruin our business. Who wants to hire someone to clean is house when he can't trust them with his possessions?"

Sarah squeezed Agatha's hand gently while Maggie brought over a dusty blanket. She shook it out, then tucked it around Agatha.

"I'm sorry," Sarah said as Agatha nodded her thanks, "if my questions caused you so much distress. Why don't you rest here? I'll get Ethan, and he—"

"Don't bother him. Before we leave tonight, he wants to finish off the room he's working on downstairs." Her weak smile returned. "He doesn't like to leave things half done."

"Are you sure you don't want me to get him?"

Agatha nodded. "He's very protective, and he gets upset when I have an asthma attack."

"Can't I do anything for you?" When Sarah saw Agatha hesitate, she said, "Go ahead. I want to help."

Agatha met Sarah's eyes. "I left my cleaning supplies in the other room. I can't go back and get them. If I ask Ethan, he'll know I didn't tell him about my attack."

Sarah nodded. "It should only take a moment. You rest here. I'll put your supplies in the kitchen, so they'll be there when you're ready for them. As soon as I get back, Maggie and I will help you downstairs."

"Okay."

Maggie perched gingerly on the bed. "I'll stay with Agatha until she's ready to go back downstairs."

Agatha looked from Maggie to Sarah. "Thank you for doing this, and for believing Ethan and I are innocent."

Sarah said nothing because she didn't want to speak the truth. She knew Agatha wasn't a thief, but Ethan remained on Sarah's list of suspects. Saying that would hurt Agatha further, and Sarah wasn't going to accuse anyone openly until she had more facts. Once she got Agatha's supplies, she would continue the search for the truth.

Sarah went into the room where she had found Agatha struggling to breathe. Like many of the rooms on the second floor, it had a dresser and a bare bed on a simple carpet.

She saw Agatha's bucket and a pair of sponges not far from the door. A wet circle marked where water had splashed out when Agatha collapsed.

Sarah picked up the sponges and tossed them into the pail. She reached to grab the bucket's handle along with the small container holding towels and a squirt bottle. She paused when she saw something else on the rug by the bed.

It wasn't on the rug. It was *in* the rug. A whitish spot. It looked like someone had dropped bleach on the rug and left it to eat away the color. She bent to smell it. Definitely lemons. Whatever smelled of lemons must be a bleaching agent.

She looked around. There was more than one spot. They made a trail toward the bed. Had the bleach been carried to the bed or away from it?

Sarah went to the bed and bent to look under it. Something was pushed only a short distance beneath it. She grabbed the item and pulled it out.

"Oh dear," she said.

It was Don's notebook. She recognized it even before she saw his name on the cover.

But it was so bulky. It hadn't been that thick when he had it at Neil's office.

She undid the latch and opened the cover. Something tumbled onto the floor. She picked it up. It was tightly rolled and held together with a pair of rubber bands. She carefully slid the rubber bands off each end and opened it. She stared at the small tapestry of St. George fighting the dragon. It was the one that had hung downstairs.

A sick feeling filled her at the thought of Don stealing from Neil and Reginald. How was that possible? He had followed Neil up here today.

But he had been on his own a lot since then. He had been off by himself while she, Maggie, Irene, and Neil had tried to return to Maple Hill. He hadn't been around after they returned. And he had been alone when Sarah had found him looking for this very notebook. Had he been anxious to find it because of his notes, or because he feared someone would discover the tapestry rolled up inside?

She couldn't forget how at ease Don seemed in the house, wandering farther and more confidently than the rest of them had. She remembered how he had spoken of gardens around the outbuildings, gardens that none of them had visited. Had Neil really told him about them, or was this not Don's first trip to the house on Lookout Mountain?

CHAPTER SEVENTEEN

Sarah tucked the notebook and the tapestry under her arm so she could also carry the cleaning supplies, then she returned to the first floor.

She found Reginald first. He was in the dining room, admiring the silver Maggie and Chester had taken out of the sideboard. She told him that she wanted to speak with him and Neil. Alone. Questions glistened in his eyes, but he didn't ask, he just led her to the formal parlor.

Neil was making an inventory of the furniture. "Sarah, are you okay?" Neil asked as he crossed the room toward her.

"I'm fine, but..." She didn't finish. "I need to show you what I found upstairs." She opened the notebook and drew out the tapestry. "I don't know if you recognize it, but it's one of two small tapestries that hung near the dining room. The other one had a unicorn on it."

Neil took the tapestry. Turning it one way and then the other, he said, "I wonder how it got upstairs."

Sarah quickly explained how she had noticed some items weren't where they had been during her first visit. "I thought they might have been moved."

"The Kramers," Reginald said.

"I asked them if they'd seen them, and they said no."

"But didn't you say two tapestries were gone? Where's the other one?"

"Reginald," Neil said. "Just let her tell the story."

Sarah waited a moment, but Reginald glared at Neil. When she realized neither man was going to capitulate, she told them how she had offered to get the cleaning supplies for Agatha. She didn't mention Agatha's asthma attack or the bleached spots on the rug that had led to her discovery. Just that she had gone into the room and found the tapestry under the bed.

"What's that other thing you have?" asked Reginald as soon as she finished.

Sarah swallowed her annoyance at his demanding tone. She flipped the notebook over to reveal Don's name on the cover.

"The tapestry was in this," Sarah said.

Both men stared at it in silence, then Reginald muttered something under his breath as he went to look out the window. Sarah decided she would be better off not to ask him to repeat it more loudly.

Reginald spun to face Neil. "I thought you said this kid was okay."

"I thought he was." Neil spread out his hands. "His credentials look genuine, and he sounds like he knows what he's talking about."

"And he conned his way in here, so he could help himself to my stuff." His face reddened. "I mean our stuff."

Neil waved away his words. "I don't think that's what happened. He arrived after the rest of us. Except for you, Reginald."

"None of that matters if he came up here before today. Is that possible?"

Sarah was glad that he aimed the question at his business partner. She didn't want to condemn Don until she had more facts. Apparently Neil didn't want to either. He stayed silent.

Reginald walked back to them. "Don't you think it's pretty coincidental that Don showed up right after we purchased the house?"

"Yes," Neil said with reluctance.

"I think so too." Sarah tried to keep her tone neutral. "However, I've learned that coincidences happen a lot. Our lives aren't nicely ordered, and sometimes we read into things where it's just coincidence. Other times we don't see the obvious right in front of our faces. Only God sees the whole pattern of our lives and the lives of those around us."

But Reginald wasn't going to be soothed by reason. He stormed off to find Don, taking the tapestry with him.

Sarah exchanged a glance with Neil, and they followed. They didn't go far because Don came walking along the hall. He smiled as they approached.

"Why did you steal my tapestry?" Reginald asked, shaking it at him.

Don's smile fell. Sarah instantly regretted not speaking with Don before she showed the tapestry to Reginald and Neil. Don jammed his hands in his pockets and locked eyes with Reginald.

"Which tapestry?" Don gave a tense laugh. "There are a lot of them in the house." He tilted his head to get a better view of it. "Is that St. George?"

"You know it is because you stole it!" Reginald insisted.

"I know it because the dragon and the red cross on a white surplice are a dead giveaway that it's St. George. But I haven't seen this particular tapestry before."

"Then how did Sarah find it in your notebook?"

"My notebook?" He whirled to Sarah, hope bright in his eyes. "You found my notebook?"

She smiled and held it out. He took it and hugged it to his chest as if it were a long lost child. He thanked her before opening it and paging through it.

"Is it all there?" Sarah asked.

Don closed the book and smiled. "It looks like it's all in there."

"Along with the tapestry," Neil said quietly. "Do you have any idea how that could have happened?"

"Other than he tried to steal it?" asked Reginald.

Don drew in a deep breath, then released it. Whatever retort he had been tempted to fire at Reginald, he didn't. He looked from one of them to the next, holding Sarah's eyes as he said, "Whoever took this set me up. The real thief took my notebook and left it where it could be found along with the tapestry."

"Or you could have arranged the whole scenario so you could claim you were framed." Reginald wasn't going to back down. "In the meantime, you've hidden the other things and can slip them out of here when you leave."

"What other things?" Again Don looked at Sarah. "Have other things gone missing?"

She explained as she had to the others. Don's face lengthened in what looked like honest dismay.

"Where did you stash them?" Reginald asked, jabbing a finger into Don's chest.

Don batted his hand aside. "Watch it, Carruthers. I'm outta here. And as you can see, I don't have your misplaced items with me." He shoved the notebook under his arm and strode away.

"Good riddance," Reginald said.

Sarah turned to Neil. "I'm going to try to talk some sense into Don. Why don't you do the same with your business partner? Try reminding him how helpful Don has been with trying to solve the mystery of our missing family."

"All right," Neil agreed.

She went after Don. She didn't want him to make a bad decision like trying to leave while it was still storming.

Don was in the entrance foyer by the time Sarah caught up with him. He stared at the sheets of rain running down the big windows, then reached for the doorknob.

"Don!" she called. "Wait a minute."

He looked over his shoulder, then lowered his hand. "Don't waste your breath, Mrs. Hart. I know you mean well, but I didn't take anything from this house. To be honest, I wish the rest of you would leave and let me look at everything first. Every time you move something, a bit of information is lost that might help figure this out."

Sarah hadn't considered that. "Why haven't you said something?"

"What good would it have done? We're acting like kids at an Easter egg hunt, looking for the next big prize." His shoulders slumped. "And I'm as guilty of that as anyone else, but it's the only thing I'm guilty of. I'm not going to stay here and listen to that idiot!" He reached for the door again.

"Where are you going?"

"Out of here."

She put her hand on his arm. "That tree is still across the road. You won't be able to drive past it."

"I'd rather walk to Maple Hill than listen to Carruthers for one more minute."

"Don't be silly. The road crew will get the tree out of the way soon, and we all can leave."

He sighed and nodded. "You're right. I'm just so ticked ... " He looked past her.

Sarah turned to see Neil and Reginald coming into the foyer.

Neil spoke first. "Don, we need to apologize. Circumstantial evidence and conjecture aren't enough to label someone a thief."

"They aren't enough either," Reginald said, "to let someone claim he's innocent when the facts point to his guilt."

"Reginald, I thought we agreed to—" But Reginald didn't let Neil finish his sentence; he just spun and stomped down the hallway.

Instead of following him, Neil said, "Don, you've got to admit the evidence is weighted against you."

Don glanced at Sarah, then met Neil's gaze without flinching. "I can assure you, Mr. Lawton, that I didn't take anything."

"I wish you could prove it."

"But I can't." Don nodded. "Okay, let me be honest with you about something I should have told you right from the beginning. I came up here before I went to your office to meet you."

Sarah sat on the lowest riser. Don was confirming her suspicions, but she still was surprised.

"When?" Neil's voice had hardened again.

"About a month ago. I'd just found out about Walter Ackermann and the fact that he had bought property here. I wanted to see it. I couldn't get past the briar patch on the driveway, so I left my car and came in to look around. I couldn't see much of the house because everything was shuttered up. Most of the outbuildings didn't look safe to go in."

"I wanted to *see* the place. I walked around and looked at the gardens and enjoyed the view of the valley," Don said. "Now, from what I've learned from you, he may never even have lived here. The Johnsons did." Clasping his hands in front of him, he said, "I'm sorry, Mr. Lawton. I should have been up-front right from the beginning. I was afraid if I did, I'd lose out on the chance to see inside the house. At the time, I thought it mattered."

Neil stared at him for a long moment, then said, "Thanks for being honest, even belatedly. Let's keep everything on the up-and-up from now on. Okay?"

"Okay. And I appreciate your giving me a chance to explain."

"In the meantime," Sarah said as she pushed herself to her feet, "let's work together to solve the puzzle about the family who lived here. All of us together should be able to figure this out."

"Not all of us." Neil's gaze followed the path his disgruntled business partner had taken.

He didn't say anything more. Sarah imagined Neil was very sorry he had ever entered into this partnership.

CHAPTER EIGHTEEN

Sarah was determined to find the lemon-scented bleach. She had smelled it at the scene of the missing items and where she had found the tapestry and Don's notebook. There had to be a connection.

Agatha had been sure she didn't have any lemon cleanser with her supplies in the laundry room, so Sarah started her search in the kitchen.

The kitchen had two huge pantries and more cupboards than a big-box home improvement store. The only way to find the lemon-scented bleach was to search the cupboards one at a time.

Sarah went to the first bank of cupboards. It was good that she wasn't bothered by mice. By the time she had opened the fourth set of doors, she had seen plenty of droppings and even heard a fleeing mouse. She hoped that Neil and Reginald planned to bring in an exterminator. Their to-do list must be a mile long.

An hour later, Sarah accepted that she wasn't going to find a bottle of lemon bleach in the kitchen. A second storm that had followed quickly after the first was throwing itself at the mountain. It had less wind, but more rain. Dripping water plopped from various leaks around the house.

"How's it going?" Don asked as he came into the kitchen, soaked through.

"You didn't change your mind and try to walk down the mountain, did you?" asked Sarah, tossing him a roll of paper towels.

"Thanks." He pulled off a half dozen, wrapped them around his right hand, and rubbed his head. It stopped the water from running off, but left his hair spiked. He reminded Sarah of Jason when he was younger, and she said a quick prayer for his safety, along with the twins'.

Dropping the wet towels onto a table, Don said, "No, I didn't try to walk down the mountain. When it stopped raining for a few minutes, I figured I'd go out and look around."

"In the dark?"

"I took a flashlight. Too bad I didn't get back inside in time."

She noticed his hands were trembling. His eyes were bright, and they didn't meet hers.

"Did you find something?" Sarah asked.

"How about you?"

He was evading her question by asking another. A trick Sarah herself had used.

"You're shaking like a leaf. You might be cold, but you look excited to me," Sarah said.

"You're right. During a lull in the wind, I'm pretty sure I heard chain saws. It sounds like we might be freed soon."

"That's great news."

Don smiled, then walked past her to get a cup of coffee. Was that gas she smelled on him? He opened the backdoor and called out to Ethan who was checking the generator. The gas odor got stronger.

Sarah reminded herself she was chasing the lemon scent, not gas fumes coming from the generator.

First, she headed back to the living room where she had first noticed the smell. She walked in and took a deep breath. The scent was almost too faint for her to sense it. She looked around, but everything was just as she had last seen it. Nothing else had been moved or gone missing.

She decided to head back to the scene of the crime—or in this case, the scene of the scent. She went up to the bedroom where Agatha had collapsed, stood in the middle of the room, and took a deep breath. She smelled the lemony aroma and tried to remember every facet of it, so she could follow it to its source.

She stepped into the hall and turned left, then right. The smell was a tiny bit stronger to the right. She needed Murphy. Liam's dog could ferret out the smallest crumb of a dog treat from ten feet away.

Sarah headed right. She paused every half-dozen steps and sniffed again. The smell was growing fainter but was still distinctly lemon.

Then it was gone. She stood on a landing for a staircase that connected all three floors. Had the scent risen up the stairs? Or had whoever was using it gone down the stairs?

Dead end. She didn't have Murphy's sense of smell, and her human one wasn't equal to the task. This wasn't getting her anywhere but frustrated. She would have to wait until she found another room with the lemon scent in it or saw more bleached spots.

Yawning, Sarah continued past the stairs. It must be close to midnight. She hurried along the hall. She hadn't been in this section of the house before but the Kramers must have. The carpets had been vacuumed, and the floorboards weren't topped with a thick frosting of dust and cobwebs.

Papers rattled in a nearby room. She paused and saw Reginald by a desk in the room.

"Hi!" Sarah said.

He visibly startled, then looked up.

"Oh, Sarah," he said as if she hadn't just witnessed his ugly confrontation with Don, "I didn't hear you coming along the hall."

"I'm sorry. Find anything interesting?"

"Not yet." He scanned the pages scattered on the desk. "I've been reading these, hoping to uncover some clue to our Ackermann-Johnsons. I've found bills and correspondence but nothing with a name."

Sarah picked up a few pages. "What about dates? Have you seen anything later than December 1941?"

"Nothing so far." He opened one of the drawers and pointed to stacks of envelopes. "I've barely scratched the surface." He dropped the page he had been holding into a nearby wastebasket.

Little pieces of paper flew out, and he grimaced. Sarah bent to pick up one that was about the length and breadth of her thumb.

"Just toss it," Reginald said. "I found a lot of pieces of ripped newspapers in one drawer. I'd hoped they were information torn out of the letters. No such luck." He frowned. "Do you think there's something in the articles that could help us?"

"Why don't you give them to me? I'll sort them out."

"Are you sure?" He glanced at the wastebasket. "There's a bunch."

"Then I'd better get started."

Sarah pulled an extra chair over to a low table. Rain splattered on the glass fitfully, and she hoped that was a sign the second storm was ready to move past. No stars or moon shone past the clouds. She clicked on a gooseneck lamp on the table. The bulb had a low wattage, but it would have to do.

Reginald dumped the pieces onto the table. Two large wads bounced across the floor.

Sarah ignored the crumpled papers as she concentrated on the tiny pieces. There were dozens. She began separating them by shape and size. It went more quickly than she had expected. They clearly hadn't been torn at random.

When the pieces were sorted, she rubbed her tired eyes, then grimaced. The newsprint ink was going to leave her looking like a raccoon. She reached into her pocket for a tissue, then froze.

Her gaze focused on the pieces in the pile closest to her. Each piece had tiny holes torn along the edges. Could they have been sewn to fabric? Some seamstresses used pieces of paper to stiffen tiny areas in an intricate quilt pattern. When the quilt block was finished, the paper was gently ripped away to leave a perfect pattern.

She reached for the group of the largest pieces and began to arrange them with the tiny holes along the edges lining up. The pattern of the design was clear. More than two dozen pieces had been stitched together in a medallion pattern. These pieces of paper might have been used in making one of the quilts she had found on her first visit to the house.

Picking up a crumpled page from the floor, she realized the piecing hadn't been done just with the scraps of paper. This full page also had tiny holes. She opened it with care and spread the paper on the table.

There were about a dozen squares outlined on the page, each about three inches square. The same size as the odd patchwork blocks sewn on the missing tapestries.

Each square had a different design. Like the teaching quilt, the squares were decorated with simple animal figures and other shapes. One might have been a sunflower because a large circle was set atop a narrow shaft, but she didn't see any petals.

Then her eyes were caught by the words on the page. Words that weren't English. The page had been taken out of a newspaper.

"Reginald," Sarah asked, "did you notice that the newspapers these pieces were cut from aren't in English? Look at the date. March first, 1939, Whoever lived here was getting German-language newspapers."

Reginald snatched one off the table and flattened it. She warned him to be careful as he scanned the page. "It looks like German. If you want to know what it says, why don't you ask your buddy Don?"

Sarah ignored his sarcasm. "This was published in New York City." She pointed to the tiny print next to the date. "Don's told us that there were a lot of German-born immigrants in the United States in the thirties, so it makes sense they'd read newspapers in their own language."

"So would a spy."

"We don't know for sure that a spy lived in this house."

His eyes twinkled as he went back to emptying the drawer. "But it would be a great selling point for the hotel. We could theme the whole place with gadgets and codes."

Again Sarah focused on the mystery. She couldn't help feeling that she was on the cusp of something important.

"Reginald," she asked, "are there more of these pierced papers in the desk?"

He pointed to the wastebasket. "Everything I found is in there. Why are you so interested in ripped newspapers?"

"These aren't just scraps. They are used for making intricate patchwork patterns."

"Uh-huh." He was reading a page he had taken out of an envelope. With a frown, he crumpled it before tossing it into the wastebasket. He reached for the next envelope.

Sarah stood. "I'm going to leave these here for now. I'll be back later to get them. Okay?"

"Okay." Again he didn't look at her.

"Reginald?"

He frowned at her. "What?"

"Could you make sure the papers aren't moved? I'll be back to get them later."

"I heard you the first time." Irritation laced through his words.

Sarah decided to make a hasty retreat. She took the two large pieces of newsprint and headed for the dining room. Nobody else was in there, so she didn't have to explain what she was doing when she held the paper up against the blocks sewn to the bottom of one of the remaining tapestries.

The blocks were identical in size. Sarah cautioned herself not to get excited. It was a fairly standard size. She ran her fingers along the edges of the appliquéd figure in the first block, trying to identify it as one of the patterns on the paper. Was it supposed to be a horse or a cow, or was it the dog outlined on the paper? It didn't matter because she couldn't find anything like it traced onto the paper. She found a tri-angle on the faded blocks, but the other shapes eluded her.

Sarah went next to the toy room. Again the blocks on the bottom of the tapestry were the same size, but none of the designs matched those on the pierced paper. She was dis-couraged, even though she believed that she was on the right track.

Were there other pierced papers with the patterns on these blocks? If she could find more pages, she would have a greater chance of putting a pattern together with the proper block, and she might understand why someone had sewn the blocks on the tapestries in the first place. She had to hope that once she started making matches, an explanation would emerge.

When she returned to the office, it was empty. Reginald must have given up looking through the envelopes and let-ters. Sarah hesitated, wondering if she should open the desk drawers without permission. Neil wouldn't mind, but she didn't want Reginald's short fuse exploding at her. But didn't he want an answer to the questions too?

Reginald had tossed out the pages he had gone through. She hoped he wasn't being too hasty. Don might find some-thing useful in the paperwork. She put the wastebasket in the room's closet where it should be safe until she had a chance to tell Don about the papers.

Sarah returned to the desk. Two rows of drawers were on either side of a shallow knee well. There wasn't a mid-dle drawer. She began with the left-hand drawers, but

Reginald—or someone else—had already emptied them. She opened the top drawer on the right-hand side and gave a silent cheer.

It was full of the paper pieces. She couldn't get through them all tonight. She would have to take them back to Maple Hill. There were too many to fit into her purse. She smiled as she thought of Irene's large bag. There should be room for the pierced papers with Irene's computer.

She found four more full-size pages and put them on top of the desk before opening the next lower drawer. It was filled with spools of threads and a pin cushion. The bottommost drawer was empty except for a single book. Opening it, she saw it was handwritten in what she guessed was German. Another possible clue to be translated. She paged through it, hoping for anything that might reveal what it was. Each page was dated, so it could be a journal. If so, it could be the best clue they had found yet. The most recent date was December 1939, so the writer had stopped using the journal two years before the last entry in the logbook. Was that significant? She set it on top of the desk, determined to find out with Don's help.

But why would someone store quilt-piecing papers and sewing supplies in a desk?

Sarah knelt to examine the desk and discovered it was an elegant sewing table. She saw a hinge next to each row of drawers, and she swung them out and away from each other. An old-fashioned sewing machine with a knee pedal was encased in the center. Putting the book and large pierced papers on the floor, she lifted the top. It contained slots to hold scissors and bobbins and other tools. The name Pfaff was inlaid with marquetry.

She was familiar with Pfaff's excellent sewing machines. They had been made in the United States since the 1930s, but the company's headquarters was in Germany. She closed the top and gathered up the book and papers.

The lady of the house must have spent a lot of time here, sewing and handling household accounts. Sarah understood why when she looked out the window and saw the magnificent view of the distant lights of Maple Hill below.

She put the book into the top right drawer and covered it with the tiny pierced papers. She would give Don the book later.

Smoothing the large pieces on the table, she stepped back, hoping she would be able to see the complete pattern better at a distance as she had with the quilts in the toy room. It worked. The bottom left square had the definite shape of a Christmas tree. Could that be the triangle she had felt on one of the squares in the dining room?

Sarah took the page and went back to the dining room. Irene, Maggie, and Don sat at the table talking in low voices. They looked up as one, and she saw them relax when they realized who had come in.

"Am I interrupting something important?" Sarah asked.

"Just brainstorming." Irene motioned to the chair beside her. "We could use your keen mind, Sarah."

"Sure." She told Don about the book she had found and where it was hidden.

"I'll get started translating it right now." He grinned as he stood. "Thanks, Mrs. Hart, for asking me."

"You're our German language expert."

"I know, but..." He left the unspoken words hanging as he rushed out.

"He's taking Reginald's accusations hard." Maggie smiled at Sarah. "Your request is exactly what he needed. Why don't you go over our meager clues with us?"

Sarah smiled back. "I'm chasing a clue of my own right now."

She crossed the room to the tapestry. Holding up the piece of paper, she ran her fingers along the Christmas tree shape. She touched the first block sewn to the tapestry. It wasn't the one.

"What are you doing?" asked Maggie as she came over.

Sarah explained as she stroked the second block. Not that one either. She reached for the third. There was the triangle! She laid the Christmas tree block over the fabric, and the outlines were identical.

"Look, Maggie!" Sarah said. "It's a match. That block was made from this paper pattern."

Irene asked, "What do you think it means?"

"I can't tell yet," Sarah said, "but I'm going to try to match the shapes from this page to the blocks sewn on the tapestries. I'm hoping once I get home, I'll be able to use a tracing wheel to help."

"A tracing wheel?" asked Maggie. "What's that?"

"It's a small serrated wheel used for marking darts in clothes-making. If I put chalk on the wheel and then run it over these pierced papers, I should be able to get a clear image."

"What a great idea!" Maggie gave her a quick hug. "Then we can come back and find the blocks that match each one. Maybe something about how they're arranged will give us a clue. Just like the alphabet on the teaching quilts."

"Irene, do you have room in your bag?" Sarah asked. "I've got a lot of pierced pieces to take home."

Irene handed her brightly colored bag to Sarah. "Use all the space you want. I can carry my laptop and camera if I need to."

Sarah thanked her and returned to the sewing room. Don was waiting there, pacing.

"The book is in the top drawer." She opened the drawer and got the book out.

He held out a sealed envelope. "I wanted to give you this without everyone seeing. If you want to share it with Mr. Lawton and his partner, go ahead. That'll be your decision."

She took it. "What is it?"

"A list of the names our ham radio operator mentioned in his logbook."

"You translated the whole logbook?"

He shrugged as if it weren't a big deal. "Most of it contained weather reports and questions about how so-and-so was. I wrote down those names. I don't know if they're the people he contacted or other people."

"Or code names."

"I didn't see anything in the logbook that would suggest there was a German spy here. But we can't be completely sure until you figure out who these people were."

Sarah turned the envelope over in her hands. It wasn't very thick. It probably held only a single piece of paper. "Are you going to compare these names to your research?"

"I don't think so."

"I would have thought that you'd want to chase down every connection to Walter Ackermann."

"The house belonged to the Johnsons, not to Ackermann. I think I've learned everything I can here." He looked at the book she held. "Why don't we hold off on that until you trace down the names? If you need me to translate it, I can. Otherwise, you can use one of the translating programs on the Internet."

Sarah didn't understand. "If you're giving up because of what Reginald said—"

"It's not that." He started to add more, then walked out without another word.

Suddenly Don had become as cryptic as the clues to the family's disappearance, and he wasn't interested in chasing down any other clues. He might be so angry with Reginald that he wanted to wash his hands of all of them.

Sarah went to work gathering the pieces of newspaper. She had chased down the last scrap of paper when an amber light flashed outside. She looked out the window and heard cheers downstairs as a DPW truck stopped in front of the house. She twisted the handle on the window, opening it in time to hear Neil call a greeting to the men in the truck.

A window rolled down on the truck, and a man shouted, "We've got the road cleared. Everyone okay up here?"

"Yes," Neil yelled back. "Especially now that we can get back to Maple Hill."

"What is this place?"

Sarah closed the window as rain came in. She wasn't interested in hearing Neil's explanation. All she wanted now was to get home. They had been stuck here over twelve hours.

"Did you hear?" asked Maggie, grinning from ear to ear as she met Sarah in the hallway. "The road's open."

"I heard." Sarah looked at her borrowed outfit as they walked to the entry foyer. "I doubt our clothes are dry yet, but I'm sure Neil won't mind if we borrow these a bit longer."

Irene and Chester were in the entry already. Chester gave them a thumbs-up before stifling a yawn. Sarah had to hide her own. Now that they were headed home, the long day was settling on her like a heavy blanket around her shoulders.

Neil came into the foyer to announce that he would get his car out of the garage and pull it as close as possible to the house. None of them wanted to get drenched again. The rain was still falling, and he wanted to get down the mountainside before the road washed out. Don offered to help with the garage door, but Reginald called him aside. Chester went with Neil to the garage instead. Don's gaze followed them, his mouth tightening.

Reginald made a big show of thanking them for coming, then wished them a safe trip down the mountain. He motioned for Don to come with him over by the stairs. Sarah couldn't hear what either man said because their voices were muted, but Don bristled.

Neil's car pulled under the porte cochere, and Sarah went out on the porch with Irene and Maggie. She started down the steps, but paused when Don came out, slamming the door behind him.

"Carruthers told me not to come back," Don said when Sarah asked if he was okay.

"I'm sorry, Don."

"You don't have anything to be sorry for." He walked away before Sarah could say anything else.

She wondered what she could have said. Reginald was rude, and he didn't think before spouting vitriol. She wondered how long Neil would put up with it.

CHAPTER NINETEEN

I t was past two o'clock in the morning when Sarah opened her front door. It had been a slow, harrowing drive down Lookout Mountain. She doubted she had ever been happier to get home. As she shrugged off her wet coat in her own hall, she took a deep breath. No lemon scent. Instead she smelled an undeniably chocolate aroma. It was a wonderful way to be greeted at such an unreasonable hour.

Lucie popped out of the kitchen, pot holders on her hands and a chocolate-stained apron wrapped around her. "Sarah! You're home."

"I hope you haven't been worried."

"No. Your son stopped by to let me know that you were marooned in the mountains because trees were down." She grinned as she held up her hands. "Okay, I was a little worried. I always bake when I'm anxious, so there are brownies and chocolate cake and chocolate chip cookies and apple crisp."

"Not chocolate apple crisp?" Sarah teased her boarder.

Lucie's dimples accented her smile. "I haven't figured out a way to make apple crisp with chocolate yet. Give me time." She glanced toward the table with the phone on it. "You've got a couple of messages on the answering machine. And Mrs. Maplethorpe stopped by earlier."

"In this storm?" She would definitely have done the same if Martha hadn't answered her phone. Even so, she appreciated her dear friend's concern.

"She asked me to ask you to call her when you got home."

"Thanks." She combed her fingers back through her damp hair, then yawned. "I'll wait until the morning. Well, later in the morning, that is. You really didn't need to stay up until I got home."

"The storms kept me awake. And once I got baking, I couldn't stop. I hope you don't mind that I used a packet of your chocolate chips," Lucie said.

"Not as long as you saved a few cookies for me." She yawned again.

Lucie took Sarah by the shoulders and turned her toward the stairs. "You go upstairs and get ready for bed. I'll bring warm cookies and milk up for you. Just the perfect thing for a damp, rainy night." Her dimples reappeared when she smiled. "And I'll bring some for me too."

Sarah thanked her for her kindness and climbed the steps. Her bedroom waited, fresh smelling and inviting. The rain pattering against the window no longer seemed malevolent. By the time she had changed into her nightgown and robe, Lucie was knocking on her door. Sarah gratefully took the tray with two cookies, a brownie, and a generous piece of cake. A large glass of fresh milk was there to wash it down. She wondered if Lucie had any idea that there hadn't been any food up on the mountain.

Sarah ate the cookies and half the brownie and a few bites of cake while she read her evening verses to the song of rain on the roof. She drank the milk while she turned to Psalm 121. The first two verses gave her special comfort: "I will lift up mine eyes unto the hills, from whence comes my help. My help comes from the Lord, who made heaven and earth."

Closing her Bible, she put it on the bedside table. She said a prayer, asking for blessings for her family and friends. She then set the alarm for seven, barely four hours from then, because she wanted to let Martha know she was okay. That was her last thought before she surrendered to sleep.

Martha answered the phone on the first ring and said, "Sarah, it's about time you called. When did you get home?"

"It was almost three o'clock in the morning by the time I got to sleep." Sarah glanced out the window at the sunshine that jeweled the raindrops clinging to the window screens. "I'm too exhausted to think clearly."

"You should go back to sleep." Martha's voice brooked no discussion. "Just tell me two things."

"I'll try."

"First, is everyone okay?"

Sarah couldn't help thinking of Agatha's asthma attack and Don's pained expression when he left the house, but Martha didn't mean that, so Sarah said, "Yes, everyone's okay."

"Did you find anything interesting?"

"Yes…or at least I think so. I've got some work to do on what I found. Once I get my brain working again."

"Tell me about it when you've caught up on sleep."

"All right." She tried to stifle a yawn but couldn't.

Martha laughed. "Go back to bed!"

Sarah hung up the phone and did.

Sarah woke just past noon, feeling disoriented as she did whenever she slept in the middle of the day. But she also felt more human. Her stomach growled, and she remembered how little she had eaten the day before.

It didn't take her long to shower and dress. She called Maggie to check on everyone, and Jason answered the phone to tell her that Maggie had gone to work for a few hours. Sarah made a quick sandwich and took it into her sewing room where she booted up her computer. While she ate, she went through her sewing supplies to see if she could find her tracing wheel. She didn't use it often but remembered its plastic handle was a vivid blue. She found it in a box at the back of her closet after her sandwich was gone and the computer was up and running, in a box at the back of her closet. She thought wistfully of the Pfaff sewing machine table and its many slots for tools. She could use one like it.

Although she was curious about the designs on the papers, Sarah decided to check on the envelope Don had given to her. The single page didn't contain many names. Twenty. It shouldn't take long to find matches on the Internet.

Fifteen minutes later, she didn't have a single lead on any of the names. She had found almost every name, but only for current Web sites or Facebook pages. She began again, putting in each name and following it with *1930s*. Again she came up empty-handed. A third time through she tried every name and *Germany*.

That led her to a census for Germany in 1938. Her hopes spiraled skyward but were dashed when she realized the census was only for non-Germans in German territory. Even so, she checked each name, including Walter Ackermann's.

Nothing.

How about the Maple Hill census? She found it online and opened up the 1930 census. She searched for the names, again coming up empty-handed. She got the same result for the census from 1940.

Maybe there still was some local connection. She would take the list over to the historical society when she went into town and ask Irene to help her check other town records.

Sarah heard someone at the front door. Getting up, she wondered if it was Irene stopping by to pick up her computer bag. She could give Irene a copy of the list now.

It wasn't Irene. Ethan Kramer stood on the porch. He wore his work-stained trousers and boots.

"Ethan!" Sarah said, throwing the door open wider and reveling in the cooler temperatures outside. "Come in. How about a cup of coffee?"

He shook his head as he stepped into the foyer. He glanced around before his gaze settled on her. "Thanks, but no. I've had more coffee in the past twenty-four hours than I usually have in a month."

"I know what you mean. What can I do for you?"

He looked toward the living room, and Sarah invited him in to sit. He perched on the very edge of the sofa.

When she sat in her rocker, Ethan said, "I don't know if you know, but Mr. Carruthers fired us last night. He hardly waited for Mr. Lawton's taillights to disappear before he told us to get out and not come back."

"Oh dear. Did he say why?"

"Isn't that obvious?" He spread out his hands and sighed. "He thinks we stole those missing antiques. I didn't realize you had told him about the items that weren't there any more."

Sarah hesitated, then said, "But I thought he blamed Don for the missing items."

"He must have changed his mind because he sent us packing too." He clenched his fists on his knees, then spread his fingers out. "Agatha didn't want me to bother you, but to be honest, if potential employers find out we were fired, we'll never get another job." He shuffled his feet, clearly uncomfortable. She guessed he wasn't used to asking for help. "I'm hoping you'll ask Mr. Lawton to give us another chance."

"Why me?"

"You didn't jump to conclusions about us or anyone else. You listened." He leaned toward her, his expression beseeching. "I'm not asking you to ask Mr. Lawton for our job back. Just if you'd ask him to give me a chance to speak with him."

"I'm sure he'd speak with you at his office."

Ethan's mouth twisted. "I'm not sure of that. Mr. Carruthers told us not to contact either him or Mr. Lawton again. He said Mr. Lawton would send us our final paychecks."

"Wait here." Sarah stood and went into the hall. She picked up the phone while she looked up Neil's number. She had written it down after he had asked her to come up to the house.

Nancy, his secretary, answered, and Sarah was put right through to Neil. Without explaining why, she asked if Neil had a few minutes now to see her and Ethan. He agreed, and she sensed his anticipation. If he thought they had found out something about the family, he was going to be disappointed.

Ethan drove Sarah in his battered car and parked not far from Neil's office.

"Maple Hill looks like a nice town," Ethan said as he stepped around a deep puddle.

"I think so," Sarah said, "but then again I've lived here my whole life."

He nodded, but didn't say anything else until they were ushered into Neil's starkly decorated office. Sarah saw Ethan's distaste with the strange furniture, though he masked it by the time Neil rose to greet them.

"To what do I owe the pleasure?" asked Neil.

Ethan didn't beat around the bush. "Mr. Carruthers fired us."

"He didn't say anything to me about that. Hold on a second." Neil held up one finger and turned to his computer. He tapped a few keys, paused, then looked at Ethan with a frown. "He e-mailed me that you wouldn't be working for us any longer, but he didn't say he'd fired you."

"I don't want a rumor getting around that Agatha and I could be thieves," Ethan said. "It would destroy our business."

"Of course. I would never say anything without proof."

"Maybe you wouldn't, but what about Mr. Carruthers?"

Neil hemmed and hawed, unable to find words that would reassure Ethan and still be the truth. He looked to Sarah for assistance. She wondered what he thought she could do. He was the one who had a loose cannon for a business partner.

"Have you contacted the police, Neil?" Sarah asked.

"Not yet."

"Has Reginald?"

"I don't think so. To be honest, I couldn't remember exactly what was gone."

Sarah pulled her camera out of her purse and clicked it on. "I'll show you the two pictures. The one I took the first time we were up there, then the one I took this time." She pushed the button to bring the photos up on the screen.

Nothing happened. The screen flickered, then went black with two words in white: NO IMAGE.

"They're gone!" She turned the camera off and then on again. Same message. "My photos are all gone."

"It's easy to erase them by mistake," Neil said.

She remembered a time the year before when she had nearly done so. "No, it's not easy. I have to go through three prompts before I can erase them." A cold quiver trickled down her back. "Someone else erased them. On purpose."

"Sarah, you had your camera with you all the time."

"No, I didn't." She might not have gotten much sleep, but her memory was clear. "I left my camera in the dining room while I helped you and Chester siphon gas for the generator."

Ethan said quietly, "It sounds like someone didn't want you comparing those photos again."

Neil's brows lowered as he stood. "Someone like you?"

"Here." Ethan dropped a plain white envelope on Neil's desk. "Maybe this will prove that we're honest."

"What's this?" asked Neil as he reached for it.

"I found it in the big dining room. We'd started cleaning in there just before we found out the tree had been cleared away." He lowered his eyes. "I didn't show it to Agatha. She loves old letters, and I wasn't sure if she'd want me to pass it along."

"She would have kept it?" Sarah asked, astonished.

"Not for good, but she would have wanted to make a copy of it for her collection of old letters."

Sarah shrugged and looked at Neil.

Neil said nothing.

"I was going to give it to Mr. Carruthers," Ethan said, "but he didn't give me a chance to do anything but get out." He jammed his hands into his pockets. "So I decided to bring it to you."

"While you asked for your job back?"

Ethan stood straighter. "We'd like to finish the job, Mr. Lawton, but I'm not going to beg. I know we're honest, and I know we do a good job."

"Well, you have done a great job so far, and I appreciate the extra effort to come to Maple Hill to give this to me."

"What is it?" asked Sarah when her curiosity wouldn't let her remain silent any longer.

Neil opened it and pulled out a typewritten sheet. It was, Sarah realized, a carbon copy.

The page nearly slipped out of Neil's hands, and he gripped it tighter. "It's dated May 1940 and it was written by Walter Ackermann!"

Sarah stared at the page. Walter Ackermann really had existed, or at least someone had used the name when writing a letter. "Who's it addressed to?"

"A Mr. Charles Garfield in the office of the Secretary of War. Hmm ... I didn't know we had a Secretary of War."

"I think that's the same as our current Secretary of Defense," Sarah said. "What does it say?"

Neil began reading aloud. The letter had been written in very formal English. "'My dear Mr. Garfield, I am in receipt of your correspondence of Tuesday past. Allow me to express my gratitude for your continuing attention to this matter. I want to impress upon you again the gravity of the situation. The valuable item I have in my possession at this address—'" Neil stopped reading to say, "The address is the house on Lookout Mountain. 'The valuable item I have in my possession at this address should be of great interest to the government of the United States of America. As I previously informed you, the leaders of the Third Reich are searching for this item. They believe, quite rightly, it is vital to their plans to conquer Europe and the rest of the civilized world. I look forward to receiving your counsel on how to remove this item from my possession and into the safekeeping of your department. I remain your humble servant...' And it's signed with Walter Ackermann's name."

"But who is Walter Ackermann?" Sarah asked. "A spy? A double agent maybe?"

Neil put the letter on his desk. "We can only assume the letter was sent, because this is a carbon copy."

"So what does this have to do with the family who lived there?" Sarah asked. "Were they part of Walter Ackermann's family, or were the Johnsons completely unrelated?"

Neil raised his hands. "Maybe they were a front for Ackermann's work." He tapped his finger on his chin. "I wonder what he was referring to and if it's still at the house." He answered his own question before Ethan or Sarah could. "No, I'm sure he took it with him. But did he leave before the Johnsons or after them?"

"Or with them," Sarah said.

Ethan cleared his throat, and Neil looked at him. "Right. Your job. Did you look at this letter before you brought it to Reginald and me?"

"Yes. I thought it looked pretty important, so I got it to you right away."

Sarah remained silent. From Neil's expression, she knew his thoughts were following the same path as her own. Once Ethan had read the letter, he must have realized he could have sold it for big bucks. Such a letter would be prized by anyone who collected World War II memorabilia.

"I'd like you and Agatha to finish the job." Neil slid the letter back in its envelope. "I'll understand if you don't want to, and I'll be glad to give you a good reference for any future employers. No strings attached."

As Ethan and Neil shook hands, Sarah smiled. Ethan and Agatha moved further down her list of suspects. Even if Agatha might not have given up the letter right away, Ethan Kramer had proven their honesty by bringing the letter to Neil.

But who had deleted her photos? It must be the thief, and the items must really have been stolen. Who'd had the chance to slip the items out of the house?

Chester had been in the house alone. Don had admitted that he had been to the house before, but claimed he hadn't been inside. Neil and Reginald had been up there between her visits. Something about the business partners' shock at the state of the house didn't ring true to her. Neil Lawton was one of the most savvy businessmen she knew, and apparently Reginald Carruthers was skilled in making business deals. So why had neither of them checked the house more closely before getting involved in what might be a very bad investment?

And why hadn't either of them called the police about the theft?

Quietly, she said, "Neil, I think you should call Chief Webber now."

Sarah remained in the office until Neil had given a report to Maple Hill's chief of police. She watched Neil's face as he answered questions. She saw no sign that he was hiding anything. Was he a better actor than she would have guessed? She didn't like to have friends among her suspects, but the list of possible thieves was dwindling fast, and she didn't have an answer.

CHAPTER TWENTY

lone figure sat on Sarah's front steps when Sarah
returned home from Neil's office. It was Amy. She
took her earbuds out when Sarah came up the walk.
"Hi, Grandma," she said with a grin.

"How are you doing, kiddo?" Sarah gave her granddaughter a hug before unlocking the door.

Amy shed her backpack and sweatshirt. "Mmm...smells
like chocolate in here."

"Lucie went on a baking spree." Sarah put her arm
around Amy's shoulders as they walked to the kitchen. She
couldn't help noticing how much taller Amy was than even
a few months ago. "Do you want to sample some of the
treats?"

"I'm a girl, and it's chocolate. I'd like to sample *all* the
treats." Amy giggled.

Sarah joined in. It was good to see her granddaughter laughing and joking and happy. She sent up a heartfelt

prayer of gratitude that Amy was sharing a bit of that joy with her grandmother.

Amy sampled the cookies, the brownies, the cake, and some warmed-up apple crisp. She announced them all excellent. "Almost as good as yours, Grandma." The twinkle in her eyes reminded Sarah of her late husband's.

She was so blessed that Jason and his family had returned to Maple Hill. No one could fill the places in her heart where Gerry and her parents had been, and there always would be a sting of sorrow when she thought of them. Yet, with her children's families and her dear friends and her quilting—and the occasional mystery to unravel—she had a very good life.

"I'm glad to hear that they're only almost as good as mine." Sarah kept her voice stern, but Amy would know she was teasing. "After all, Lucie's only here for a couple more weeks, and then you'll have to suffer through my cooking again."

"I'll do my best." Amy didn't pause as she changed the subject. "Could you teach me and Audrey to hem dresses?"

"I'd be glad to do it for you, if you want."

Amy reached for another brownie. "Mom said it'd be better if I learned to do it for myself."

"She's right. Is this your new dress for the dance?"

That was the last thing Sarah got to say for the next fifteen minutes while Amy described her dress and then Audrey's. The middle school was hosting its own homecoming dance, and Maggie had shared with Sarah that both Amy and Audrey were going with friends.

When Amy was finished, Sarah offered to take both twins to her friend Vanessa's fabric shop to find thread to match their dresses.

"Mom is going to take us there tomorrow. Can we get started on Saturday?"

"Perfect. Bring your dresses and the thread over. I'll help pin up your hems, then you can do the sewing."

"Cool!" Amy jumped up and gave Sarah a big hug. Waving good-bye, she ran out of the kitchen, scooped up her backpack, and went racing down the front steps.

Sarah watched from the doorway. She couldn't believe Amy was that excited about learning to hem a dress. Did Amy have her eye on a boy? Maybe the one Sarah had seen her *not* talking to at the field hockey game?

She remembered Maggie saying she had heard the girls talking about what they wanted to wear and who was going and which boys were taking which girls. They were at that age.

As she closed the front door, Sarah chuckled. Jason and Maggie were in for an exciting—and challenging—few years.

Sarah wasn't surprised when Chief Webber called the next morning and asked her to come to the police station. The chief wanted her to make a statement to accompany Neil's robbery report. She told the chief that she would be there within half an hour.

The police department was quiet when Sarah went to the counter on the half wall and asked the officer behind it to let Chief Webber know that she had arrived. She sat on the bench by the door while she waited until the busy chief could see her.

She looked up when the door in the half wall opened and Irene walked out. Sarah stood to greet her friend who was carrying her laptop under her right arm.

"I wondered if I'd see you here," Irene said. "Chief Webber said he's talking with all of us who were at the house."

"He's always very thorough."

"I'll say." She tapped her computer lightly. "He wanted to see my photos and the lists I made while I was there. We uploaded what I have onto a disk for him to put in the investigation file. I'm not sure how a list of inedible groceries in the pantry will help, though."

Sarah laughed with her friend, then reached into her purse to pull out the page with the names that Don had given her. Explaining her fruitless search, she asked Irene if she would check at the historical society to see if she could find a match for any of the names.

"Has Don had any luck finding out anything about these people?" Irene asked.

"Don isn't going to be helping us find out about the Johnsons any longer." At Irene's questioning look, Sarah said, "He told me it's because he's interested solely in Walter Ackermann, not the Johnson family."

"Okay," Irene said, "but I don't think we've seen the last of Don Monroe."

"I think you're right."

Irene waved good-bye as an officer came to escort Sarah to the chief's office.

Sarah recognized Officer Hopkins whom she had seen on previous visits to the police station. She greeted him, and he made friendly conversation on the way back to Chief Webber's office.

Chief Webber was staring at his computer screen when Sarah walked into his office. He hadn't served in the military police in more than a decade, but he still had that stern and controlled demeanor he had gained in the army.

"Good morning, Mrs. Hart," he said as he stood and motioned for her to take the chair in front of his desk. "I appreciate your coming in on such short notice."

"I can't say I was surprised to get your call," Sarah said.

"Yes, Mr. Lawton told me that you were at his office when he called. I got the distinct impression from him that you weren't leaving until he contacted us." His lips twitched, but his eyes remained serious. "Why don't you tell me in your own words what happened. I'll just take some notes."

Sarah started at the beginning: the first conversation with Neil on the phone. Chief Webber scribbled notes, but didn't halt her until she mentioned that she had taken her camera with her.

"Do you have the photos with you?" he asked.

"My photos were deleted by someone. I suspect it was the thief, who didn't want proof that the items had been moved."

Chief Webber noted that. "That's too bad. The other photos I've seen were mostly taken on cell phones, and they're not as good as I would have liked. Okay. We'll have to do this the old-fashioned way. Tell me which items you noticed were missing. Not what anyone else noticed and told you. Just the ones you yourself noticed were missing."

"I understand." She listed the antiques that were now gone.

"Did you notice anything unusual about the items?"

Sarah told him about the patchwork blocks sewn onto the tapestries in each room. Taking an envelope of the small pierced pieces out of her purse, she spread them across his desk and explained what they were and how they were used.

He examined several, nodding when Sarah pointed out that a German-language newspaper had been used. "May I keep these?" he asked.

"I was hoping to use them to rebuild the actual designs that were created. I thought I might find a pattern that would lead to more clues."

"I see." Disappointment deepened his voice. "Could we make copies of the papers?"

"Of course," Sarah said. "But I'll warn you that these are a small sample of what I found, and individually they may not make much sense."

He carefully put them back into the envelope. "For the time being, I'll let you keep them. We're certainly going to make neither hide nor hair of them without your help. What do you plan to do with them?"

"I'm going to use a tracing wheel. The chalk will trace the designs on plain paper, and I should have a clear picture of each design. I'll be glad to make you a set as well."

"Now *that* would be helpful."

"I'll bring them over when I've got them finished." Sarah put the envelope in her purse while Chief Webber scanned through his notes. "There was one other odd thing."

"Yes?" Chief Webber asked.

"Has anyone mentioned a lemon scent to you?"

He picked up his pen again. "Why don't you tell me about it?"

Sarah did, not leaving out Agatha's asthma attack or the spots Sarah had found on the rug in the bedroom. Chief Webber said nothing when she was done other than to ask if there was anything else she would like to add. She had told him everything she could remember. He had her read through the notes he had taken to see if he had made any errors. He hadn't, so she stood, shook his hand, and left with the promise to bring in the pierced paper designs as soon as she finished tracing them. The chief's thanks went with her, but she couldn't help feeling that she had overlooked something important, something that had been right in front of her eyes.

After Sarah went to the store to pick up some groceries and the chalk, she decided to make another stop before she headed home. She had realized while going through the list of names from the logbook that she didn't know much about ham radios and their operators. She headed for the library.

Spencer greeted her when she came in. "Glad to see you home and safe after your adventure up on Lookout Mountain," he said.

"It's one adventure I don't want to repeat." Surely wandering through the old house had been fascinating. It had been like stepping into a seventy-year-old snapshot, a virtual reality image where she could turn 360 degrees and touch, hear, and smell every item. She hoped Neil would invite her back to continue exploring the house. "I need a book on ham radios during the 1930s and forties. Do you have something like that?"

With a smile, he crooked a finger for her to follow him. He didn't hesitate as he turned into one alcove of shelves and reached for a book. She wondered if he knew exactly where every book was. He had an unfailing ability to find a book without glancing along a shelf.

"Here's one that should help." He handed it to her.

Sarah tilted it so she could read the title. *Amateur Radio Operations During World War II.*

"That looks perfect." She couldn't wait to get home and read through it. "Thanks, Spencer."

"I figured you'd be looking for something on that subject after hearing everyone talking about how there was a German spy up on Lookout Mountain during the war."

"What?" asked Sarah. "Who said that?"

"I heard about it at the post office this morning. Everyone is excited about it."

Sarah took the book after he had checked it out for her. Who had started that rumor? Had it been on purpose? She couldn't forget how Reginald had hoped to use the possibility as a marketing tool. But she couldn't stand that a man, a family, could have their reputation tarnished if the rumors proved to be false.

She looked down at the book she held. The only way she could halt the rumors was to prove that there hadn't been a spy—German or otherwise—at the house on Lookout Mountain. She needed to get to work.

An hour later, Sarah put down the book on ham radio operators and sighed. Clearly the logbook had ended shortly after the attack on Pearl Harbor because it had to. Ham radio operators were banned from broadcasting during the early months of the war. A few—very few—radio operators returned to their sets later, working with the military to provide a network that could reach places where the government didn't have operatives. But the casual user was kept off the airwaves until after the war was over.

Had they been misled by the logbook into thinking that the family had disappeared around the beginning of the war? No, she couldn't assume that. The tax records had been switched over to the tax accountants in Maryland around that time too. Nothing in the house was newer than those dates.

And she couldn't help thinking about Walter Ackermann's letter and its mention of an item in the house that was vital to the Nazis. Was it an actual thing, or had it been information sent via the radio to the house on Lookout Mountain?

But then he might have been a spy.

Sarah shook her head and laughed. She needed to stop playing "what if?" and "why?" It was time to do something, and she knew exactly what.

Sarah left the book by her computer and took some sheets of white paper from under her printer. Putting the paper and box of chalk on her sewing table, she drew out one of the large pages of pierced paper. She went into the laundry room and got a can of spray starch. She set it on the table beside the paper before she ground one piece of blue chalk in a small bowl and ran the points of the tracing wheel through it.

Setting a sheet of paper beneath the newsprint, she settled her glasses on her nose. She slowly traced the lines in the centers of two blocks. She peeled back the newsprint and smiled at the chalky outline of a blue dog and a blue flower. Holding the spray starch high above the white paper, she squirted a fine mist. It settled onto the paper, gluing the chalk in place. Now she wouldn't have to worry about the chalk shifting when she moved the page. She considered what she could place between the sheets to transport them without the pages sticking together, and decided to try cotton remnants from her rag bag once the starch was fully dry.

By the time she had completed one large piece of newsprint, she had four sheets of paper with two designs on each. In addition to the dog and flower, she had traced a horse, a little girl, and the Christmas tree. She wasn't quite as certain what the other designs were supposed to represent.

Maybe if she showed them to Neil, he would have some idea. He had spent more time at the house than she had. She picked up two sheets and was on her way out when the phone rang.

Irene hadn't found any matches for the names on Don's list. "Another dead end," she said.

"One of these clues is going to lead to the answer," Sarah said after sharing what she had learned from the library book.

"I hope so."

Sarah did too. After hanging up, she carried the sheets out to her car, making sure the cool breeze didn't snatch them from her fingers. She placed them carefully on the backseat before getting behind the wheel.

Traffic was busy around the town green, and Sarah had to park almost the green's length from Neil's office. The breeze fought to pull the pages out of her hand the whole way. Autumn had arrived with the storms, and had sent summer away for another six months.

Sarah nodded to friends and neighbors as she walked toward Neil's office, passing Maggie's store and Liam's café.

She paused when she heard her name called with a cheery, "Look who's returned from the mountain!"

Liam waved at her from his door.

She walked back to the café. A serving of his spiced chai latte as well as a dose of his good humor couldn't hurt. "We all survived," Sarah said as she reached the door. "What about you, Liam?"

"Well, I'm much better now that I see you're all right and well." He held the door open in an invitation to come in. "How was it on the mountain?"

Sarah crouched to ruffle Murphy's fur as he rushed up to welcome her. "Wet." She smiled when Liam chuckled. "It was interesting and frustrating. The interesting part was seeing more of the house."

"And the frustrating part?" he asked as they walked to Sarah's favorite table in the empty café. Karen must have the afternoon off.

"Still not finding a keystone clue that could explain everything, the clue that would make the answer obvious. I keep coming back to the strange patchwork squares on the tapestries." She explained what she had found. "I can't help thinking that if I could find a way to match the paper blocks with the cloth ones, I would see a pattern that would lead us to the truth."

He pointed to the pages. "Is that what those are?"

"Yes, tracings of the pierced papers." She set them on the table. "This is a dog, and this one is some sort of flower. I have no idea what the other two are."

Liam turned the page toward him, then gave it another quarter turn. "Look. This one is skis and ski poles."

"So it is." She smiled at him. "I should have guessed that not all the orientations would be identical." She tapped her finger next to the fourth square. "And this one is an old-fashioned camera, the kind with the accordion pleats when it was open. Thanks, Liam! You've got a good eye for details."

He hooked a thumb to his own chest. "We Irishmen have a good eye for lots of things, especially the charming *cailíní*. And my good eye tells me that you'd like a warm drink."

"You're right." She sat and put the pages on the windowsill beside her, so there was no chance of anything spilling on them.

Liam brought over a steaming cup and put it on the table. "So what do you think of these rumors that there was a spy up in that isolated old house?"

Sarah drew in the spiced chai's fragrance. "Spencer told me that everyone's talking about how a spy used to live up there. I don't know who's telling these tales."

"Neil told me this morning, but in confidence, so I don't know how it's gotten around town. I didn't tell anyone."

"I think I know who might be spreading the story around." She wasn't going to name Reginald as the culprit, but he had been the only one excited about repeating the story.

"Neil also said he was disappointed that Chief Webber didn't consider the spy something worth the police investigating," Liam said.

Sarah took a cautious sip of her latte, then put the cup on its saucer. "Even if there had been a spy, it was a long time ago. I don't think espionage is part of the Maple Hill police department's jurisdiction."

"That's what I told Neil. He didn't seem too happy." Liam pulled out a chair and sat. "To be honest, Sarah, he seemed pretty miserable about everything."

"That house is a big project. I'd be overwhelmed." She was eager to speak of something other than Neil's private business. She glanced at the papers on the sill. "I'm still baffled as to why anyone would sew patchwork squares onto the bottom of tapestries."

"Spies have always used a variety of ways to hide or convey messages."

"Let's forget about spies for a minute. People other than spies use quilts to send messages," she said, thinking back on what she had learned from quilts while restoring them and investigating other mysteries.

Liam stood and walked along the counter to where he kept the pies. He took out a coconut cream and sliced two generous pieces. Carrying them back to the table, he put one piece in front of Sarah along with a fork. He dug a fork into the other piece as he sat.

"Sarah," he said, "you look pretty troubled too."

Trust Liam to see past her busy work and see the concern she was trying to hide.

"Liam, I feel terrible about . . . well, I don't know—"

"You shouldn't feel terrible if you're in pursuit of the truth, and I know you're always honest."

"Certain items have been stolen from the house." She put her fork on her plate without tasting the pie. "My list of suspects is down to Don, Neil, Reginald, and Chester."

"Chester?" He pushed his plate aside and folded his arms on the table. "Why do you suspect Chester? I thought you two were friends."

Sarah wanted to throw her arms around him and give him a big hug. She was glad to hear Liam speak so matter-of-factly about Chester. While Chester seemed to feel he was vying for her attention, Liam accepted that—at least for now—Sarah wanted to spend time with Chester. No big competition. She had created something different in her mind, but she was more than ready to toss that scenario aside and enjoy Liam's company.

"Chester and I *are* friends," she said, "and I've known Neil since we were kids, but they both had the opportunity to take the items."

"But why would they do it?"

She sighed and rested her chin on her palm. "That's what's got me stumped. If I could figure out a motive, I'd probably know who the thief is."

He put his hand on hers. "You need to be careful, Sarah, especially if you think a friend is guilty of a crime. You may overlook something that would give you the answer because you don't want to see it."

"I know. That bothers me."

Liam lifted her hand from the table and held it gently. "What worries me is eventually you'll be going back up to that house."

"It's not as if I'd go alone."

"No, but you might go with someone you suspect is a thief. Promise me, Sarah, that you'll be careful."

"You know I will." She patted his hand. "And I appreciate your concern, Liam. I'll let you know before I go up there again. I hope I'm wrong, and that there's an obvious suspect that I've missed."

"But what if there isn't?"

CHAPTER TWENTY-ONE

L iam's question stayed with Sarah while she waited in the outer room to Neil's office. She prayed for guidance and to be able to see everything clearly, undistorted by friendship or a lack of it. She mustn't let personal feelings sway her, just as Chief Webber didn't let others' opinions lead his investigation in a different direction. She needed to focus on facts.

It was a fact that Chester had been in the house by himself. She didn't know how long he had been there before the Kramers arrived, but it wouldn't take long to grab those few things.

It was a fact that the St. George tapestry had been found with Don's notebook. Maybe someone had tried to frame him. Maybe not.

It was a fact that both Neil and Reginald could have gone to the house at any time, together or separately. They each had a set of keys to the house.

And it was a fact that she had no idea if the thefts were related to the family who had lived there.

"Sarah," said Neil from his office doorway. "Come on in. Sorry to keep you waiting. I had a chatty client, and I couldn't get off the phone."

"It's not a problem. I'm sorry to interrupt your workday." She walked into his office and sat when he did. "I wanted to give you an update. As you probably know, Chief Webber asked us to make statements to go with your robbery report."

He leaned back in his chair and crossed one leg over the opposite knee. "I appreciate your doing that. I'm not sure how much it will help."

Sarah told him how she had found the match for one square on the smaller dining room's tapestry. She put the sheets of paper with the traced designs on Neil's immaculate desk as one light began blinking on his phone to let him know a caller was waiting.

"And that's all I've discovered so far," Sarah said as another light blinked along with the first. "Maybe with these traced designs, I'll have better luck, but I don't know how matching them will get us any answers about the Johnsons or Mr. Ackermann."

Neil sighed. "A family can't simply vanish. Someone must know where they went. Both Reginald and I are stumped about what it was the Nazis wanted. There are a lot of German things in the house."

"Maybe we should go back up and investigate further."

"Not right now." He glanced at the lights blinking on his phone. "Sarah, I hate to be rude, but I've got clients waiting. Maybe we can get up there next week if there's a lull in the work on the house."

"Neil, have you heard the buzz around Maple Hill about a spy having lived in your house? If we don't get this nipped in the bud, you're going to have a bunch of looky-loos hanging around while you're trying to get the hotel ready to open."

A third light came on just as his secretary Karen buzzed him.

"Sarah, I'm sorry." He reached for the phone, and Sarah got up and walked out.

Maybe she was going about this the wrong way. Instead of looking for the thief, maybe they should be looking for the antiques. The thief probably hadn't taken them because he wanted to keep them. He most likely took them to sell.

She smiled. If that were so, the thief had made a big mistake. The items were unique. There couldn't be many medieval unicorn tapestries or authentic German jugs available for sale in the Berkshires. She would ask Maggie to help. Maggie had contacts in the antiques business throughout the Northeast.

She thought for a moment about asking Chester to help as well. If he helped her find the antiques, she could take him off her suspect list.

Sarah went to Neil's secretary's desk. "Nancy, can you get me a couple of copies of the police report Neil made?" It had Neil's descriptions of the stolen items. Having it could help.

Nancy made the copies for Sarah. Taking them, she put them in her purse.

"Thanks, Nancy."

"I hope they help."

"Me too."

Sarah opened the door to Maggie's store after she had stopped by the police station and dropped off a copy of the traced designs. She hadn't talked to Chief Webber because he had been busy. She knew he would call her if he had any questions.

Two customers were discussing blue willow export china with Maggie in the left-hand corner of the store, so Sarah wandered to the right. She pretended to admire samplers on the wall, but her mind was too focused on finding that all-important clue to pay any attention to the elegant stitches.

Maggie came over as soon as she finished with the women who had each purchased a teacup and saucer in the charming blue pattern.

"You look ready to burst," Maggie said. "What's up?"

Sarah told her about her idea that the thief might have made arrangements to sell the missing antiques to legitimate dealers. Maggie listened, nodding.

"If the thief went to someone who buys stolen goods," Sarah said, "we're out of luck. But none of our possible suspects is a professional thief. Whoever took the antiques probably did it because he had the opportunity."

Maggie walked to the counter and grabbed the phone. "Let me start calling other antique shops in the area. Maybe one of our missing items has been brought in for sale. Even if it hasn't, I can alert the owners to keep an eye out for them. Why don't you check online auction sites?"

"That's an excellent idea." She pulled out a copy of the police report and gave it to Maggie. "Thank you."

"Neil is your friend, and I want to help him." She met Sarah's eyes steadily. "And thank you for agreeing to help Amy and Audrey with their dresses for the homecoming dance."

"I'm looking forward to it."

"So are they." She smiled. "All of a sudden, they're back to being the sweet girls they used to be. I don't know how long it'll last, but I'm enjoying it while I can." Maggie pulled a blue-covered book from under the counter and opened it to a list of phone numbers for other nearby antique stores. "I've been hearing about a Mike quite a bit lately, so I'm pretty sure Amy's got a crush on him. It's really cute."

"How about Audrey?" Sarah thought about the boy who had stared at her granddaughter with obvious affection at the game.

"The only way Audrey would notice a boy is if he's in a scene with her in the play. I don't think she even planned to go to the homecoming dance until Amy pleaded with her to go."

Sarah left Maggie to her calls and headed home. As soon as she got in, she phoned Chester. She got his voice mail and asked him to give her a call as soon as he had a chance.

She looked up the stairs and noticed Lucie's door was closed, so she must not have gotten home from school yet. The young girl was dedicated to her students, even though she would be moving on next month. Whoever had her for a teacher would be lucky.

Sarah went into her sewing room and looked at the pierced papers and ground chalk. If only the patterns could give her the answers she needed.

"I know things must happen in your time, Lord," she prayed while turning on her computer. "But please help me see the truth and guide me to it."

Sarah couldn't help smiling as she recalled how Gerry had teased her about trying to persuade God to heed such prayers. Gerry had understood that patience was a difficult virtue for Sarah. So many times he had told her how he loved her willingness to rush in where angels feared to tread. She wondered if he and her father were watching her now along with the angels. She hoped so.

Sarah began her search. She was astonished at how many online auction sites she found. Even when she limited her search to sites that handled antiques, there were hundreds.

Before she could formulate a plan of action, she heard someone at the door. She got up and opened it. "Chester! Did you get my message?"

"Which message?" he asked as he came in.

"I called to ask for your help in contacting antique stores. We need to alert them in case someone tries to sell our missing antiques." She took his coat and hung it in the hall closet. "If you didn't get my call, why are you here?"

"I wanted to make sure you were okay after our strange visit to Lookout Mountain."

"It was bizarre, wasn't it?" Sarah's smile met his. "Lightning and thunder and a huge, mysterious house on a mountain."

Chester rested his elbow on the newel post. "Well, now I know you're all right, I'd be glad to make a few calls to alert other antique aficionados."

"You might want to coordinate with Maggie. She's already contacting her network. There's no need for you to call the same people."

He took out his cell. "What's her number?"

Sarah gave it to him, and he put it in his phone. "In the meantime," she said, "I've started looking online. There are about a billion auction sites. Any ideas how to make the search simpler?"

He stuck the phone in his pocket. "The easiest way is to set up watch requests on the major sites. Many smaller sites feed into the biggies. You can arrange on those major sites to be alerted by e-mail if a certain item comes up for bid. It'll save you a lot of time."

"Can you show me how to do it?"

"Sure. Where's your computer?"

"Back here." Sarah led the way toward the rear of the house. She ignored the niggling thought that Chester was on her suspect list. He easily could have said he didn't know any shortcuts for searching Web sites if he were the thief.

Chester sat and began typing with two fingers. He had Sarah create a sign-in name and a password for each site.

She used *Lookout* as her password because it was one she wasn't likely to forget on this case. Next, he created search parameters. It was slightly different on each site, but within fifteen minutes, he had created accounts and searches for her on the major sites as well as on a few smaller ones.

"You'll need to check your e-mail regularly," Chester said, "to see what alerts you get. I tried to make the searches broad enough so you won't miss an item if it does come up for auction, but narrow enough so you aren't inundated with e-mails." He pushed back from the desk. "That's all we can do other than wait to see if you get any hits."

"How about brick and mortar auction houses? The thief may avoid online sites if he realizes that we can watch for the items to come up for bid."

Chester smiled as he opened another screen. "Most auction houses have Web sites. Some allow you to bid in real time. Let's get you set up on the ones within a hundred mile radius. The items aren't worth millions, so I doubt the thief will drive too far to sell them."

"And the longer he has them, the more likely he is to get caught," Sarah said.

"You'd think so, wouldn't you?" He grew serious as he met her eyes steadily. "That's conventional wisdom, but if the thief never tries to sell what he's stolen, he might never be caught. Big art heists are often done that way."

Sarah looked at the computer screen as he began typing again. "Let's hope our thief wants to make a profit from his ill-gotten gains."

Chester set up accounts for her with auction houses in Pittsfield and Springfield, Massachusetts; Albany, Schenectady, and Troy, New York; and Bennington and Rutland, Vermont. If she didn't get any hits in a week, he suggested that she expand the radius of her search.

"I'll send you some links to other auction houses when I get home," Chester said. "These are the ones I know off the top of my head."

"These will be good to start." Sarah stepped aside as Chester stood up.

"It's still a long shot," he said.

"I know, but a long shot's better than no shot at all."

He chuckled. "Now that that's all set, how about me taking you out to dinner?"

Sarah's smile wavered. "Thanks, Chester, but I've got to say no."

"Still recovering from our trip to Lookout Mountain?"

Sarah wanted to say that was the reason, but she wouldn't lie. "It just has to be a no right now. Can we leave it at that?" Her words sounded as stilted as if they were strangers, but she couldn't explain her developing relationship with Liam.

Chester looked disappointed, but didn't press. He simply asked her to let him know if she got a hit on her searches.

As Sarah walked him to the door, she asked, "Chester, would you mind looking at something for me and telling me if it seems familiar?"

"What is it?"

"Something from the house on Lookout Mountain." She collected the designs she had traced and let him study each one. He shook his head as he handed them back to her.

"I don't recognize them. The patterns are very primitive, and most of the items in the house are very sophisticated," he said.

Sarah nodded. That was true. The art and the furnishings in the house were not the country style that most people preferred in western Massachusetts. So why had someone added these simple squares to beautiful tapestries?

"You're the textile maven," Chester said with a smile after she had asked that question out loud. "If you don't know, the rest of us don't stand a chance of figuring it out."

"No pressure," she said wryly.

He chuckled and wished her good luck before he left.

CHAPTER TWENTY-TWO

Sarah's head ached when she got up the next morning. She wished she could have shut her mind down earlier last night, but she had tossed and turned until the wee hours of the morning.

When Martha called and asked her to drive to Williamstown for a lecture by a local author, Sarah took the opportunity to put the mystery out of her mind. Soon she and Martha were on their way, laughing about the misadventures of one of Martha's younger grandchildren who had gotten the idea of putting on a backyard circus last Sunday afternoon. The plan had been to raise money for charity, but the so-called performing dog wouldn't do anything but sleep and the clowns used real water instead of confetti in the buckets they aimed at the audience.

"Luckily the only people who got wet were other kids." Martha laughed. "And Pastor John, though he was a good sport."

Sarah happily listened to the everyday events. It was a delight to hear about families that didn't vanish into thin air.

When they passed Bradford Manor where her father had lived his last years, Sarah couldn't help staring at the place she had visited so often. Martha herself began talking about Sarah's parents and how patient they had been with two young girls' misadventures. Sarah was even more grateful for Martha's compassion and company.

They avoided talking about the house on Lookout Mountain. Martha didn't mention it on the way to Williamstown, or when they went into a small lecture hall at Williams College, or on the return trip after the excellent lecture about regional flowers.

When Martha pulled up in front of Sarah's house, Sarah opened her door and got out. Turning, she said, "Thanks, Martha. This morning was exactly what I needed."

"I thought you could use a few hours off." Martha's grin was warm. "I've got to take Ernie to the doctor this afternoon, but maybe tomorrow we can get together for lunch at Liam's, and then you can tell me everything that's been going on."

"It's a date. I'll see you at noon."

"Make it eleven thirty. I can't wait much longer to hear about your latest adventure."

Sarah laughed as she closed the door and stepped back from the car. She waved as Martha drove along the street.

The house was quiet when Sarah came in. She took a deep breath and savored the peace. Martha was such a dear friend, knowing what Sarah needed even before Sarah knew herself.

After hanging up her coat, Sarah started her computer and went in the kitchen for a mug of warm cider, which she sprinkled with cinnamon. It smelled like autumn: apples and spices.

Sarah cautiously sipped the hot cider as she checked her e-mail.

One address was unfamiliar. It was an e-mail alert from an auction site. She clicked on the link, and the auction site page opened. At the top was the name of a brick and mortar auction house in Pittsfield.

She paged down and gasped when she saw a unicorn tapestry. She read the description of the bright gilt and red ribbon woven around the unicorn's neck and the crosses on the maiden's faded green gown. It had to be the one from the Lookout Mountain house.

Her phone rang. Still reading the description, she picked up the phone and said, "Hello."

"Sarah." It was Chester. "Turn on your computer."

"The unicorn tapestry?" She guessed the reason for his call as she clicked on the magnifying glass icon to zoom in on the crosses. They were exactly like the ones she had seen at the house. "If it's not the one from Neil's and Reginald's house, it's an identical twin."

Chester didn't answer for a moment. "Tapestries weren't mass-produced in the Middle Ages, so this may be our missing unicorn." She heard him shift the phone. "I think we should go look at it. I'm getting the directions to the auction house now. I'll stop by and pick you up. You're on my way to Pittsfield."

"If you take the scenic route." She smiled, glad their friendship remained after she had turned down his offer for dinner. "While you drive over here, I'll call the auction house."

"Tell them we'll be there in about an hour."

Sarah hung up and looked at her computer screen. The tapestry was scheduled to be auctioned tonight. She breathed a prayer of thanks to God for guiding them in this direction before the tapestry could be sold and vanish as completely as the family.

Pittsfield proudly displayed the remnants of its past as a mill town, the streets reflecting the hierarchy of the mills. Tightly bunched houses once lodged the mill workers, while middle management lived in the small Victorians. Mill owners had a street of grand Queen Anne mansions for their families.

The auction house had originally been a carriage house for a Victorian mansion. When Chester drove around to the back, Sarah saw that every small porch and eave was decorated with ornate gingerbread.

The carriage house was almost as fancy. Painted a New England barn red, the building boasted a big sign that gently rocked in the breeze, announcing this was Hollingsworth's Auction Barn. She saw a couple of trucks with the same logo painted on their sides.

"Their site says they pick up and deliver throughout Berkshire County," Chester said. "I probably should have checked them out before now. I've picked up some nice pieces at auctions over the years."

A strident beep went off when Sarah and Chester walked in, announcing visitors to employees at the back who couldn't see the door. The huge space was filled with furniture and statues and artwork and books and boxes of tools or china or anything else Sarah could imagine.

"Which way?" Chester asked.

"Your guess is as good as mine." She pointed past a pine hutch. "How about that way?"

They walked around the hutch, and Chester halted before he ran into a heavyset man with a full white beard. The man wasn't very tall. If he had been wearing a red suit instead of jeans and a flannel shirt, Sarah would have thought they had come face-to-face with Santa Claus.

He smiled broadly. "Kurt Hollingsworth," he said, offering his hand to Chester, then to Sarah. "I assume you're the people who called to view the tapestry. Mr. Winslow and Mrs. Hart, right?"

"That's right," Sarah said. "We're afraid the tapestry may have been stolen from a friend of ours."

Sarah drew out a copy of the statement Neil had given to the police.

Mr. Hollingsworth's practiced smile vanished as he took the paperwork and read it slowly. His breath sifted out past his clenched teeth as he looked from the form to Sarah and Chester.

"I haven't seen any of these other items, but you're right. The description of the unicorn tapestry matches the one we have."

"Can you tell us who brought it and when?" asked Sarah.

"I'll have to check our records." He motioned for them to come with him toward the rear of the building.

It was tempting to stop and admire the furniture and the stacks of plates in both rare and commonplace patterns. Two crazy quilts sat on a burgundy mohair davenport that resembled the one in the Lookout Mountain house. Beside her, Chester's head swiveled frantically as he tried to take in all the antiques at once.

"I've definitely got to get back to attending auctions," he said as they followed Mr. Hollingsworth. He stopped by a headboard and dresser. "Look at this painted furniture."

Sarah glanced at the pale yellow furniture decorated with finely drawn flowers and vines. She took Chester by the arm when he reached to open a dresser drawer.

"Look at them *after* we see the tapestry," she said with mock sternness.

"Yes, ma'am." He smiled as they wound through the crowded space to catch up to Mr. Hollingsworth walking past the auction stage.

Sarah glanced at the podium on a dais. The auction-eer would stand there, where everyone could see him, his hammer ready to knock down the sales. More impor-tant, he could see the participants and not miss a single bid.

Mr. Hollingsworth's office was cramped. A table in one corner was draped with light blue satin. Beside it, a camera waited on a tripod. Sarah guessed that was where they took photos for their catalog and online.

Mr. Hollingsworth offered them a seat while he went to get the tapestry and its paperwork. Sarah was too anxious to sit. She paced the small room, but had only gone back and forth twice before Mr. Hollingsworth returned.

With care, he set the tapestry on the fabric-draped table. "Is this the one you're looking for?"

A single glance was enough for Sarah, but she raised the lower corner to look at the back of the tapestry. She wished she had her photos, but it looked just as she remembered.

She smoothed the tapestry's corner down again. "Yes. I'm sure it is. How long have you had it?"

"It came in last weekend," Mr. Hollingsworth said. "We normally wouldn't have listed so quickly, because we like to do marketing on our unique pieces to draw in bidders, but the owner was insistent that it be sold as soon as possible. We have an auction every other week, so this was the first night we could sell it."

Sarah exchanged a glance with Chester. The thief had been determined to get rid of the tapestry before anyone no-ticed it was missing.

"Was it given to you on consignment?" Chester asked.

"All our items are," Mr. Hollingsworth said.

"So you must have a phone number to contact the owner."

The auctioneer opened the file folder he had brought with him. He mumbled as he paged through the papers inside. "Ah, here it is." He pulled it out and frowned. "Odd. There's no contact information. It simply says that the owner will return within a week of the auction to pick up a check."

"Is there a name?" asked Sarah.

"Yes. Walter Ackermann. With two ens."

Sarah wasn't sure whether to laugh or shriek with frustration. "The man who left the tapestry with you was using a fake name," she said.

Chester asked, "Could you describe him?"

Mr. Hollingsworth shook his head. "My assistant met with him, and she's out today with a sick child, so I don't want to disturb her at home. I could ask her when she gets back tomorrow or the next day. It sounds like I need to call the Pittsfield police," Mr. Hollingsworth added, sighing. "It's a shame. There was a lot of interest in this lot."

"Do you mind if I call Chief Webber at the Maple Hill police department?" Sarah asked. "He's a good friend, and he took the initial robbery report."

Mr. Hollingsworth glanced again at the tapestry, then nodded. "Go ahead. I'm sure the local department will contact him anyhow as soon as I'm done with them."

Chester remained in the office while Sarah went out into the main room. A few workers were testing the microphones and getting the auction house ready for the evening's sale. She found a quiet corner and called the Maple Hill police station. It didn't take long to connect, and she was put right through to the chief.

"Mrs. Hart, how can I help you today?" Chief Webber's voice boomed through the phone.

She explained what she and Chester had found and where they were.

"The local authorities have been contacted?" he asked, all business.

"Mr. Hollingsworth is calling them now, but I thought I'd give you a heads-up. Also, I have a copy of the police report Neil filed with you. Do you want me to pass that along to the officer who comes to take Mr. Hollingsworth's report?"

Chief Webber didn't hesitate. "No, but let the officer know I'll be glad to fax over a copy upon request." His voice eased from its professional sternness. "It's best to keep everything in official channels, Mrs. Hart. You and Mr. Winslow did a good job in finding the tapestry, but I have to ask you to—"

"Stay out of your investigation," Sarah said with a laugh. She didn't add that she had another mystery to solve, one that the police didn't even know about other than a passing mention in her statement. She needed to figure out why the real Walter Ackermann and the Johnsons had vanished.

Chester and Sarah went directly to Neil's office upon their return to Maple Hill. Sarah wasn't sure when the police would contact Neil about the tapestry, but she had promised to keep him informed about what she discovered. Plus, she wanted to see Neil's face when she gave him the news. She still hoped that Neil wasn't the thief, but if he was, his reaction could reveal the truth.

The cool sprinkle that had begun shortly after they left Pittsfield was now a steadier rain. That didn't keep four different people from stopping Sarah and Chester and quizzing them about the spy who had lived on Lookout Mountain as they walked to Neil's office.

Nobody wanted to hear that there probably hadn't been any spies. Instead they wondered if Sarah knew when Neil and his business partner would be opening the house for spy tours. Nothing Sarah said could convince them that there was nothing worthy of a "spy tour" up there.

Chester looped his arm through Sarah's and hurried her along the sidewalk. It was a relief to go into the building where Neil had his office. Chester shook his head in disbelief and then again to get the rain out of his hair.

Sarah was glad when they were shown into Neil's office.

Neil stood and came around his desk with a smile. "Chester, good to see you. Sarah, I was just about to call you. I got the deed from my attorney today. It's got interesting information on it." He reached for a legal-size folder on his desk.

Sarah held up her hand. "Before we get to that, Chester and I have some news. We found the unicorn tapestry."

"That's fabulous! Where?"

She couldn't see any hint of subterfuge on his happy face. Unless Neil was a better actor than she would have guessed, he was truly excited.

"At an auction house in Pittsfield," she said.

"Amazing!" He gave her a hug, startling her, before pumping Chester's hand. "I can't wait to tell Reginald it's been recovered. Let me see if I can get him now." He placed the call, then hung up and dialed again. His smile faded when he set the phone in its cradle. "He's not answering. When do you think we'll get the tapestry back?"

"You'll have to ask Chief Webber about that," Sarah said. "He'll have to hold on to it for evidence."

Neil nodded. "I should have guessed that. Do they have any leads?"

Sarah let Chester answer as she watched Neil's reactions. His eagerness to have the tapestry back was greater than she had expected.

"I guess I'll have to be patient," Neil said when Chester finished. "In the meantime, take a look at the deed." He picked up the folder. "Here it is."

Sarah opened the thick folder. It had information she hadn't seen in her investigations online and at the library. Seeing the size of the document, she realized she had been looking at only extracts. She hadn't thought to ask if there were more complete documents. Not that it mattered now that she had the file. The information she had been eager to see was on the second page. There was no mention of Walter Ackermann. The Johnsons were the first owners listed. Someone named Ian Fields had purchased the house from the Johnsons in 1960.

"It sold almost twenty years *after* the date we think the family went missing," Sarah said.

"Unless we're wrong about when they left." Neil shook his head. "I'm not sure what to think at this point."

"The latest date we've found on anything at the house is 1941, and that was in the logbook," Sarah said. "I wonder how long Mr. Fields owned it. When I checked online, I saw that the most recent owners were a family trust and then Berkshire Properties Management. How about if we give your Realtor a call? Maybe Ms. Richards has some information that can help us."

Neil scooted around his desk and opened a personal phonebook. He paged through, then picked up the phone and called. He tapped a button on the phone. "I'm putting it on speaker."

Sarah heard a ringing tone, then a pleasant voice said, "Berkshire Properties Management. This is Harriet Richards. How may I help you?"

"Harriet, it's Neil Lawton. I've got you on speaker phone because I have two friends here with me. Sarah Hart and Chester Winslow. They've been helping Reginald and me learn more about the contents of the house."

Ms. Richards's chuckle was as warm as her voice. "You two have a big job ahead of you. That house is packed to the rafters with stuff. So, Neil, what can I do for you today?"

"I just got the deed back from the Register of Deeds, and we were looking it over. I was wondering if you could tell us anything about the Meadowlands Family Trust."

"That was set up by Ian Fields, who's listed as the previous owner. Berkshire Properties Management was hired to oversee the property for the trust."

"Do you know," Neil asked, "how we can contact Mr. Fields?"

Sarah held her breath. The truth they had been searching for might be only a single answer away.

Ms. Richards's voice echoed oddly through the speaker. "Neil, I'm afraid Ian Fields passed away."

Again Sarah's hopes fell flat. Chester slapped his hand in frustration on the back of a chair.

"I'm sorry," Neil said.

"Thank you, Neil, but I didn't know the man. He used Berkshire Properties Management, but I wasn't the agent managing it. That's why I was surprised when, out of the blue, I got the call."

"What call?" Sarah spoke up. "This is Sarah Hart."

"Hi, Mrs. Hart. I was informed that the property had been left to me with the proviso that I sell it and take my commission, then give the rest to a charity of my choice. I remembered Reginald had been looking for such a property, so I contacted him. I'm sorry that's all I know about it."

"Thanks, Harriet," Neil said. "We appreciate what you've told us. Maybe it'll help us with figuring out some of the stuff in the house." He clicked a button, ending the call. He sighed. "Well, I guess that's that."

Sarah wasn't ready to give up. "Can I use your computer, Neil?"

"Sure. Let me save what I've found so far." He tapped a few keys as he said, "I've been trying to learn more about Nazi research at the time, anything that might be connected to that letter Ethan found."

"Any luck?" Chester asked.

"Not a lot. I've been reading about their innovations during the late 1930s and early forties. Most had to do with weapons."

"What types of weapons?"

"What you'd expect, but many were developed to help the Third Reich gain control of seaports so they could keep oil flowing into their refineries. They needed fuel for their war vehicles. That doesn't help us." Neil looked out at the rain now sliding down the window. "Why is it that every time we take a step forward, we don't get any closer to solving this blasted mystery?"

"Let me try something," Sarah said. "I've got an idea that might get us somewhere."

Neil chuckled at her enthusiasm. "I'm glad Reginald suggested you be on our dream team of experts."

Sarah halted in midstep. "Reginald suggested me? He didn't know me before this project."

"He suggested we have a team of experts help us go through the house." Neil sat on the edge of his desk and watched as Sarah pulled out his chair. "Neither of us had any idea where to begin. We didn't know what was valuable and what was junk."

Sarah sat and glanced across the room to where Chester was perched on one of the strange chairs. He met her gaze, and she saw he was as unsettled by Neil's words as she was.

"So did you go up to the house before you invested in it, Neil?" Chester asked.

"It was a busy time. I had a couple of clients being audited by the IRS, and they were demanding every accounting line back to the beginning of time. We were working flat out." A flush rose from his collar. "I know what you're thinking. I'm a money guy, helping other people handle their money, and I didn't do the work I should have before investing."

Sarah felt sorry for Neil, so she changed the subject. "Let's see what we can find about Ian Fields."

"He owned the house long after the Johnsons left." Neil looked puzzled. "Why is he of interest?"

"He must have bought the house from the Johnsons or their representative. There may be some connection."

"I didn't think of that."

Chester gave him a hearty slap on the shoulder. "When you hang around Sarah, you'll be endlessly surprised at how many different ways she can look at a problem. And solve it."

Sarah looked at the sites for her search. When she saw an obituary for an Ian Fields in the Washington, DC, area, she clicked on it. The tax accounting firm, Lehrer and Sons, was just outside of DC in Maryland. Maybe they were related.

It took several frustrating steps before Sarah could access the newspaper's archives. Finally the page rendered a two-year-old obituary. Sarah called the men to look over her shoulder when she saw that Ian Fields's obituary reported that he had been born in Germany and had come to the United States in the 1930s.

"It says here," Sarah said, "that Mr. Fields lived in Massachusetts before relocating to the DC area in the forties."

"Then why did he buy a house in Massachusetts twenty years later?" asked Neil.

Sarah scanned through the obituary. Mr. Fields had worked as an automobile engineer, rising high in the ranks and retiring a wealthy man. That didn't make the connection she needed.

Clicking back to the search results page, she said, "Let me try something else."

She clicked on the *images* link. Dozens appeared, but she focused on the few that were of people. The rest were farm scenes, and she realized the search had picked up on the word "fields."

The first photo was too recent, taken last year. She double-clicked the next one, and it linked her back to the obituary. This time, a photo popped up in the upper left-hand corner. It must have been an old photo, because the man in it looked no more than thirty. Sarah zoomed in on the photo and gasped.

"I know him!" Sarah said.

"How?" asked Neil.

Sarah looked over her shoulder. "Last week, I did some research at the library. I told you that I'd gone through the newspaper archives and found a photo of the Johnsons at your house, Neil. The man in this photo looks enough like the Mr. Johnson in that photo to be his twin. Ian Fields may just be Carl Johnson himself."

CHAPTER TWENTY-THREE

S arah listened to Neil's and Chester's excitement while she read the obituary more thoroughly. Mr. Fields was survived by a daughter named Tanya Poulter.

It didn't take Sarah long to find a social networking page for a Tanya Poulter in the Washington, DC, area. She glanced at the photo of a woman close to her own age. Had this woman been one of the children in the newspaper picture? Sarah wrote an e-mail message explaining briefly why she was contacting Mrs. Poulter. It was worth a shot.

Sending the e-mail off, Sarah stood. One thing was clear. She wasn't going to get any further answers about Mr. Fields/Mr. Johnson in Maple Hill. She needed to go back to the house on Lookout Mountain. When she voiced her need, the worried furrows in Neil's forehead became deeper.

"It's raining pretty hard, Sarah," Neil said. "I'd hate for you to get stuck up there again."

"But we're close to the answer." She looked out the window. "It's already getting lighter over the mountains. I need to check those designs I traced from the pierced papers too. I found one match, and I want to see what else I can find. Maybe they'll lead to the answer."

"It's worth a try," Neil said, relenting. "We haven't been making much progress in other directions."

"Mind if I go with you, Sarah?" Chester asked. "If you want, I'll drive."

"Sounds good. Neil, do you want to come too?"

He shook his head. "I need to get some work done on the item the Nazis were after." He hesitated, then said, "I told Reginald that I wouldn't let any of you up there without us." His mouth straightened as he pulled a key ring out of his pocket. "But I trust you, Sarah. Just make sure you lock up if you stay after the Kramers go home."

Sarah took the keys, thanked him, and left with Chester. She paused in the hallway outside of Neil's office. Chester held the door to the street half open, but he closed it as Sarah pulled out her cell.

"I told Liam that I'd call him before I went back up to the house."

"Because he's worried about you?" Chester asked.

Sarah hoped her face wasn't as red-hot as it felt. "A lot of people were worried last time we went up there and couldn't get back."

"Is Liam the reason you didn't want to go out to dinner with me last night?" Chester waved the question away before she could answer. "I'm sorry, Sarah. I shouldn't have asked that. I don't mean to pry." A smile lightened his expression. "Okay, I obviously did mean to. But let's pretend I didn't ask."

"That's fine with me." She returned his smile. "You're a good friend, Chester."

"And I don't want to do anything to ruin our friendship." He pointed to her cell. "Make your call. I'll wait in the car."

"Thanks, Chester." Sarah watched him leave, then dialed Liam's café. She was lucky to have good friends like Martha and Chester.

The phone rang and rang. Sarah was about to hang up when she heard, "Spotted Dog Café. This is Karen. How can I help you?"

Sarah smiled. "Hi, Karen. It's Sarah. Is Liam there?"

"Nope. He has the afternoon off. Why don't you try him at his place?"

"I will. Thanks." She hung up and called Liam's home number. Again it rang and rang before the answering machine picked up. At the beep, she said, "Liam, it's Sarah. Chester and I are going up to Neil's house. I'll call you later with an update." She put the phone in her purse.

Sarah and Chester stopped at her house long enough to collect the traced designs and her boots.

"If you want my opinion," Chester said after they had driven out of Maple Hill, "Neil is avoiding the house. Chasing down the Nazi angle is an excuse not to come with us."

Sarah's thoughts had been going in the same direction, but she couldn't help wondering if Neil hadn't wanted to go with them because he feared they would discover he had a part in the thefts. She didn't want to voice her suspicions until she had more facts.

"Neil doesn't like mysteries," she said. "He likes everything to fit in nice, neat columns. He's always been that way."

Chester flipped the turn signal, looked in both directions, then drove onto the narrow mountain road. "It may be, too, that he's mad at himself for making what may turn out to be a very bad investment."

That made a lot of sense. "Maybe the house won't work as a luxury hotel, but it *is* a lovely property."

"On a road that's impassable in the winter and won't be much better in the spring until the mud dries up." He eased carefully into the first hairpin turn.

The road grew steeper and steeper. Sarah's seat belt caught as they went around a particularly sharp corner, even though Chester was driving slowly. Sunshine burst from the clouds, making the wet leaves and branches glitter.

Everything Chester had said made complete sense. But if Neil wasn't the thief, there were only two names on her list: Reginald Carruthers and Don Monroe.

Chester didn't say anything else until they reached the gate. Sarah wasn't sure if he wanted to concentrate on driving the treacherous road or if he was lost in thought. She released the breath she had been holding when they drove through the gate. When Chester chuckled, she did too.

"I can't help it," Sarah said. "These mountain roads always make me nervous."

"You're not the only one happy to see that gate."

Sarah couldn't silence the feeling that the pierced paper designs were her final chance to solve the puzzle about the family. They might be if she didn't hear back from Ian Fields's daughter.

Chester parked the car near the house, the muddy parking area clearly showing where at least one other car had come and gone recently. Sarah pulled on her gardening boots and fought through the clinging mud to the porch. She drew them off and left them by the front door.

"They need to spread some gravel around here," Chester said. "Tracking mud in will ruin the nice floors." He lifted one foot to remove his shoe, but wobbled and put his hand on the door to steady himself.

The door swung open. Sarah grabbed one of his windmilling arms and kept him from falling.

She went inside and called Ethan's and Agatha's names. She didn't get an answer. Chester followed her into the kitchen, and she threw open the cupboard where they kept their supplies. Everything was stored neatly, mops, brooms, cleaning supplies, and the vacuum. She reached for her cell.

"Maybe we should call Neil," Chester said.

Her phone showed a single bar. She hoped it was enough. Finding Neil's number on her call list, she put the phone to her ear and listened to it ring. As soon as he answered, she said, "Neil, we're at the house. The door was open, and we don't see any sign of the Kramers."

"I'm sorry," Neil said. "I should have called you as soon as I got off the phone with Ethan. He called right after you left. Agatha had a bad asthma attack. He wanted to get her to the doctor right away."

"Maybe we got here in time to find the scent that triggered the attack." She told him about Agatha's previous asthma attack. Chester listened without comment. "That lemon bleach might have some connection to the thief. Did Ethan say where it was?"

"No," Neil said. "Maybe you and Chester should get out of there. You don't want to run into the thief if he's still in the house."

"There isn't another car up here. If the thief was here, he's long gone."

"It's more likely," Chester said, "that Ethan didn't check if the door was locked because he was too worried about Agatha." He held out his hand, and Sarah handed him the phone. He repeated what he had said, then added, "I checked the door. The dead bolt looks like it was thrown, but the door wasn't closed all the way." He paused, then said, "Okay. We'll let you know if we find anything." He closed the phone and handed it back to Sarah. "Where do you want to start?"

"With the blocks on the tapestries while we still have good light."

"I'm going upstairs to see if I can learn anything more about the radio."

"Good idea," Sarah agreed. "Let me know if you get a whiff of lemon. It might give us a clue about where the thief's been."

"Will do."

Chester headed for the stairs while Sarah decided to start in the smaller dining room. She had already found one matching square there.

She spread the traced designs on the table. Selecting the page with the Christmas tree shape on it, she examined the rest of the patterns. One looked like a candle in a simple candlestick holder. Another was shaped like a teapot. The other three were a dog shape, a flower shape, and the outline of what she guessed was a chair.

Sarah ran her fingers along the four blocks on the bottom of the tapestry on the wall, then realized she was going about this the wrong way. She pulled a chair over and climbed onto it to lift the tapestry off its hook. With care, she carried it to the table and set it beside her traced pages. She was accustomed to working at this angle.

Suddenly the sewing lines were easier to see. There! The block farthest to the right had been appliquéd with what looked like the teapot. She set the page over it and ran her finger along the shape she had traced. They were a perfect match.

The other two blocks had a candlestick and a chair. Leaving the tapestry on the table, she took her traced designs and went to the toy room. Someone had hung up the tapestry that had been lying on the back of the rocking horse. She tested the toy box to make sure it would hold her, then climbed up to get the tapestry down. Once it was on the floor, she knelt and matched the three blocks on it. A dog, a girl, and a horse.

Sarah sat back on her heels. Matching the blocks was good, but did it mean anything? It was like learning a new language, but she didn't have any idea what the words meant.

A dog, a girl, and a horse.

Did they refer to something in German? Don might still be willing to help her. But as she reached for her phone, she froze at an odd angle as she stared at the rocking horse and the doll she had propped against it.

A horse.

A girl.

A dog?

Sarah scanned the room. Her gaze alighted on the black stuffed dog Maggie had put on the bookshelf. Standing, she took the dog off the shelf and carried it to the rocking horse and the doll. She checked the dog for any sort of label. Her eyes widened when she felt a button in its ear. She didn't have to be an antiques expert to recognize the symbol of a Steiff toy.

The doll had a porcelain head, hands, and feet, but a rag body. Her eyes were glass, and one had come loose enough to rattle when Sarah turned the doll over to look for a manufacturer's name. Small letters on the back of the doll's head spelled out Kämmer and Reinhardt. The names were very German.

One of the teaching quilts was folded on the back of the horse. Sarah moved it to the toy chest, then examined the horse. Its maker's name had once been hidden beneath its mane. With the mohair gnawed away, it was easy for Sarah to find the words Bauer & Krause. More German names.

A rocking horse.

A girl doll.

A black stuffed dog.

Each one made in Germany. Each one in this room along with the tapestry blocks. There had to be some sort of connection, but what could it be?

Sarah put the teaching quilt back on the horse and ran her fingers over the alphabet letters and the pictures, then along the quilting lines. She closed her eyes and imagined the young mother from the newspaper photo sitting in this room with her children. She was teaching them their ABCs with the quilt. That much was clear. How did the tapestry blocks fit in?

Sarah decided to keep matching the traced patterns to items in real life in hopes of finding the answer. She paused in the smaller dining room, and she found a teapot in the sideboard along with a candlestick holder. The tree stumped her until she noticed that a tree in the garden was framed by the large window.

The unmistakable lemon scent tickled Sarah's nose when she went into the huge dining room to look at that tapestry. In the daylight, the chamber was even more impressive. The lacing of rafters and the small windows in the gables at either end must be twenty-five feet above the floor. She walked past the table with more than twenty chairs, looking for the spot where the odor was the strongest. It grew fainter and fainter. When she saw the room's windows were open, she guessed Ethan had hoped to air out the room before he and Agatha came back.

Sarah heard footsteps. She imagined the thief coming back and fought down a pulse of panic. Whoever was walking in her direction wasn't trying to be stealthy. Even so, she breathed a sigh of relief when Chester came into the room.

"Here you are!" he said. "I didn't learn anything new about the radio. Any luck with the blocks?"

"Each of the blocks matches something in the room." She pointed at the tapestry. "See? That's a lamp on the first block. Just like the one on the sideboard."

"They look a lot alike, but could it be a coincidence?"

"No, it's the same in other rooms. See the flowers on this block? They match the pattern on the platter in the middle of the table."

Chester peered at the next block. "But what about these two dogs?"

She looked around the room. "There were some china dogs on the sideboard when I came in here before. A pair of pugs, one fawn-colored and the other black."

He walked to the sideboard. "Look here."

On top of the sideboard, the dust was still thick, except for two spots. Each would match the base of a china dog.

"Someone took them," she said. "Not very long ago."

She returned to look at the next block on the tapestry when she noticed the rug beneath the tapestry. Pale spots had erased the color in the carpet.

"Chester, come and see this." When he did, she said, "We need to follow these spots. Our thief may have been using the lemon-scented cleanser to conceal his fingerprints. It's time we turned the tables and used the splotches to track him."

CHAPTER TWENTY-FOUR

E xcellent idea, Sarah." Chester pulled a flashlight out of his back pocket. "I brought it along in case the power went out again." He turned it on and aimed it at the spots on the carpet.

They leaped to life in the light, making the trail easy to follow. It led into the kitchen. And stopped.

Sarah looked across the room. The linoleum showed no spots. No odor of the cleanser told her which direction to take now.

"There." Chester pointed at the braided rug by the sink. "Isn't that a bleached spot?"

Sarah took Chester's flashlight and aimed it at the rug and smiled. A pair of pale blotches marked where bleach had dripped.

"If the thief went this way," Chester said, "he must have been going to the pantry or the laundry or outside."

Standing beside the braided rug, she looked back at where they had come into the kitchen and then in the other directions. She bent down again.

"What are you doing?" Chester asked.

"Trying to figure out what direction the person carrying the bleach took." She leaned forward so the two blotches were lined up with the door they had entered. "This way."

"Which way?"

"To the backdoor." Sarah opened it and was struck by the lemon scent, stronger than she had ever smelled it before. She bent toward a small puddle. She drew in a quick breath and coughed. "It's the lemon cleanser. Don't step in it."

Chester edged past her. "What's out here?"

Sarah heard a sharp thud. Had someone dropped something or slammed a door? "What's that? Did you hear that?"

"I didn't hear anything." He looked at a small shed in the back garden. "Did it come from there?"

"I'm not sure." Sarah glanced over her shoulder. "I thought it was behind us, but maybe I was wrong."

"Let's check out this shed, then we'll look in the house."

Weeds reached almost to Sarah's knees in places, but other areas had been knocked down as if someone else had trampled through earlier. Who had been wandering around back here?

Chester opened the shed's door and went in. Sarah followed. Her foot struck something. It clattered on the wooden floor.

"It's the missing camera!" she said. "And isn't that one of the jugs that you and Maggie looked at on our first visit?"

He examined the jug on the floor beside the camera. "Yes. How did it get out here?" He switched on the flashlight.

Sarah started as light sparked off a set of eyes. Chester reaimed the flashlight, and she saw a familiar face.

"Reginald!" She looked from the stolen items to him. He stood behind a table and held two books in one hand. In the other was a mailing envelope addressed to an auction house in Bennington, Vermont. "You're the thief!"

"How can I be a thief when these are my things?" he asked in his pleasant, well-cultured voice.

"Yours *and* Neil's. You're stealing from him." Sarah was glad that Neil hadn't been involved in the thefts, but he was going to be wretched that he had been betrayed by his erstwhile friend.

Reginald snorted rudely. "Neil has no imagination. All he could think about was turning this white elephant into a luxury hotel. He didn't see the other possibilities."

"And you did?" asked Sarah. From the corner of her eye, she watched Chester inch to Reginald's left. She wasn't sure what Chester planned, but she prayed neither man would get hurt.

"After I found the letter from Walter Ackermann." His smile became a sneer as he moved toward her. Not her, she realized, but the door. He intended to make a break for it. "Neil never suspected the true treasure up here."

Sarah matched his motions, staying between him and the door. Chester, stymied by Reginald's shifting, eased toward her.

"You found the letter before you decided to buy the house," Sarah said. "You didn't have enough money, so you convinced Neil to go in with you, never telling him the truth about why you wanted the property."

"He had his plans for the house. I had mine."

"But then you lost the letter, didn't you? That's what you were looking for when you were going through the correspondence in the sewing machine table. When did you misplace the letter? When you were setting up Don to take the fall for your crimes?"

"You don't know what you're talking about." His voice rose on each word, growing louder and more strident.

"Actually, I know all about the letter." She spoke slowly and gently as if dealing with a child. "Neil has it. He knows about the item that Mr. Ackermann wanted to protect and that it might still be in the house."

"Good luck finding it." Reginald stepped out from behind the table.

Sarah wondered if he meant that he had already found it, or that he suspected it was gone. Or never existed. Her gaze flicked to the bleached spots on his trousers. He must not have noticed them.

"Is that why," Chester asked when Sarah didn't speak, "you decided to steal from your business partner? To make up for a bad investment?"

"You can't prove anything," Reginald said.

"Why?" asked Sarah. "Because your fingerprints aren't on these items? You used the lemon cleanser to make sure of that." She sniffed the air. "All I can smell is your cologne. You let it hide that you'd been using the cleanser."

"You're crazy!"

"I don't think she is." Liam's deep voice came from behind Sarah. "Unless you like polka-dot pants."

Reginald glanced at his trousers, then ran toward the door. Sarah moved to halt him, but Liam grabbed Reginald's arm. Chester rushed over and seized Reginald's other arm. They walked him to a chair by the table and sat him down.

Sarah pulled out her cell and called Chief Webber. The police chief said he would be up as quickly as he could. When she had finished the call, Liam came over to her. He kept his eyes focused on Reginald who was glowering at them.

"Are you okay, *cailín*?" Liam asked.

"Yes."

"As soon as I got your message, I headed up here." He gave her a lopsided grin. "Then I got lost trying to find my way through the house. I heard that fool shouting, so I got here just in time to make a grand entrance and save the pretty *cailín* and the day."

Sarah couldn't help smiling. "I think I heard your car door slamming."

"So much for my sneaking up on the thief." He folded his arms over his chest and stood in the doorway until the police arrived far more quickly than Sarah had expected.

Neil was with them. He looked as if he had aged a decade. Chief Webber questioned all of them, including Reginald. Sarah drew Neil to one side while the police arrested Reginald on suspicion of theft from his business partner and read him his rights.

"I never suspected he was the thief," Neil said. "I knew he'd lied to me about a lot of things to do with the house, but I thought he was trying to make the best of a bad situation."

Chester gripped Neil's shoulder. "I don't think any of us suspected him. I was shocked to see him with the stolen items."

"I think one of us knew," Neil said, turning to Sarah. "Did you suspect me too?"

"Of course." She smiled to soften her words. "I didn't want to, but I had to keep you on my list of suspects. If it makes you feel any better, Chester was on it too."

They chuckled, but the sound faded as Reginald was put into the police car. Chief Webber came over to ask if Neil wanted a ride back to Maple Hill.

"I'll get a ride with my friends," Neil said.

"All of you will need to come into the police station to make another statement," Chief Webber said. "The sooner, the better." When they nodded, he got into the second police car. It followed the first along the dirt road.

"Reginald might have gotten away with it," Sarah said quietly, "if he'd been more careful with the bleach."

"The irony," Liam said, "is that the police never would have questioned his fingerprints on any of the items because he was the co-owner."

Sarah noticed a car coming toward the house. "Who's that?"

"It looks like Don Monroe's car," Neil said. "What's he doing here today?"

"Maybe he's come to take the spy tour," Liam said with a straight face.

Neil grumbled under his breath. "We've got to put a stop to those rumors right away. Poor Nancy! She's answering dozens of calls every hour from people interested in visiting here. Just before I left, she was fielding calls from reporters wanting to get the scoop. I don't know how to stop the story. It seems to have taken on a life of its own."

Don pulled his car in next to Chester's. Getting out, he smiled when he saw them standing on the porch. "I'm glad you're still here, Neil. Your secretary told me where you were." He climbed the steps. "She didn't want to tell me at first, but I convinced her when I gave her one of these." He pulled four business cards out from under his coat.

Sarah looked at the one he had handed her. Under Don's name was printed *Private Investigator*.

"So you're not a grad student," Neil said in his iciest voice.

"No, that was my cover story. I'm sorry not to have been honest with you."

"What did you tell us that *was* true?" asked Sarah.

He leaned against the porch railing, then straightened when it creaked. "I've been trying to find information about Walter Ackermann. Not for a thesis, but because I was hired about six months ago to find a missing car. A Bugatti Type

56. It was thought until recently that there were only six in the whole world. Then my employer discovered there might have been a seventh car made in Alsace in the thirties. I've been looking for it." A smile flashed across his face. "I believe I've found it in your garage, Mr. Lawton, but I can't be sure because each time I've tried to get in the garage, it's been locked. My one chance to help you get your car out the other night was halted by Carruthers when he decided to read me the riot act and toss me out on my ear."

"Did he know what you were really doing?" Sarah asked.

"Not that I know of. He never mentioned it. He was too busy blaming me for the missing antiques. I don't know why."

Sarah exchanged a glance with Liam, Chester, and Neil, but didn't explain. "You were excited when you came into the kitchen just before we were rescued. Had you found the car then?"

"Yes, I'd looked in the garage window, and one of the cars looked like the Bugatti."

Neil stared at Don for a long minute, then motioned for the young man to follow him. Don's eyes sparkled with anticipation, but they all waited until Sarah had put her boots on.

Nobody spoke as Neil pulled out his keys and unlocked the side door. The lights came on when he flipped the switch.

Don's smile was almost too wide for his face as he strode over to the Bugatti. He ran his hand along its side and squatted down to look at the nameplate.

"Mr. Lawton, this is the car I've been looking for." He stood and patted the top of one headlight. "Too bad it's been sitting so long. If it actually ran..."

"Why don't we see?" asked Chester, opening the curved door and getting in. He pushed the starter. The vehicle bucked a couple of times as if it still had horses connected to it, then the engine turned over. It hummed like a high tension wire instead of chugging like a petroleum engine.

"Knock me over with a feather," Neil said, his voice regaining some of its usual good humor. "Who would have guessed that those old batteries would recharge after all these years?"

Sarah watched the men crowd around the battery compartment and the engine. Now Chester's and Neil's grins were as broad as Don's. "Those batteries must be something special," Sarah said. "That's it!"

"What?" asked Liam, looking over the hood at her.

"I've figured out what Walter Ackermann was referring to in his letter."

"You did?" Chester turned off the car. "Spill it."

Sarah sat in the passenger seat and admired the simple dash. "Neil, you said the Nazis feared they'd run out of oil. They had to have been interested in alternative technologies."

"Like this car." Neil stared at it as if he had never seen it before.

"Chester," Sarah said, "you told me that Bugatti was established in Alsace. It was part of France before the war, but a little thing like a border didn't stop the Nazis. They must have been desperate to get their hands on any nonpetroleum technology."

Chester still stared at the car. "Those batteries were a breakthrough in electric car technology. A breakthrough that carmakers may have forgotten. The batteries charged after sitting idle for more than seventy years." He smiled at them. "But how did this car get here?"

"Walter Ackermann stole the prototype when he fled from Alsace," Don said as he walked around the Bugatti, admiring it from every angle. "At least that's what I was told when I was hired to find it."

"And once the Nazis learned it was gone," Sarah said, "they wanted it back. They wouldn't have been hesitant about threatening Mr. Ackermann, which may explain why he turned to the United States government for protection."

"But why," Chester asked, "would the Nazis threaten their own spy?"

"Because he wasn't a Nazi spy. Nobody here was." Sarah got out of the car and closed the door. She walked with the men out of the garage. As Neil locked and checked the door, she said, "The radio was used to keep in touch with family and friends in Europe, as you believed, Don. That's why we couldn't find information about any of the names you found in the logbook. They were regular folks." She looked at the massive house, wishing the last piece of the puzzle would fall into place. "But how do the Johnsons and Mr. Ackermann fit together?"

Before anyone else could speak, Don turned to Neil. "My employer would be willing to pay you and your partner well for that Bugatti, Mr. Lawton."

Neil considered the offer for a moment, then shook his head. "I'm going to contact Bugatti and the Department of Energy to see if it's a lost technology. If it is, it could be as valuable today as before World War II. The alternative fuels market is hot right now, and if these batteries are superspecial, they should be available to everyone." He offered his hand to Don. "However, if we do decide to sell the car itself, you'll be the first one we call."

"Fair enough." He shook Neil's hand, then Sarah's. "Mrs. Hart, if you ever want a job as a private investigator, let me know. I could use your quick mind."

"Thanks," Sarah said with a chuckle, "but I'll stick to quilting."

Don got in his car and waved as he drove toward the gate.

"We should go, too," Liam said. "Chief Webber is waiting to talk with us."

"And I've got to figure out a way to stop these spy rumors." Neil sighed. "Once people find out about the Bugatti, they'll be coming up in droves to see the spy's car. Any ideas how to dampen the excitement?"

Sarah wished she had one, but she didn't. No one would believe Mr. Ackermann hadn't been a spy, unless there was solid proof that he'd had another reason for taking the car.

"I need to get my tracings." Sarah climbed up the porch steps and took off her boots. "I left them inside."

While she led the way to the grand dining room, Neil said, "So the patchwork blocks weren't part of this at all."

She recalled her image of the young mother teaching her children with the letters on the quilt. That same mother had sewn the blocks and affixed them to the tapestries. But why?

To teach the children about...Germany!

The answer was so obvious Sarah wondered how she could have missed it before. Probably because she had been looking for something with the huge impact of a ring of spies. She had overlooked the struggle of refugees who wanted their children to know about the homeland that soon would be at war with their new country. That meant that the Johnsons had come from Germany too. Was that a link between them and Walter Ackermann?

Sarah explained her insight to the others. They nodded and then smiled as they saw how the blocks connected to articles in the room.

Liam examined the dining room's large tapestry. "So the code wasn't in the radio messages home. It was in the patchwork blocks."

"Yes," she said. "We know more about the family, but we may never know why they left, where they went, and what happened to them."

Sarah was the last out of the room. She turned off the light, but looked over her shoulder. A ray of sunshine spotlighted the tapestry. The words of a psalm filled her mind: Thy word is a lamp unto my feet, and a light unto my path.

God would have been with the family when they came to this property and when they left upon the path they had been given. Wherever they had gone, they had never truly been alone. She smiled as she hurried to catch up with the others.

CHAPTER TWENTY-FIVE

S o you've solved the mystery once again," Martha said as soon as she came into Sarah's house the next day.

Martha had called a half hour before and said she would drop by before heading to Liam's.

Sarah shook her head as Martha closed her umbrella and set it by the door. "We didn't solve it completely. We did figure out who was taking the items from the house and we learned more about the cars in the garage, but the most important questions haven't been answered. Who were Walter Ackermann and the Johnsons? Why did the Johnsons vanish apparently without a trace?"

"Because they were spies." Martha laughed. "At least that's what everyone in Maple Hill thinks."

"So I've heard. People are driving Neil crazy with calls about wanting to go to the house. I don't think there were any spies, but I don't have proof."

"I assume you're going to keep looking." Martha walked with Sarah into the kitchen and poured herself a cup of tea. "You don't give up."

"Now that you're not so busy, maybe you can help me." She took a sip from her own mug.

"Where should I start?" Martha leaned back against the counter.

Sarah shook her head. "I don't know. I've chased down every clue we've found, and they haven't helped answer those two vital questions."

"So you've hit a brick wall."

Moving the tea kettle off the hot burner, Sarah went to the table and sat. "I've sent an e-mail to a woman whose father bought the house from the Johnsons in the sixties. Maybe he mentioned something about them to her." She grimaced. "It's a real long shot."

"Did you check your e-mail today?"

"Yes, just this morning."

"Not since then?" Martha put down her cup and took Sarah by the arm. "Well, let's give it a shot."

Sarah laughed as they crossed the hall to her sewing room. "Don't get your hopes up. She might not even open my e-mail, and if she does, she'll probably think I'm a kook."

"That's defeatist talk." Martha pulled out Sarah's chair and bowed toward it.

Sarah sat and shifted her mouse to bring her screen back to life. She had three new e-mails, but her eyes focused on one. The sender was Tanya Poulter.

"Martha, you were right."

She clicked to open it, holding her breath. She began to read the note from Tanya Poulter aloud:

"As you can imagine, Mrs. Hart, I was astounded to receive your e-mail with your questions. Let me explain what I know and why I was surprised. I never knew my father as other than Ian Fields until a few days before his death. I never suspected he ever had a different name. He wanted me to know our real history, not the one my parents created when they sought sanctuary in the United States with my sister and my brothers.

"The truth is, Mrs. Hart, that my father was both a patriot and a traitor. Before I was born, he worked for Ettore Bugatti, the famous car designer. When Mr. Bugatti turned his mind to designing a racing airplane, my father was put in charge of a team working on an electric car. Their experiments caught the attention of Hitler's government. Papa was determined that the car never fall into Nazi hands. He made his plans with care. First he sent Mama and my sister and brothers and many of the family's belongings ahead of him to America. Germans weren't welcome in Alsace then, so he had no trouble getting them out and across the Atlantic. He bided his time, then one day drove the electric car prototype away from the factory. He had help to get himself and the car to where he could catch a ship too. But someone betrayed him, and the Nazis discovered where Papa and the car were. At that point, he appealed to the United States government.

"Mrs. Hart, my father's true name was Walter Ackermann, but he changed it shortly after he arrived in Massachusetts. We became the Johnson family until we had to flee our beautiful home. Papa went to work for the War Department, and we were told our last name now was Fields. I was very young when we left our Massachusetts home, but I remember our house was wondrous. Until now, I never was certain where it was. My parents always avoided questions about those years. Now I understand why. When Papa died, the house was left to a stranger because Papa feared something bad might happen to us if we returned there. Of course, it won't, but I didn't contest his final wishes even though I would have loved to return to live in my first home. Papa believed that nothing was more precious than his family. He considered nothing—not his homeland, not the house that he and Mama built here in the states—more important than keeping us safe.

"I hope this helps answer your questions. If you have any others, please let me know. I hope you will return the favor and allow me to ask you questions about Maple Hill. Maybe one of these days, I'll pay a visit."

Sarah turned in her chair. Martha's eyes were riveted on the screen, and she kept shaking her head in amazement. Leaning past Sarah, she rolled the screen back up so she could read it again from the beginning.

"I need to call Neil," Sarah said, standing and slipping past Martha. She dialed Neil's number at his office.

Nancy answered the phone. "He's with a client. Could I have him call you back?"

"I need to speak with him immediately. It's about the family from the house on Lookout Mountain."

"Just a minute. Let me check with him."

Sarah tapped her foot in beat with the music now playing in her ear. It halted abruptly, and she heard Neil ask, "What have you found out, Sarah?"

"I just received an e-mail from Tanya Poulter, Ian Fields's daughter." She walked back to her computer. Martha moved aside to let her sit again.

"What did it say?"

She read the e-mail over the phone.

"Wow!" he said when she finished. "We were on the right track, but I never guessed that all three families were the same one."

"Kind of a World War II witness protection program. Neil, it sounds as if she'd be interested in purchasing the house."

Relief sifted through Neil's voice. "I'd be more than happy to sell it to her for what we paid for it, and I think I can convince Reginald to agree to sell too. But Mrs. Poulter needs to understand that the house needs a ton of work."

Sarah wondered how she could ever have doubted Neil's integrity. Instead of being eager to unload the house quickly or at a profit, he wanted to do the right thing.

"I'm sure it'd be a labor of love for her," Sarah said. "If it's okay with you, I'll send your e-mail address to her and hers to you, and the two of you can work this out. And, Neil?"

"Yes?"

"This is the proof that there weren't any spies. You can put out a statement with the facts, and the looky-loos should leave you alone."

Neil thanked her and hung up.

Sarah smiled at Martha. "I love it when everything comes together perfectly."

"You can see how God's pattern weaves through it all," Martha said.

"It's so good to know when I'm stumbling about that someone with a greater vision than mine sees the beginning, middle, and end of the story."

Martha started to answer, but Amy's voice called from the hall, "Grandma!"

"Back here," Sarah said as she exchanged a glance with Martha, who smiled and said, "Today's an in-service day. Half day for the kids."

"Hi, Amy," Sarah said when her granddaughter rushed into the sewing room. Amy's eyes were as bright as on Christmas morning.

"Grandma...Oh, hi, Mrs. Maplethorpe." Amy was trying to be polite, but her impatience was revealed when she bounced from one foot to the other.

Martha smiled. "Hi, Amy. Sarah, why don't I meet you at Liam's?" She winked at Sarah before leaving.

Amy didn't speak until the front door closed. "Guess what, Grandma?" She didn't give Sarah a chance to reply. "Mike asked me to the homecoming dance!"

"Mike? Is he the boy who was talking to you at the hockey game?"

"Grandma, were you spying on me?"

Sarah laughed and raised her hands. "No more talk about spies, okay? So did you say yes?"

"Of course! And Mom and Dad said I could meet him there. They even said if Mike and I and Audrey and a few other friends wanted to go together, everyone could meet at our house and they'd drive us. How cool is that?"

"Positively cool," Sarah said, grinning.

Amy laughed before flinging her arms around Sarah and hugging her. "Grandma, thank you so much. If you hadn't told me about how shy you were, I don't think I would have dared to say a single word to Mike."

Sarah held her granddaughter close. She was happy that Amy was facing challenges and conquering them. "You know that boy I told you about was your grandpa, don't you?"

"Of course I knew. All your best stories are about you and Grandpa Gerry." Amy laughed again before asking if she could heat up some cider.

Telling Amy to go ahead, Sarah got up. Mrs. Poulter's e-mail caught her eye.

Mrs. Poulter had written: *Papa believed that nothing was more precious than his family.*

Sarah agreed with Mr. Ackermann/Johnson/Fields. Nothing was more important or precious than family.

ABOUT THE AUTHOR

Jo Ann Brown has published more than eighty titles under various names. Her most recent title was the novelization for Thomas Kinkade's *Christmas Cottage* movie. Raised in a small town, she served as a US Army officer. She has lived in New England most of her life with her husband, her three children and two very spoiled cats.

TO HAVE AND TO HIDE

BY CAMY TANG

 CHAPTER ONE

Sarah Hart smiled as she swept aside the playful streamers falling from the decorative crown over Roseanna Walsh's front door. She knocked briskly on the glossy white-painted wood, shivering a little in the October air.

Sarah's best friend Martha Maplethorpe grinned at her as they heard the girlish giggling and chatter filtering through the door. "Sounds like the party's already started."

"Wait for me," came a huffing voice behind them.

Sarah turned to see Angela Miller, a friend from church, hurrying up the walk toward them.

"We're only a couple minutes late," Sarah assured her.

They saw a figure through the glass panes on the door a split second before it opened to Roseanna's round figure and wide smile. "Come on in! Everybody's in the living room."

"We're not the last ones, are we?" Angela asked.

"No." Roseanna stepped aside so they could enter the front hall of the Georgian colonial home. "We're still waiting for the bride."

"Caitlin isn't here yet?" Martha asked.

"She called me half an hour ago to say she was on her way," Roseanna said. "Maybe she had car trouble? Although I hope not. It's getting a bit cold to be stuck changing a tire." Roseanna glanced out the door before she shut it, then said to Angela, "Aunt Imogene isn't with you?"

Angela shook her head. "No, she's not coming."

"Imogene Dowling?" Sarah said. "She's my next-door neighbor. I didn't realize she was your aunt. I would have volunteered to bring her."

"She's not really my aunt," Roseanna said. "She and my mom were cousins."

"Imogene is my aunt," Angela said. "She and my mom were sisters. But Roseanna and I grew up like cousins."

"I can't believe I've gone to church with you all these years and didn't know you were cousins with Roseanna," Martha said to Angela.

Angela shrugged. "Since Roseanna and I go to different churches, there's hardly ever a situation where we mention it to other people."

"Why isn't Aunt Imogene coming?" Roseanna asked Angela.

"I was on my way to her house when she called to tell me that Uncle Elmer tripped on his way down the front steps.

She thinks he sprained his ankle, but she wanted to take him to the emergency room just in case."

"Poor Elmer. This will cut into his fishing time." Sarah shifted the covered pie dish in her arms while keeping hold of the gift bag slung over her wrist.

"Oh my goodness, and here we are just standing and talking. Let me help you." Roseanna took the covered dish and headed through the open doorway on Sarah's left into the spacious dining room. As Sarah entered the room, she smelled roast chicken wafting from the open doorway that led into the kitchen at the other end of the dining room. A fire had been laid in the large fireplace, with colorful autumn leaves artfully arranged around a pumpkin on the wide mantel.

The long, elaborately carved dining table groaned under the weight of food ranging from appetizers and salads to breads and pies. With the efficiency of a general, Roseanna had told each guest what type of dish to bring, whether appetizer, side dish, or dessert, while she took care of the main course.

"Gracious, Roseanna." Martha laid her bowl of green salad on the table. "There's enough to feed an army."

"You know people in Maple Hill." Roseanna laid Sarah's lattice-top apple pie down on the other end of the table, next to an orange chiffon cake. "I told each person to bring a dish to feed eight to ten people, but everyone brought a dish big enough to feed twenty."

Sarah eyed her twenty-four-inch pie plate. Guilty as charged.

"Where do we put our gifts?" Martha held up her pink frilly gift bag.

"This way." Roseanna led the way back into the central hall and straight through into the open doorway to the living room, where several women were gathered. Some perched on the edges of antique Victorian chairs while others tried to find a comfortable spot on the narrow Regency couches. But the laughter echoing off the silk wallpaper showed the women cared less about the comfort of the furniture and more about spending time together.

An end table was buried under bridal shower gifts, so Angela, Sarah, and Martha laid theirs on the Turkish carpet underneath, where other gifts already rested.

The doorbell rang, and without waiting for Roseanna to answer it, the door opened. A slender girl rushed inside with the scent of crisp fall air and a hint of smoke from burning fireplaces.

"Hello, Caitlin." Roseanna gave her a light hug. "Caitlin, you know my cousin Angela Miller—you met her at the family party last week."

"Hi again," Caitlin said with a smile.

Roseanna continued, "And you've met Sarah Hart and Martha Maplethorpe, haven't you? They're friends of your father."

Caitlin turned to Sarah with bright green eyes, the same color as her father's though her eyes were shaped just like her mother Jeannie's. "Hi, Sarah. I didn't really know you well while I was growing up, but Dad said that recently you've been getting close."

Sarah smiled. That was a good way to put it. It seemed a little silly to say she was "dating" Liam. "I hope we'll get a chance to know each other better soon," Sarah said. "This is my friend Martha. I don't think you've met."

Caitlin shook hands with Martha, then turned to Roseanna. "Sorry I'm late." She pulled her colorful wool cap from her head, loosing a riot of long, red-gold curls. "I couldn't get my car trunk to close for some reason. It kept popping open every time I slammed it shut."

"Is everything okay?" Roseanna asked.

"Oh yeah, I finally got it to latch." Caitlin gave Sarah a grin. "But I also knew you couldn't start without me."

"Well, you're just in time." Roseanna took Caitlin's coat. "The chicken has only a few more minutes in the oven before we can all start eating. Then we'll do the gifts, and then I'll give my special gift to you."

"Special gift?" Caitlin's green eyes lit up like emeralds. "Roseanna, you shouldn't have."

"Of course I should have." Roseanna's brown eyes crinkled as she smiled. "I'll be your mother-in-law in a month, so that gives me license to spoil you silly."

Liam had told Sarah that while Caitlin and her fiancé Travis were both from Maple Hill, they had become close while working in Concord, so Caitlin hadn't really gotten to know her future mother-in-law until recently, when she had become engaged. Sarah hoped Caitlin would eventually become as close to Roseanna as Maggie was with Sarah.

Sarah asked Caitlin, "So have you decided where you and Travis are going to live?"

Caitlin described their cozy cottage just outside Concord, and only three hours away from Maple Hill. "It was a great price, even though Travis's commute into Concord is going to be a little long."

"How about your commute?" Angela asked. "Where's the hospital where you work?"

"It's just outside Concord, so my commute will be only about fifteen minutes."

The five of them wandered toward the living room, where the bride was greeted with a friendly chorus of voices. Angela bustled after Roseanna, who greeted a few other women on the other side of the room.

Tiffany Henderson, Caitlin's maid of honor and a nurse at Bradford Manor, approached them. Sarah liked Tiffany for the gentle care she had given Sarah's late father, but the sight of the nurse sent a pang through her. How she missed Dad, especially at happy gatherings like this. He loved hearing about who was getting married, who attended the party, how people were doing.

"Hi, Mrs. Hart, Mrs. Maplethorpe. Caitlin, come meet some of Travis's cousins."

As Tiffany took Caitlin to a group of young people in the far corner, Martha touched Sarah's arm. "Are you okay? For a moment you looked sad."

"I'm fine. I'm just missing Dad." Sarah took a deep breath. "But I don't want to be a downer at a happy gathering like this."

Martha squeezed her hand before they started making their way through the living room, saying hello to friends.

Kathy Earhart, Vanessa's young assistant at the Wild Goose Chase fabric store, laughed with Alana Marquez and Missy Johnson. Alana had helped Sarah with her late husband Gerry's funeral years before, and Missy's grandmother Myra had shown Sarah a quilted dress back in April. All three women attended Congregational Church with Caitlin and Liam.

Sarah and Martha sat next to Karen Bancroft, one of the waitresses at The Spotted Dog. "So Liam let you escape today, did he?" Martha asked with a wink.

Karen laughed. "Considering that as of tomorrow, I'll be working a lot more hours for the next few weeks, he owed me at least one afternoon off."

"Where exactly is Liam going?" Martha asked.

"He's going to a Christian men's retreat in some mountain cabin for about seven days," Sarah said. "From there, he's going to drive to an invitation-only event at a publishing house, and from there to a weeklong booksellers' convention. But he'll be back a week before the wedding."

"Poor Caitlin, to think she has to plan everything without him," Karen said.

"What do you mean, 'poor Caitlin'?" Martha snorted. "I wish my father had been out of town while Ernie and I planned our wedding. Then I wouldn't have had to hear him sigh and moan over every single penny we spent."

Sarah chuckled. "Actually, most of the preparations are done by now, according to Liam. And he's had the retreat and the business trips planned for a while. Caitlin knew when she set the wedding date, and she made sure Liam was okay with it. She said she didn't mind he'd be gone for so long just before the wedding, if he didn't."

"Do you know anything about the special gift Roseanna has for Caitlin?" Karen asked.

Both women shook their heads. "It must be fantastic. At least, Roseanna seems very excited about it, and she never does anything halfway."

Roseanna called them to the dining room to start eating, and once Sarah and Martha were back in the living room with their heaping plates, Tiffany Henderson sat down next to them. "Hi ladies whoops!" She caught her sweet roll before it fell off her overloaded plate.

"I don't think you got enough food," Sarah teased.

"I could eat a house," Tiffany said. "Who knew being a maid of honor took so much work?"

"You've done a great job."

"Thanks, Mrs. Hart." She pushed a lock of straight brown hair over her ear, and the silver bracelet on her wrist gleamed.

"That's lovely. Is it new?" Martha asked.

Tiffany held it out so they could see. "My boyfriend just gave it to me for my birthday."

The silver bracelet shone with a glossy patina, indicating exquisite purity and a high price tag.

"How beautiful," Martha said. "So modern. Did he get it in Concord? Or Boston?"

"No, he got it at the jeweler's shop right here in Maple Hill."

"Really? I thought Les McLean retired this year."

Not to mention this very trendy piece didn't seem like something Les McLean would have at his staid jeweler's shop, which had been open in Maple Hill for over fifty years.

"Mr. McLean let his grandson Aiden take over the shop, and it's gotten really busy the past couple of months," Tiffany said. "Aiden has been bringing in some really neat pieces. Travis and Caitlin got their wedding bands there too."

Jason had asked Sarah earlier this week about helping him find something nice for Maggie for Christmas. Maybe the "new and improved" McLean Jewelers was just the place for him to go.

Roseanna got everyone's attention and they played a couple of shower games that had them all laughing. Then came time to open gifts. The gaily colored packages were being transported from the table to the area around Caitlin, although Roseanna objected, "Just a few at a time. Don't crowd her."

Caitlin and the rest of the women oohed and aahed over the gifts. Martha had given her a delicately crocheted lace shawl made of fine mohair yarn, and Sarah had made a small quilt in the Courthouse Steps pattern. Caitlin also got kitchen towels and pretty sleepwear sets.

After the last package was opened and the giver thanked, Roseanna rose to her feet in exultation. "And now, Caitlin, for my gift to you." She reached behind her chair for a large box covered in white embossed wrapping paper with an elaborate silver bow. Sarah leaned forward in her seat.

Caitlin opened the package carefully, then gave a small gasp. "Thank you, Roseanna. It's exquisite."

She lifted out a quilt which had been folded so that an intricately embroidered patch lay on top, with "Caitlin Connolly m. Travis Walsh, November 2011" stitched in flowing letters. Sarah caught her breath at the clusters of embroidered flowers in a riot of colors that decorated the edges of the patch. She knew Roseanna enjoyed doing fine embroidery, but Sarah had never seen any of Roseanna's work until now. It was breathtaking.

Just as interesting as the patch was the quilt. When Caitlin unfolded it to see the front side, the scent of lavender tickled Sarah's nose. She saw that it was a Double Wedding Ring pattern. Each ring was a different color, red or pink or green, and each ring had been pieced from many different fabrics, ranging from solids to prints to stripes. The colors created the impression of a flower garden on the white background of the quilt top.

"I know this quilt," Caitlin said in surprise. "It used to belong to Mom."

Roseanna nodded. "Your father took it out of storage and intended to give it to you for your wedding, but I convinced him to give it to me first to attach the patch on the backing."

"It was Jeannie's quilt? I didn't realize she used to quilt," Sarah whispered to Martha.

"I don't think she did," Martha said. "Maybe it was given to her."

The quilt was passed around, and as Sarah touched the hand-quilted top, she realized the quilt was very old. Perhaps not a hundred years old, but not made recently either. It was also a difficult pattern that had been constructed very well.

If Jeannie had made it, she would have been young, in her teens or twenties, and she would have had to have been very proficient in quilting.

Sarah flipped the quilt over to gaze at the patch again, and caught her breath at the lovely embroidery. It had been appliquéd on the bottom right-hand side of the quilt's backing, and positioned exactly an inch from each edge.

As they passed the quilt to Tiffany, sitting on the other sofa, Martha turned to Sarah. "What are you going to wear to the wedding?"

Sarah thought about her wardrobe. "Actually, I don't know. The silver and gray dress I wore to Jason's and Jenna's weddings got a terrible rip at the waistline when a relative stepped on the skirt at Jenna's reception."

"You can't fix it?"

"The rip isn't on a seam, so I'm afraid any repair would make the fabric pucker."

"Well, you'll have to buy something, then." Martha grinned. "I suppose I could make some time to shop with you."

Sarah smiled. "Such a sacrifice."

"Anything for my friend. I'll pick you up Monday morning at ten o'clock."

On Monday morning, Sarah flipped through her closet again. Her clothes were by and large comfortable and neat, and she had never owned many fancy dresses. She had that black crepe skirt…but it was too light and summery for a late fall wedding. Besides, she also didn't have any appropriate tops to pair it with, so she would have to go shopping either way.

Besides, the black crepe skirt was only so-so. She wanted something extra special. She wanted something that would make Liam's eyes light up when he saw her.

The doorbell rang downstairs. She glanced at the clock—only nine. Too early for it to be Martha. The bell rang again as she was heading down the stairs. Who would be so insistent?

She opened the door to Caitlin's white face. "Caitlin! What's wrong?"

"I think it's ruined!" Caitlin held out a large open box, and inside was her mother's quilt, darkened with muddy water. "Dad said you restore antique quilts, so when this happened, I couldn't think of anywhere else to go."

"Oh goodness. Come in." Sarah led the way to the dining room where she quickly laid out some old towels on the table. "Lay it down here."

"Do you remember how my car trunk wouldn't latch on Saturday? It popped open when I was driving to Dad's house today and the box fell out—upside-down—into a puddle."

Sarah carefully lifted the quilt from the box.

"I don't know why I didn't bother to put the cover back on the box after the bridal shower." Caitlin wrung her hands. "I liked looking at it, I guess, every time I opened the trunk. I was going to take it to our new house today."

"Don't worry. It's only a little wet and dirty. We can clean that up with a little tender care, and it'll be good as new."

But as she unfolded the quilt, she realized the part that had landed flat in the puddle had been the corner with the embroidered patch. While the quilt was cotton, Roseanna had used silk embroidery floss and fabric for the patch. The delicate weave of the fabric and the extreme cold temperature of the water was making the fabric tighten and shrink slightly, which would normally not be much of a problem in a garment. But because of the embroidery, the fabric was starting to wrinkle. There was also a large mud stain. She would need to take extra care that the patch wasn't ruined.

The tightening silk was causing the patch to pull away from the stitches on the edges where Roseanna had sewn it to the quilt, and Sarah worried the silk would continue to pull away and rip if she tried to rub the mud stain out without first taking the patch off.

"I'll need to remove the patch," she told Caitlin.

"That's fine, as long as you can put it back on," Caitlin said. "I hope you can fix it. I remember Mom telling me that one of my great-aunts made this quilt and it's a family heirloom. I'll die if I've ruined it."

"It'll be fine," Sarah assured her.

"I hope I didn't interrupt you this morning. I was panicked, plus I'm late for a nine o'clock premarital counseling session at church."

"Oh, don't let me keep you. I'll take care of this and call you when it's fixed."

"Really? Oh, thank you so much," Caitlin said. She leaned in and gave Sarah a quick hug. "I hope we get a chance to spend some time together before the wedding. Dad has told me so much about you."

Sarah waved good-bye as Caitlin drove away, then hurried back inside to take care of the quilt.

She got a bowl and filled it with lukewarm water, then went into the laundry room to get a bottle of baby shampoo from under the sink. She squirted some into the bowl and headed back through the kitchen.

Sarah went to her sewing room and got her seam ripper, a measuring tape, a small gooseprobe table lamp for extra light, and a cloth rag. She set the lamp up on the dining room table and started carefully ripping out the stitches that held the patch to the backing, starting from the bottom left corner and working her way around all four sides. When she was done, she picked up the patch carefully so as not to rip the silk by accidentally pulling at an embroidery stitch.

But as she took the patch up, she saw something written on the quilt backing itself, underneath the patch.

"Liam Connolly" had been written in faded black ink on the cotton fabric in a flowing cursive hand. Then beneath it were embroidered letters:

"M. Fiona Hamill."

A NOTE FROM THE EDITORS

We hope you enjoy Patchwork Mysteries, created by the Books and Inspirational Media Division of Guideposts, a nonprofit organization that touches millions of lives every day through products and services that inspire, encourage, help you grow in your faith, and celebrate God's love in every aspect of your daily life.

Thank you for making a difference with your purchase of this book, which helps fund our many outreach programs to military personnel, prisons, hospitals, nursing homes, and educational institutions. To learn more, visit GuidepostsFoundation.org.

We also maintain many useful and uplifting online resources. Visit Guideposts.org to read true stories of hope and inspiration, access OurPrayer network, sign up for free newsletters, download free e-books, join our Facebook community, and follow our stimulating blogs.

To learn about other Guideposts publications, including the best-selling devotional *Daily Guideposts*, go to ShopGuideposts.org, call (800) 932-2145, or write to Guideposts, PO Box 5815, Harlan, Iowa 51593.